*Too Late
American Boyhood
Blues*

TEN STORIES

Too Late
American Boyhood
Blues

Frederick Busch

DAVID R. GODINE, PUBLISHER · BOSTON

First published in 1984 by

David R. Godine, Publisher, Inc.
306 Dartmouth Street
Boston, Massachusetts 02116

LIBRARY OF CONGRESS CATALOGING IN PUBLICATION DATA

Busch, Frederick, 1941–
   Too late American boyhood blues.

   1. Boys – Fiction. I. Title.
   PS3552.U814T6 1984   813'.54   83-48895
   ISBN 0-87923-511-X

"Defense" and "Critics" appeared in *Conjunctions*, "Time is Money" (as "The Too Late American Boyhood Blues") in *New Directions*, Part 1 of "Stand, and Be Recognized" (as "The Right Address") in *Columbia*, "The New Honesty" (as "The Falls") in *Crazy Horse*, "A History of Small Ideas" in *Carolina Quarterly*, and "The Settlement of Mars" in *Tri-Quarterly*.

Half of these stories were written on a Solomon R. Guggenheim Memorial Foundation Fellowship. Most of the rest were written with the support of the Ingram Merrill Foundation. I am very grateful to the kind people who gave me the gift of so much time.

PRINTED IN THE UNITED STATES OF AMERICA

For Ben

*Look at the beggar now, Wilson
thought. It's that some of them
stay little boys so long, Wilson
thought. Sometimes all their lives.
Their figures stay boyish when
they're fifty. The great American
boy-men. Damned strange people.*

— ERNEST HEMINGWAY, *"The Short
Happy Life of Francis Macomber"* ·

Contents

*Too Late
American Boyhood
Blues*

The Settlement of Mars

I t began for me in a woman's bed, and my father was there though she wasn't. I was nine years old, and starting to age. "Separate vacations," then, meant only adventure to me. My bespectacled mother would travel west to attend a conference about birds; she would stare through heavy binoculars at what was distant and nameable. My father and I would drive through Massachusetts and New Hampshire into Maine, where he and Bill Brown, a friend from the army, would climb Mount Katahdin and I would stay behind at the Brown family's farm.

And it was adventure — in the days away from New York, and in the drive alone with my father in the light-green '49 Chevrolet, and in my mother's absence. For she seemed to be usually angry at someone, and my father struck me as usually pleased with the world, and surely with me. And though I knew enough to understand that his life was something of a secret he didn't tell me, I also knew enough at nine to accept his silence as a gift: peace, which my mother withheld by offering the truth, in codes I couldn't crack, of her discontent.

I remember the dreamy, slow progress of the car on heat-shimmered highways, and my elbow — this never was permitted when we all drove together on Long Island — permanently stuck from the high window. We slept one night in a motel that smelled like iodine, we ate lobster rolls and hot dogs, I discussed the probable settlement of Mars, and my father nodded gravely toward my knowledge of the future.

He gave me close escapes — the long, gray Hudson which almost hit us, because my father looked only ahead when he drove, never to the side or rear, as we pulled out of a service station; the time we had a flat and the jack collapsed twice, the car crashing onto the wheel hub, my father swearing — "_____ it!" — for the first time in my hearing; and the time he let the car drift into a ditch at the side of the road, pitching us nose-down, rear left-side wheel in the air, shaken and stranded until a farmer on a high tractor towed us out and sent us smiling together on our way. My father bared his teeth to say, "It's a lucky thing Mother isn't here," while I regretted the decorum I had learned from him — I was not to speak without respect of the woman with binoculars who had journeyed from us.

I thought of those binoculars as we approached the vague shapes of weathered gray buildings, wished that I could stare ahead through them and see what my life, for the next little while, might offer. But the black Zeiss 12 x 50s were thousands of miles from us, and really further than that: they were in my memory of silent bruised field trips, when my father's interest would be in covering ground, and my mother's would be expressed in the spraddle-legged stiffness with which she stared at birds up a slope I knew my father wanted to be climbing.

Bill Brown was short and mild in silver-rimmed glasses. He wore a striped engineer's cap with a long bill, and he smiled at everything my father said. Molly Brown was taller than Bill, and was enormously fat, with wobbling arm flesh and shaking jowls and perpetual streaked flushes on her soft round cheeks. Their daughter, Paula, was fourteen and tall and lean and beautiful. She had breasts. Sweat, such an intimate fact to me, stained the underarms of her sleeveless shirt. She wore dungarees that clung to her buttocks. She rolled the cuffs to just below her knees, and I saw the dusk sun light up golden hairs on her shins. She had been assigned to babysit me for the visit. I could not imagine being babysat by so much of everything I had heard rumored, and was beginning to notice in playgrounds, secrets of the other world.

We ate mashed potatoes and a roast that seemed to heat the kitchen, which, like the other rooms in the house, smelled of unwashed bodies and damp earth. I slept that first night on a cot in Paula's room, and I was too tired even to be embarrassed, much less thrilled, by the proximity; I slept in purest fatigue, as if I had journeyed on foot for weeks to another country, in which the air was thin. Next day, we walked the Browns' land — I could not take my eyes from Paula's spiny back and strong thighs as we climbed fences, as she helped me, her child-assignment, up and over and down — and we ate too much hot food, and drank Kool-Aid (forbidden, because too sugary, at home), and we sat around a lot. I rejoiced in such purposelessness, and I suspected that my father enjoyed it too, for our weekend days at home were slanted toward mission; starting each Saturday morning, we tumbled down the long tilted surfaces of the day into weeding and pruning and sweeping and traveling in the silent car to far-off fields to see if something my mother knew to be special was fluttering over marshes in New Jersey or forests in upstate New York.

My father, who made radio advertisements, spoke a little

about his work, and Bill Brown said in his pleased soft voice that he had heard my father's ads. But when Bill said, "Where do you get those crazy ideas, Frank?" my father turned the conversation to potato farming, and the moth collection which Bill and Molly kept together, and the maintenance of trucks. I knew that my father understood nothing about engines. He was being generous again, and he was hiding again while someone else talked of nothing that mattered to the private man who had taught me how to throw a baseball, and how to pack a knapsack, and how — I know this now — to shelter inside other people's words. And there was Paula, too, smoking cigarettes without reprimand, swinging beside me on the high-backed wooden bench that was fastened by chains to the ceiling of their porch. I breathed her smoke as now I'd breathe in perfume on smooth, heated skin.

In reply to a question, my father said, "Angie's in Colorado."

"All the way out there," Molly said.

Bill said, "Well."

"Yes, she had a fine opportunity," my father said. "They gave her a scholarship to this conference about bird migration, I guess it is, and she just couldn't say no."

"I'd like to go there sometime," Paula said, sighing smoke out.

"Wouldn't you, though?" Molly growled in her rich voice. "Meet some Colorado boys and such, I suspect?"

"Give them a chance to meet a State of Maine *girl*, don't forget," Paula said. "Uncle Frank, didn't you want to go to Colorado?"

My father's deep voice rumbled softly. "Not when I can meet a State of Maine girl right here, hon. And don't forget, your father and I already spent some time in Colorado."

"Amen that it's over," Bill said.

"I saw your father learn his manners from a mule out there, didn't I, Bill?"

"Son of a bitch stepped so hard on my foot, he broke every damned bone inside it. Just squatted there, Frank, you remember? Son of a bitch didn't have the sense to get off once he'd crushed it. It took Frank jumping up and down and kicking him just to make him wake and look down and notice he already done his worst and he could move along. Leisurely, as I remember. He must of been thinking or something. I *still* get the bowlegged limps in wet weather. I wouldn't cook a mule and eat one if I was starved to death."

"Well, didn't she —" Paula said.

"Angie," I said. I felt my father look at me across the dark porch.

"Didn't Angie want to come up here and meet us?" Paula asked.

Molly said, "Couldn't you think of any personal questions you would like for Frank to answer for you?"

"Well, I guess I'm *sorry*, then."

"That's right," Molly said.

"It was one hell of a basic training," Bill said. He said it in a rush. "They had us with this new mountain division they were starting up. Taught us every   thing you could want to know about carrying howitzers up onto mountains by muleback. How to get killed while skiing. All of it. Then, they take about three hundred of us or so and send us by boat over to some hot jungle. Ship all our gear with us too, of course. So we land there in the Philippine Islands with snowshoes, skis, camouflage parkas, light machine guns in white canvas *covers*, for gosh-sakes, and they ask us if we'd win the war for them."

"It took us a while," my father said.

"Didn't it now?"

Bill went inside and returned with a bottle and glasses. He sat down next to my father, and I heard the gurgle, then a smacking of lips and, from my father, a low groan of pleasure, of uncontrol, which I hadn't heard before. New information was promised by that sound, and I folded my arms across my chest for warmth and settled in to learn, from the invisibility darkness offered, and from the rhythm of the rattle of bottle and glass.

I was jealous that Paula wanted boys in Colorado when I was there, and I was resigned — it was like fighting gravity, I knew — to not bulking sizably enough. Their voices seemed to sink into the cold black air and the smell of Paula's cigarettes, and I heard few whole words — nothing, surely, about my vanished mother, or about my father and me — and what I knew next was the stubbly friction of my father's cheek as he kissed me goodbye and whispered that he'd see me soon. I thought that we were home and that he was putting me to bed. Then, when I heard the coarse noise of Bill's truck, I opened my eyes and saw that I was on the canvas cot in Paula's room in a bright morning in Maine. I was certain that he was leaving me there to grow up as a farmer, and I almost said aloud the first words that occurred to me: "What about school? Do I go to school *here*?" School meant breakfast, meant wearing clothes taken from the oak highboy in the room in Stony Brook, Long Island, meant coming downstairs to see my father making coffee while my mother rattled at *The Times*. The enormity of such stranding drove me in several directions as I came from the cot, "What about school?" still held, like scalding soup, behind my teeth and on my wounded tongue.

Paula, at the doorway, shaking a blouse down over her

brassiere — I could not move my eyes from the awful power of her underwear — called through the cloth, "Don't you be frightened. You fell asleep and you slept deep. Frank and Daddy're climbing, is all. Remember?" Though the cotton finally fell to hide her chest and stomach, I stared there, at strong hidden matters. We ate eggs fried in butter on a wood-fired stove while Molly drank coffee and talked about a dull moth which lived on Katahdin and which Bill might bring home. I stared at Paula's lips as they closed around corners of toast and yellow runny yolks.

We shoveled manure into the wheelbarrow Paula let me push, and we fed their dozen cows. One of them she'd named Bobo, and I held straw to Bobo's wet mouth and pretended to enjoy how her nose dripped. I listened to the running-water noises of their stomachs, and I looked at the long stringy muscles in Paula's tanned bare arms. Her face, long like her mother's, but with high cheekbones and wide light eyes, was always in repose, as if she dreamed as she worked while naming for me the nature of her chores and the functions of equipment. I watched the sweat that glistened under her arms and on her broad forehead, and she sounded then like my father, when he took me to his office on a school holiday: I was told about the surfaces of everything I saw, but not of his relation to them, and therefore their relation to me. In Jefferson, Maine, as on East Fifty-second Street in Manhattan, as in Stony Brook, New York, the world was puzzling and seductive, and I couldn't put my hands on it, and hold.

We went across a blurred meadow that vibrated with black flies and tiny white butterflies that rose and fell like tides. On the crest of a little hill, under gray trees with wide branches and no leaves or fruit, Paula lay flat, groaning as if she were old, and stared up through bug-clouds and barren limbs and harsh sun. "Here," she said, patting the sparse fine grass beside her. "Look."

I lay down next to her as tentatively as I might lie now beside a woman whom I'd know I finally couldn't hold. Her arm was almost touching mine, and I thought I could feel its heat. Then the arm rose to point, and I smelled her sweat. "Look," she said again. "He looks like he's resting awhile, but he's hanging onto the air. That's work. He's drifting for food. He'll see a mole from there and strike it too."

Squint as hard as I might, there was nothing for me but bright spots the sun made inside my eyes. I tried to change the focus, as if I looked through my mother's binoculars, but I saw only a branch above us, and it was blurry too. I blinked again; nothing looked right.

"I guess I saw enough birds in my life," I told her.

"That's right, isn't it? Your mother's a bird-watcher. In Colorado, too. I guess there's trouble *there*."

"They're taking separate vacations this year."

"They sure are. That's what I mean about trouble. Man and wife *live* together. That's why they get married. They watch birds together, if that's what they do, and they climb up mountains together, and they sleep together in the same bed. Do Frank and Angie sleep in the same bed?"

I was rigid lest our arms touch, and the question made me stiffer. "I don't see *your* mother climbing any mountains," I said.

"Well, she's too fat, honey. Otherwise she would. And if this wasn't a trip for your father and mine to take alone, a kind of special treat for them, you can bet me and Momma would be there, living out of a little canvas tent and cooking for when Daddy came back down, bug-bit and chewed up by rocks. And you won't find but one bed for the two of them. I still hear them sometimes at night. You know. Do you?"

"Oh, sure. I hear my mom and dad too." That was true: I heard them talking in the living room, or washing dishes after a party, or playing music on the Victrola. "Sure," I said, suspecting that I was soon to learn things terrible and delicious, and worried not only because I was ashamed of what I didn't hear, but because, if I *did* hear them, I wouldn't know what they meant. The tree limb was blurred, still, and I moved to rub my eyes.

Then that girl of smells — her cigarette smoke lay over the odor of the arm she'd raised — and of fleshy swellings and mysterious belly and the awesome mechanics of brassieres, the girl who knew about me and my frights, about my parents and their now-profound deficiencies, said gently, "Come on back to my room. I'll show you something."

When she stood, she took my hand; hers was rough and dry and strong. She pulled me back over field and fences, and I thrilled to the feel of flesh as much as I hated the maternity with which she towed me. But I thought, too, that something alarming was about to be disclosed. I couldn't wait to be told, though I was scared.

Molly was putting clothes through a mangle near the rain barrel, and she waved as we passed. We went through cool shadows into the room Paula had decorated with Dick Powell's picture, and Gable's, and on the far wall a blurred someone with a moustache wore tights and feathered hat and held a sword.

"My library," she said, opening the closet. "Here." And on shelves, stacked, and in shaggy feathering heaps on the closet floor, were little yellowing books and bright comics and magazines that told the truth about the life of Claudette

Colbert and Cary Grant. I doubt that she knew what I needed, for she was mostly a teenage kid on a little farm in Maine. She wasn't magical, except to me in her skin, although she was smarter than I about the life I nearly knew I led. But something made her take me from the swarm of sun and insects, the high-hanging invisible bird of prey — that place where, she possibly knew, I sensed how much of my life was a secret to me — and she installed me on the dirty floor of a dirty house, in deepening afternoon, half-inside a closet where, squinting, I fell away from the world and into pictures, words.

I read small glossy-jacketed books, little type on crumbling wartime paper, with some line drawings, about Flash Gordon and Ming the Merciless and the plight of the always-kidnapped Dale. I read about death rays and rockets that went to Mars from Venus as quickly as they had to for the sake of mild creatures with six arms who were victimized by Ming's high greed. Dale and the other women had very pointed breasts and often said, "Oh, Flash, do you really think so?"

And there was Captain Marvel, whose curling forelock was so much like Superman's, but whom I preferred because I thought we looked alike and because he never had to bother to change his clothes to get mighty: he said *Shazam!* and a lightning bolt made him muscular and capable of rescuing women with long legs. I read of Superboy, whose folks in Smallville were so proud of him. Littler worlds, manageable by me, and on my behalf by people who could change, whether in phone booths or storerooms or explosions of light, into what they needed to be: Aqua-Man, Spider Man, the Green Lantern, wide-nostriled Wonder Woman in her glass airplane, and always Flash and Dale, "Oh, Flash, do you really think so?"

For a while, Paula sat behind me, cross-legged on her bed, reading fan magazines and murmuring of Gary Cooper's wardrobe and the number of people Victor Mature could lift into the air. When she went out, she spoke and I answered, but I don't remember what we said. I leaned forward in the darkness, squinting and forgetting to worry that I had to screw my face around my eyes in order to see, and I stayed where I was, which was away.

They had a radio, and we listened to it for a while after dinner, and then Molly showed me, in a room off the kitchen, board after board on which dead moths were stiffly pegged. I squinted at them and said "Wow," and while Paula and Molly sat in sweaters on the porch and talked, I squatted in the closet's mouth, under weak yellow light, and started Edgar Rice Burroughs's *The Chessmen of Mars*. When Paula entered to change into nightclothes, I was lured from the cruel pursuit of Dejah Thoris by Gahan of Gathol, for the whisper of cloth over skin was a new music. But I went back with relief to "The dazzling sunlight of Barsoom clothed Manator in an aureole of splendor as the girl and her captors rode into the city through the Gate of Enemies."

When Paula warned me that the lights were going off, I stumbled toward my cot, and when they were out I undressed and went to sleep, telling myself stories. And next day, after breakfast and a halfhearted attempt to follow her through chores, I walked over the blurred field to the rank shade of Paula's room, and I sat in the closet doorway, reading of Martian prisons, and heroes who hacked and slew, unaware that I had neither sniffed nor stared at her, and worried only that I might not finish the book and start another before my father and Bill returned. They didn't, and we ate roast beef hash and pulpy carrots, and Molly worked in the shed on the motor of their kitchen blender while Paula listened to "Henry Aldrich" and I attended to rescues performed by the Warlord of Mars.

It was the next afternoon when my father and Bill returned in the truck. They were dirty and tired and beaming, and they smelled like woodsmoke. My father hugged me and kissed me so hard that he hurt me with his unshaved cheeks. He swatted my bottom and rubbed my shoulders with his big hands. Bill presented Molly with a dirty little moth and she clapped her hands and trilled. Paula smoked cigarettes and sat on the porch between Bill and my father, listening, as if she actually cared, to Bill's description of how well my father had done to follow him up Abel's Slide, where the chunks of stone were like steps too high to walk, too short and smooth to climb, and up which you had to spring, my father broke in to say, "Like a goat in a competition. I thought my stomach would burst, following this — this *kid*. That's you, Bill, part mountain goat and part boy. I don't know how you stayed young for so long. You were the oldest man in the outfit, and what you did was you stayed where you were and I got ancient."

"Nah. Frank, you're in pretty good shape. For someone who makes his living by sitting on his backside. I'll tell you that. You did swell."

"Well, you did better. How's that?"

Bill swallowed beer and nodded. "I'd say that's right."

And they both laughed hard, in a way the rest of us could only smile at and watch.

"Damn," my father said, smiling so wide. "*Damn!*"

My head felt hot and the skin of my face was too tight for whatever beat beneath it. They were shimmering shapes in the afternoon light, and I rubbed my eyes to make them work in some other way. But what I saw was as through a membrane. Perhaps it was Paula's cool hand on my face

14

that did it, and the surge of smells, the distant mystery of her older skin and knowledge which I suddenly remembered to be mastered by. Perhaps it was the distance my father had traveled over and from which, as I learned from the privacies of his laughter, he still had not returned. Perhaps it was Molly, sitting on the porch steps next to Bill, her hand on his thigh. Or perhaps it was the bird I couldn't see which hung over Jefferson, Maine, drifting to dive. I pushed my face against Paula's hard hand and I rubbed at my eyes and I started to weep long coughing noises which frightened me as much as they must have startled the others.

My father's hobbed climbing boots banged on the porch as he hurried to hold me, but I didn't see him because I knew that if I opened my eyes I would know how far the blindness had progressed. I didn't want to know anything more. He carried me inside while I wailed like a hysterical child — which is what I was, and what I'm sure I felt relieved to be. I listened to their voices when they'd stilled my weeping and asked me questions about pain. I swallowed aspirin with Kool-Aid and heard my father discover the comics and the books I'd read while on my separate vacation. And the relief in his voice, and the smile I heard riding on his breath, served to clench my jaw and lock my hands above my eyes. Because he knew, and they knew, and I still didn't, though I now suspected, because I always trusted him, that I wouldn't die and probably wouldn't go blind.

"Just think of your mother's glasses, love," he whispered while the others walked from the room. He sat on the bed and stroked my face around my fists, which still stayed on my eyes. "Mother has weak eyes, and these things can be passed along — the kids can get them from their parents."

"You mean I caught it from her?"

The bed I was in, Paula's bed — I smelled her on the pillow and the sheets — shook as he nodded and continued to stroke my face. "*Like* that. Just about, yes. I bet when we go home, and we go to the eye doctor, he'll put a chart up for you to read. Did you have these tests in school? He'll ask you to read the letters, and he'll say you didn't see them too clearly, and he'll tell us to get you some glasses. And that's *all*. I promise. It isn't meningitis, it isn't polio —"

"Polio?" I said. "*Polio?*"

"No," he said. "No. No, it isn't a *sick*ness. I'm sorry I said that. I was worried for a minute, but now I'm not, I promise. You hear? I'm promising you. Your eyes are weak. Your head'll feel better from the aspirin — it's just eyes-train, love. It's nothing more."

"Yeah," I said. "Some dumb vacation. I should have gone with Mommy."

I lay in a woman's bed, and in the warmth of her secrets, and in the rich smell of what was coming to me. And my father sat there as his large hands gentled my face. His hands never left me. I dropped my fists, though I kept my eyes closed tight. I felt his strong fingers, roughened by rocks, as they ran along my eyebrows, touched my cheeks, my hairline, my forehead, then eyebrows again, over and over, until, with great gentleness, they dropped upon the locked lids, and he said, "No, no, this is where you should be." So I hid beneath my father's hands, and I rested awhile.

Rise and Fall

His father rose early and climbed the attic stairs to bathe in the farthest tub of their house. He came home from work for dinner at seven o'clock. In between for Jay Reese it was school, and his mother in the late afternoons; at every hour, though, he was the kind of boy who liked living alone. But especially after the war — during which he had lived by himself with his mother — while he was being six and seven and eight, his father was the figure disappearing in the early part of the morning, and then coming home from the practice of the law while the day went dark.

He remembered his father in two weekend costumes from those days in the Midwood section of Flatbush, in Brooklyn in New York, when the old trees made the air green in summer and were a network of traps, during the autumn and early winter, for the pink Spaulding rubber ball the boys would bat, with a sawed-off broomstick, as far down the narrow street as they could. In hot weather, his father would, on Saturdays, wear one of two seersucker suits. There was a brown-and-white stripe, there was a gray-and-white stripe, and each jacket buttoned tight at the waist, and the trousers of each would cling to his father's thin calves. He always thought it was his father's garters and long hose that made the trousers cling. With the brown suit, his father would wear a Panama hat; with the gray, a fedora made of gray straw. And, often, there his father would be, emerging from the hot brown cars of the BMT subway at the elevated Avenue H station, obviously not thinking of his older son because he was always surprised to see that he had pedaled over the Avenue H footbridge down the leafy streets past the wide brick or stucco houses where, on Saturdays, so many fathers mowed lawns or clipped hedges or threw baseballs to kids. His father worked on Saturdays until Jay was nearly out of college, and his father, on so many of those Saturdays, in the early afternoon, tall and strong and bald and handsome in a way that used to be called manly, came out of the BMT and was surprised to see his son. They went home in, for the father, a march, and a slow ticking of bicycle gears for the son, who made his legs act patient as he wobbled his front wheel so that he might go slowly and not fall down. They were nearly side-by-side.

The other costume he recalled — the son was the sort of grownup who would dwell on melancholy matters and tatters torn back from the past — was his heavy winter coat. It was a camouflage coat, and his father had worn it in the Second World War. Jay spent a good deal of time in looking the coat over carefully for blood. It was an unbloodied coat, however, and on Sunday mornings in winter, after his father had looked at *The Times*, and while his mother tried to sneak into her own life in another room for a few private moments, his father, if there was snow on the ground, would tell Jay and his little brother, Jonas, to get dressed for the cold. Jay would dress himself, and his father would slide Jonas into a snowsuit that left him immobile, a two-year-old doll bundled under wool and nylon and rubber except for his nose and sad eyes and solemn mouth. Jay would wear a dull plaid mackinaw over sweater and flannel shirt, and the corduroy knickers that slid into the tops of his boots. His father, also in a mackinaw and woolen pants and boots, would add the camouflage shell, khaki on one side and snow-white on the other. His father always wore the snow-side out, and only when Jay was grown would he wonder what purpose such camouflage, in Brooklyn, New York, in the 1940s and '50s, might serve.

His father pulled Jonas on their small wooden sled, while Jay, like a warrior, carried the longer sled at port-arms across Avenue I, and toward the footbridge at Avenue H, over which pedestrians might walk while, underneath, the freight trains of the Long Island Railroad rumbled, heading for the Atlantic Avenue terminal and then out of Brooklyn to the rest of the world. It was a great concrete slab, that arching bridge, with meshwire sides and both a railed ramp and a set of concrete steps. You could stand on it and look down as the train came by, throwing heat and sound. Next to the steps was a patch of waste ground, beside a small pale apartment house. And in the area between the apartments and the bridge, fathers stood and talked easily, without intimacy, or they read their Sunday papers, swaying as though they hung onto handstraps aboard the BMT, and no trains ran below, and children — Jay, alone, and then sometimes with Jonas tucked before him, seated, or clinging prone to his back — rode shrieking down the long gradual hill to stop in the deeper snow some twenty feet or so from the double set of tracks.

And one day, in the winter, after Christmastime, Jay remembered, he and Jonas and their father went to the bridge to sled and were met by a group of puzzled fathers and children. They stood, looking at the newcomers and then back to the waste ground from which the sleds were launched, to see the new fence. There was something miraculous about it, because although children had walked and biked there, and though certain fathers, Jay's among them, had walked on the bridge twice a day all week, no one, apparently, had seen the fence erected. It was very high, and was attached, on the right, to the bridge itself, and, on the left, to a 10- or 12-foot metal pole beside the apartment house. It was a tall wire fence of the sort that keeps people out of, or trapped inside, the recess yards of public schools. Many of them stood at the fence and held the heavy, woven mesh. And then Jay's father pointed out to the others that the overhead electric wires, running beneath the bridge and above the tracks, were different — they had new hues of glass transformer, and large metal boxes of a different shape were affixed to creosoted poles, and the wire itself was a thicker and shinier black. They agreed, the fathers, while their children stamped and whined and looked about, that these were "high power lines," though no one knew the meaning of what they agreed on. To keep the children of the Avenue H neighborhood safe, their sledding ground was closed.

Of course, children learned to sneak under the fence soon enough, and to climb over the side of the bridge and hang by their hands and pull themselves, dangling in the air, to the side of the hill and then tumble until their balance was caught, and then be safely standing on what was forbidden. Some threw sleds over in winter and then climbed over the bridge — for a while, Jay was among them. Some climbed over in warmer weather to huddle under the bridge, as if it rained and they were camping, in order to have a hidden place for smoking their Old Gold cigarettes. And two boys, who came from across Ocean Avenue, climbed over and shinnied along the girders beneath the bridge and fell onto the lines and were burned to death by the electricity. A man who lived in the apartment house, a Silesian bookbinder named Jankowicz who bound Jay's mother's magazines into volumes, had reported to Jay's parents that when the police lifted the bodies up to the bridge and took them off in a long green truck, the limbs were stiff and the flesh was dark, "like they was cooked," his mother reported that Jankowicz had said. She reported it a lot. And Jay thought of roasted bellies and crusts of dark buttock and he stopped climbing over the bridge. But that was later, after the day when the fathers and sons stood interdicted by a fence in a neighborhood that was largely without such barriers. It was a witty but to him forgivable formulation, as Jay thought of it later on, waxing sentimental over his father's wardrobe and his early life in the quiet, gentle district where they'd lived: the world had, one weekend, announced to the children of children of immigrants, many of whom thought of themselves as living in the almost-prosperous not-quite-suburbs, that they could descend as swiftly as they wished, in silence or in frightened laughter; the danger, said the diamond-shapes of thick linked fence, the bright black wire, the energy that snaked within it, was in trying to rise.

Jonas, his brother, had soared. Like their father, he went to law school and then was a clerk, of sorts, in a shabby firm of men whose wages came from defending the malfeasances and tax shelters of businessmen with overseas interests. Jonas was in fact above that kind of law, at least as often as he could be. He moved on, a junior partner in a firm whose practice was exclusively international law. And then, on lower Broadway in Manhattan, across the street from Trinity Church and hard by Brooks Brothers, Jonas rented quarters for himself and a secretary and two other men, and he became Reese, Kupkind & Slatauer, and at meetings of the New York Bar Association, he served on the foreign law committee. He took taxis to work, from Yorkville, and when they spoke by telephone every few months — each might have sworn, Jay suspected, that they'd spoken within the past week — Jonas reported savagely to Jay on how, from families still in the old neighborhood, he had learned of sweeping ethnic shifts, brown skins edging out white, and rumors of voodoo practiced within three-quarters of a mile of the synagogue that Eleanor Roosevelt herself had opened with a garbled Hebrew phrase in 1953.

Jay had gone to Moravian and then to the medical college of the University of Pennsylvania. To their father, going to any out-of-town college was a step up from his own attendance at Brooklyn College. Moravian was a major school to him, therefore, and the move to Penn had been pure triumph. Jonas's acceptance, with a scholarship, by Reed, had actually made their father weep. When they were to-gether, and drinking too much, Jonas went wet at the eyes, remembering their father's tears. Jonas had come home for law school, attending Columbia while living at International House, uptown, and then moving to an apartment at 112th and Riverside. Jay had gone from Penn to a residency in Syracuse, at Upstate Hospital, and then he had moved downstate into Duchess County, near Poughkeepsie, where he practiced pediatrics and lived in a large white house that had been started in the eighteenth century and, according to Jay, had rarely been lived in since. He claimed to Jonas that most of his money went toward making up for years of rot and structural decline. He never talked about the tall, coal-colored woman he had married in Philadelphia, and had lived with for two years, and who had left him for a man in Durham, North Carolina.

Jonas married too. His wife was named Norma, their daughter Joanne, their son Joseph. The grandparents were healthy and transplanted and long-lived in Miami. The boys were men now, Jonas thirty-seven and Jay forty-two, and progress seemed assured. If they were not what might be called a successful family, and there is always someone who wants to say that, then they surely were not a failure. They lived in America and were making their way.

In the part of Duchess County from which Jay commuted to Vassar Hospital in Poughkeepsie, there were still large areas of forest, and there were dirt roads that tore a car apart in winter and that in summer were half-grown-over with weeds and hanging brush. Jay lived nearly in the woods, except for the half-acre of lawn around the house, and the long scrubby hillside climbing away to the west. He almost never mowed the lawn, so he lived within a swollen circle of meadow that, from time to time, he engaged someone with a tractor to come and cut. It was a Sunday in June, and he had driven home from morning rounds in his old crimson Alfa-Romeo with the top down. He was wearing khakis with white porch-paint on them, and was even getting some of the paint onto the four fluted pillars at the front of his house. He worked with his back to the hillside forest and the road that went through it, listening to Elgar on the big radio he'd put at the edge of his drippy brush's reach, beside the cooler in which four Beck's beer bottles glistened. Paint spattered onto the green V-necked hospital shirt he'd swiped, and it flew onto his chin and, he was sure, up into his five o'clock shadow. One more white hair, he thought, and he smiled charitably at the notion of getting old because — he caught himself and warned himself and kept on smiling anyway — he wasn't taking his whitening whiskers and aging body very seriously at all. I will pay for that, he thought. Janet Baker was singing the Elgar Sea Pictures, and, as her voice soared, he dropped his thought about age and he shouted, in a strong and utterly off-key braying, to accompany the song about horses running on a beach.

Nell drove up his hill in her very old Jeep, with the big front grille that looked like a sneer. He not only heard her above the music and his own noise, but he saw, in the corner of his vision, the plume of dusty roadbed that she trailed, like smoke, below her. He put the brush down and stood, paint-smeared fingers on his hips, to watch her arrive. He watched her all he could. She was wearing dirty jeans and boots with flat heels and a tank-top knitted shirt, and he thought again that she must have more muscles than he, and yet she looked so smooth at the shoulders. He could see the bones below the neck. Baker rose again; she sounded like a cello. Through her, Jay said, "You have the chest of a bird. I can see all of your bones."

Nell grew red, as she often did, but looked down at her body and then shook her head, as if she disapproved. She shrugged and started walking again, and soon she was there. As usual, they didn't know what to do. She pulled her hair back and refastened the clip that held it in a clump above her neck. Her hair was very close to black, and very fine, and it was always falling down. "You must be wooing me again, to talk like that."

He reached to turn the radio off and pulled the cooler to him, across the patch he'd just painted. He handed her a bottle of beer. She nodded and unscrewed the cap and started to drink. He said, "What else? I invited you to marry me, and you declined. I take that very personally."

"I would hope so," she said.

"It's a kind of combat," he said. "Do you remember this from when you were teen-aged? You'd have a crush on someone and they'd be going with somebody else, or they'd just be too obtuse to notice you, and you'd spend most of your time being cruel to them and teasing them and vilifying them because you wanted them to just react? In almost any way at all? Do you remember that? I do. I think I must have done it a lot. Forgive me."

She finished the beer too quickly and belched a little. "All right," she said. "How's the porch? Oh. Oh, that's not really good, is it?"

"Paint's paint."

"Jay, you're putting latex over enamel. And you haven't even scraped the enamel. You got paint all over everything. You're incompetent. No. It's worse than that. You don't care about this."

He handed her another beer and opened one for himself. The sweat ran down his forehead, and sap beetles whirred slowly in the sun to land on the sticky paint and die there. He heard the tapping of a woodpecker, and a lot of other birds he never bothered to identify: they called, he listened, and that was all he required.

"And," she said, frowning, looking too serious, "you got paint on your face, and you got it in your hair — Jay! You got paint all over your   hair."

"Do you love me?"

"No."

"Really. Do you *like* me?"

"No."

"So marry me, then. We'd be the Great American Marriage. Can you tolerate me in small doses?"

"I don't think so. No."

"Perfect. We can get the blood tests tomorrow. Or I can do them here, heh heh."

"Pig. Painting pig. I will not be married to you."

Then Jay said, "No. I meant it."

She slowly nodded her head.

"Okay," he said. "Now tell me what you really think about my paint job."

And she did smile, then, so they sat down on the hill below the house, their faces in the sun, and they shared the last bottle of beer while Nell complained, as usual, about the bookstore she ran in Spruce Plains — that she wasn't bankrupt yet was the best she could report — and Jay described a child in the emergency room, body covered from waist to neck with a deep gouging rash that itched and hurt simultaneously, and that his family physician couldn't cure. He had remembered the article on gypsy moth larvae as the child's mother was describing how calamine didn't stop the discomfort. He'd swabbed the crusted lotion away and rubbed on a topical cortisone cream, explaining that the larvae of gypsy moths produce histamines, and they had set up an allergic reaction in the child, who had run shirtless through chest-high grass where the moths had laid their eggs.

"Pretty nice, huh?"

"You're a good detective," she said. "I like the way you look for clues. I like the way you enjoy it when you find them."

"Me too. It's the best thing I do. It's the only fun, really, except when little kids hug me and get better."

"You should have children," she said.

"And you have one I could use. You want to do a deal with me? Nell, are you listening?"

"Yes. I am."

"Okay. I have no idea what else I should say."

She stood and she jumped on him and bore him down. She lay on top of him and kissed him crookedly, half on the mouth and half beneath his nose. Then she pushed off him and left him slanted on his hillside, and she backed her Jeep and drove down the road. He lay there a while and looked up into the light, then he rolled over onto his hands and knees, got up, and walked back up to his porch, where he dipped his brush into the wrong kind of paint and continued to apply it to the unprepared surfaces. He turned the radio on, and the Fountains of Rome played. He smacked the radio hard, and it slid into wet paint. "Baby music," he said. He took a deep breath and then he apologized to Respighi. I don't need a baby, he told himself. I have one. He paints my porch. He paints my radio. What I have to find, really, he said to himself, putting the brush into a jar of turpentine that he needed, he realized, for enamel paint, but not for the latex he'd been using, and then pressing down the paint can's cover to save the wrong paint for the rest of the job, what I have to locate around here is somebody who could pass for an adult.

He tried his brother, Jonas, who was inside Jay's house, sitting in the livingroom and reading at old copies of *Science* and *Esquire*, sitting in an armless rocker that Jay had stripped but never refinished. Jonas sat as if he were in a waiting room in a country doctor's house. Jonas wore the trousers to the suit he'd arrived in — it was a blue-and-white Brooks crisp seersucker — and the same black polished penny loafers he had worn last night, and the same wrinkled blue oxford cloth shirt that he now wore rolled to just above the elbows. He was smoking a small cigar with a filter on it, and the air around him was the color of steel. He seemed to derive no pleasure from smoking, but he worked away at it, squinting against the smoke, blowing out as if it all were distasteful to him, but necessary. Maybe it was, Jay thought. Jonas had come in a long, wide Lincoln that matched the light blue of his suit. He had come before Jay was back from his evening with Nell, and he'd been sitting, although the door was unlocked, on the unscraped and as yet unpainted front porch. Buckets and brushes were waiting to be used there, and so was the radio, and Jonas had been sitting against one of the pillars, legs crossed before him, smoke around his face like bugs, listening to jazz on some disc jockey's dawn patrol. They had said hello while Peggy Lee sang her instructions that some poor sucker had better go out and get her some money like the other men do.

Inside, though Jay had wanted to sleep, or at least not talk, they had sat up late together. They had drunk beer and had sat in the old shabby kitchen, with its damp sticky surfaces, and ants behind the long rusted sink, and mildew on the wallpaper, gashes in the linoleum — Jay liked to say that he was taking his time in bringing the house up to snuff: he had lived there for seven years — and they'd discussed how Jonas had just run away from home.

Jay asked, "Did you leave them a note or something? So they'd know you weren't dead?"

Jonas shook his head.

Jay said, "No? You didn't?"

Jonas said, "No. I didn't. Okay?"

"Did you want to talk to me or what? Because I could go upstairs and we could sit around and not say anything tomorrow, if you're busy tonight."

Jonas waved his hand at Jay's temper, then he looked at

him. This was something Jay thought lawyers did with juries — the red, wounded little-boy's eyes, peering into you. Jonas rarely pleaded trials, however, and Jay knew that. Jonas did good research and wrote fine contracts and argued before law referees, but he didn't go to trial a lot. And, anyway, his eyes this time looked enormous and brown and liquid.

Jay said, "Is it really busted, you think? The marriage?"

Jonas shrugged. "Yeah, I think, probably."

"And the kids?"

"They get hurt. You have a war, people get hurt."

"Your kids, I mean."

"Who do you think I was talking about, Jay? You think I'm doing some kind of routine here?"

"Ladies and gentlemen: take my wife. Please."

"Fuck you, Jay. Okay? Hey. I left one of my kids crying and the other one's not talking to *any*one no more. Any more. Joanne thinks every person who's a grownup, he's a, like a traitor. I'm talking like the neighborhood again, you hear me? I'm falling apart here, Jay. I'm already treating my kids like casualties. You do that and they're your kids once removed. The thing is, you end up, you have to do that. Otherwise, the pain kills you. Your heart stops from it. So you do — you turn your heart down, like a radio. Then it don't hurt so much. Doesn't. Will you listen to me? I do some divorces, you know, just for favors. Everybody's splitting up, and some of them are friends of mine. So I handle it. Every fuckin' time, you see some kid get broken, like little rocks that a truck rolls over. It's all the same parts of the kids, but it's powder. Go put that together again, right? It don't work. That's Joanne. Whatever happens, I'm afraid she's finished. She won't trust people. And —"

The big eyes ran. Jay knew that Jonas was about to speak of Joe, his son. Jay looked down at the palimpsest of white rings on his old oak dining table. He made a big brother's decision and stood to walk to the wall phone and call Manhattan to say that Jonas was here and all right.

"No," Jonas said.

"You can't just drop out of sight, you know. You have one or two responsibilities, right?"

"Oh. Excuse me. I didn't think of that, Jay. I didn't know that, about my responsibilities. I was thinking, this marriage didn't work, you could take me down to some fuckin' farm around here or something and pick me out a new one. I could marry a cow or a fuckin' pig next time. Thank you for the memo."

"Pick out a room with a bed," Jay had said on Sunday night, leaving his beer bottle half-empty on the table and going up. "Don't cut your wrists except in the bathroom, okay? I've got rounds and then I'll come home and we can talk or something. Or yell. Whatever you want. Also, fuck you too. I don't think your suffering ennobles you."

"Well, that's not why I'm doin' it, schmuck."

"Putz."

"Fuckin' asshole."

"Prick. Goodnight."

"Thank you for the bed."

Smiling, and feeling fifteen, Jay went up to bed, and he was worried that he couldn't feel more completely unhappy. Before he fell asleep, to the sounds of Jonas bumping into things in an unfamiliar house, he wondered if Jonas's dilemma pleased him. He wondered if anyone ever recovered from being a brother, especially a younger one. He was certain that being the older was far from beneficial to the soul: no matter where in the world you lived, your younger brother, on entering some place or any time, was a stranger on terrain you might already have hoisted your flag above. You could not feel such confidence about your relationship to any other person's life and still be decent, he thought. Feeling indecent, therefore, yet not so unhappy about all of it as he should, Jay fell into sleep. The whimpering woke him up almost at once. He listened hard, to be certain that Jonas was actually crying. He wasn't. It had been Jay's own noises calling him up and to the rescue. On and off, he kept himself company for long hours, or so it felt, because the sleep he fell to was so frightening, and its nature unnameable. Blinking against the dark, and rolling, rolling, he wondered whether he had taken some of Jonas's troubles onto himself. That question was the answer. Hearing the word *decent* repeated by the secret self, he finally stayed asleep.

Next day, he spent fifteen minutes in the emergency room, instead of walking his ward, in explaining to two very well-read but misinformed parents that their little girl's *herpes simplex* — the child had a lipful of cold sores — did not necessarily mean that she would come down with genital herpes and infected children and a sex life demanding a terrible precision and tact. He administered synthetic penicillin to one patient and took another off intravenous feeding. He dictated records and signed orders. He got hugged by children in pajamas and he hugged them back. He got hugged by a nurse who weighed fifty pounds more than he, and who smelled of soap, and they traded shocking stories while he helped her find the key to the drug cabinet. He fed the goldfish in the corridor of the ward and then, after checking his mail and gossiping with doctors who also drove European cars, he went toward home.

He kept going, though, and drove into Spruce Plains, which once had been a sleepy town inhabited by merchants and a few teachers from the local school and some antique dealers from New York who wanted privacy for their domestic arrangements. They all were still there, and the one or two artists who kept vacation homes. But there were also people who sold health foods, and tall bearded men who wore faded jeans and who made pots and rugs and furniture, and there was a bookstore. It had no cute name because it was Nell's. The sign outside said BOOKS. That was what she sold — no art postcards, and not even witty place-markers, and no small anthologies of religious doggerel from greeting-card companies. She sold paperback books and clothbound books and she made enough money, along with a modicum of assistance from her former husband who taught history at Williams, to feed herself and her daughter, whose name was Rachel, and who was sitting behind the cash register when Jay came in.

"Hi, Jay."

"Hi, Rachel. Where's your mom?"

The child smiled all of her teeth. "Nellie!" she called. "Nellie! A man's here for you."

Nell came through the curtains at the back of the shop, glared at Jay, then harder at Rachel, and she marched the length of the store. Standing in front of the register, as if she were about to pay for something, she said, "Apologize. Apologize to Jay and then to me. Now. *Now.*"

Rachel got down from her wooden stool and stood on the other side of the counter. "How do you think I feel, being humiliated like this? I'm thir*teen*." Her face frightened Jay because the eyes were like marbles in something shot and stuffed; only the lips and forehead moved.

"You're grounded. You're starving for a meal. Your goose is cooked, and I'm eating it. I mean it. Look at me: Do I mean it? Apologize."

Rachel said, "Jay, I'm humiliated right now, but I'm also sorry. I didn't mean to act like some adolescent creep. It just — Jay, when you come *after* her like that, you don't know how crappy it makes me feel."

"Didn't mean to make you feel crappy, Rachel. But it isn't entirely your problem. And you made me feel very peculiar when you said that. When you treated me that way."

"I'm sorry, Jay. I didn't mean to imply you were sniffing around Nellie's legs."

Nell squealed, swung at Rachel's face, missed most of it, but caught enough to make a plopping sound of skin and to send Rachel into a fast pallor. "Ma!"

"That's right," Nell said, panting. "Try calling me Nellie again real soon, won't you? And be a smart little shit in front of grownups again real soon. You think you will?"

"I apologize," Rachel said, not crying, "all right?"

Nell said, "I mean, do you have problems, or what?"

"I think either I'm jealous of Jay's affections for you or I'm unsettled by their implications for our family."

"Will you stop sounding so *gifted*?" Nell wailed. "Talk like the other kids. Talk like *me*."

"I do apologize," Rachel said. "I'll go into the house and chew gum and watch bowling now, if you'll excuse me."

"No," Nell said. "You'll go wash your face and fix your hair and do chores."

"Ma."

"Now." Rachel's face changed, some of the stillness and sullenness leaked out, and she left, waving casually to both of them. Nell said, "Can you tell, I made the mistake of giving her some Salinger stories? They took her hostage, I think."

"Is she going to stay a chowderhead like that?" Jay asked.

"Not if she wants to keep breathing. Hello."

"You want me to take care of your kid? I'll stay here and nurse her."

"She isn't sick. She's just an adolescent."

"Okay. You want me to stay here and take care of you?"

"What'd you have in mind?"

"I thought maybe one of us might want to sweep the other of us off of his or her feet."

The door opened and two women in identical straw hats came in. One of them wore a patch over her eye, and its delicate yellow tone precisely matched her gloves, bunched in her hand and waved at Nell in greeting. "So much for the leisure to sweep," Nell said, waving back.

"My brother showed up. He's running away from home. I meant to tell you, but I was thinking about getting *you* to run away from home. Anyway, he's here."

"He's younger than you?"

"He's thirty-seven, and he's running away from home."

"To live with you and be a kid brother?"

"To tell me some of his troubles, maybe. Maybe today. I don't know. Let's not count on tonight, though, all right?"

"I didn't know I *was* counting on tonight."

"If I can put up with your kid, can we live together?"

"No."

"Then we can get married?"

"No."

"Can I nibble your toes in the village square?"

Nell giggled, then stopped herself. She said, loudly, "I don't think there *is* a village square in Spruce Plains, Dr. Reese. Perhaps you had some other place in mind."

He said, also louder, "Where I can nibble?" Nell colored, the woman whose eyepatch echoed her gloves looked over, and Jay left the store, making the sounds of chomping.

Jay drove back to the clinic he shared, in Millerton, with two other doctors, and he saw private patients until four, when he remembered that he had been expected at home for lunch. It was an uncrowded day, and his partners took his patients when he left and drove too quickly home. His brother was wearing the wrinkled seersucker pants and the wrinkled oxford shirt. He sat outside with Jay's bottle of vodka and two glasses and a plate of rubbery egg-with-ketchup sandwiches. Without speaking, they ate and drank across the picnic table from one another, under the willow at the side of the house. Then Jay talked a little about his practice, and about the day, and, apologizing for his late-ness, and gesturing with his full glass that Jonas should take his too, he led him from the table up the sloping small lawn toward the field that ran west from his house. They walked slowly, for their drinks' sakes, climbed the wooden fence and then descended, walking through cowflop and high grass, through swampy ground and dense thistle and very uneven dry field, away from the house and finally uphill, toward nothing but long meadow and bright yellow flowers that Jay couldn't name.

Then they stood, sweating slightly, but cooled by the evening wind that came up, sipping small to make the drinks last, and looking at the orange sunset that told of tomorrow's humidity. A blue jay landed very close to them and bounced twice, then flew away, nagging. "This is pretty," Jonas said.

Jay nodded.

"You still like it? Out here?"

Jay nodded again.

"You got girlfriends or something? Shit. It's probably nice, being a bachelor. I don't want it, though. That part scares me, having to date girls. Date. What a terrible word.

35

You stamp them November twenty-ninth or something. But I'm the one who wants to be free. You understand the contradictions here, Jay?"

Jay said, "I have a friend, a woman, and when she puts a disciplinary move on me, really rags me and tells me exactly what I should do, I tell her she's conducting orthopedic conversations — like a brace, or a cast, say. Orthopedic. I don't intend to be doing that to you, Jonas. So you tell me when I start, all right? If I do, I don't want to. And not that I ever doubted that you would tell me. But I wanted to ask you something, all right? I wanted to ask you: Do you love Norma? How's that for a question?"

"It's always the first one I ask people if they come and ask me to handle a divorce for them. Same question. And what I learned, Jay, is — this's a good one for you to know. Though you're not getting any younger, and maybe it's time for you to make a move, you know? I learned, anyway, that loving the wife or husband is very often about the last problem they have when they're splitting up. Well, hell, Jay, you did this whole thing. It was so long ago, I almost forgot. You know what I'm talking about. Sure, they say, right? Sure, yeah, I love McSchmuck. Big deal, though. See: I can't *live* with him, they say. Right? Or: She eats my soul like a carrot stick, this one guy told me. So how is loving her supposed to help, he asks, and then of course he cries all over my desk. I wanted to tell him it sounded like a very spiritual kind of a blowjob, but I'm a tasteful guy. But it's amazing how little it counts for, love, when you got a marriage that's dying, dead, diseased, whatever you want to call it. You remember that from your —"

"Yes. I'm so dumb about that," Jay said. They strolled now, breathing unevenly because of the terrain, but still, Jay thought, like a couple of old Jewish guys in the neighborhood, walking and discussing issues of international importance and great local impact. They walked at the same pace and they discussed. "I always think that love is the thing," Jay said. "This is in spite of Elizabeth, who you may remember from my days as cuckold-to-a-culture in Philly, and in spite of other people I've known since then, including this friend of mine now, who's also divorced. You know someone who isn't? But I keep thinking *love*, anyway. Everybody is talking *strain* and *need* and *alienation* and the timelessly popular *self*, and this one, which is Nell's current favorite: *erosion*. She says you can get eroded, and down to bedrock, and then you have to move on or you're washed away."

"That's it," Jonas said. "She knows."

"Does Norma love you?"

Jonas nodded. He was wet-eyed again. A swallow was near them, raging in clicks behind and in front of them. Bugs flew up, and mosquitoes clung to their arms and faces and necks. Jonas kept trying to light one of his cigars, but the matches blew out. He threw the unsmoked cigar into high grass.

Jay asked, "And is everybody — faithful to everybody?"

Jonas smiled, as if this time Jay were the younger one. "Yeah. So far as I know, neither party has entered into adulterous relationships."

"You sound like Pop."

"Who, me?"

"The time they had all the trouble."

"What trouble?"

"When I was in college, away at school? You don't remember? They almost split up, Jonas. You remember."

"Never happened. That has to be your imagination. Never happened, Jay."

"Jonas, it happened."

"No way. Not them. That's a *couple*. Bullshit, Jay."

"Bullshit back, Jonas. It's true."

They had stopped again, no longer old men outside the synagogue, though, but boys in an argument. Jonas's voice went higher. "Jay," he shouted, "you don't think I woulda known if the old man and Mom nearly got a divorce?"

"Well, you did know once. You cried at night. I heard you when I came for the weekend, to study for exams, I think. I came in and I asked you what was wrong, and after you told me to drop dead, you said it was on account of them."

"Never."

"Okay. Never."

"Jay. Really?"

"No, never, I was lying."

"Jay, come on. Tell me. Really?"

"No."

"*Jay.*"

"You're a baby, Jonas, you wiped it off your mind because you didn't want it there. What the hell. You were young. That's true, you know? You were young. I was seventeen, maybe eighteen. But I think it happened in my first year of school. I was seventeen. So you were twelve? Almost thirteen? It's a disgusting age. I realized that earlier today. You were thirteen. And you wiped it out. Amazing. Domestic amnesia, you could call it."

"Hey, *doc*tor. You want me to make an appointment so you could tell me about it? All it is, it's only my parents. If it gets important, you could send me a registered letter, huh?"

"It's simple. It's so simple. You know them. They wouldn't

let us hear it or see it. Which is why you probably don't remember it."

"*Defi*nitely don't remember it," Jonas said. "Am I a liar? *Plus* amnesia? Look at this, around here. You're practicing medicine in an office, you carpet it with cowshit. You know why?"

"All it was," Jay said, "was that Mom flew out to Aunt Anna's and Pop freaked out when she was late coming home. I mean by a *day*. He went out to the airport and she never showed up. That night — can you see her making him eat it like that all day? That night, it was in some hot month this happened, I think. That night, she telephones, and I don't know what she said, but it slams him down into his chair and keeps him there until she's done talking. I remember we were eating dinner. Horrible gray hamburgers and that peas-and-carrots mix from a can? He turned around to me. He was wearing those thin glasses with gold rims at that time. He turned while you were shoving the food in, and he said, 'Mother will probably be home tomorrow,' he said. I remember that. His eyes looked like yours do. Excuse me. They were all wet and they looked like yours. He knew something about her, or about them both, and he didn't want to. I think that was a lot of whatever he was feeling. He didn't want to have to deal with the information. Whatever the information was, he hated having to know it. And he must have hated what it meant. So out we go the next day. Kennedy was called Idlewild in those days. He took us there. He made you wear the school assembly clothes, blue pants and white shirt and red tie. He combed your hair so hard, you cried before we left. He was scared. He was *white*. We're standing there someplace at the field, and there's her plane, and people keep

39

getting off it. For him, Pop's a mess. He's turning his Palm Beach hat around and around, he's fingering the summer silk tie from Brooks. He was wearing the brown seersucker with the stripes. Do you remember that?" Jonas shook his head. "It was a suit he wore a lot. Anyway, all of a sudden, there she is. She must have waited until the plane was empty. It was quite an appearance. She stands up there in the door of the airplane like a conquering warrior. Oh, they knew some stuff we didn't, boy. At that minute, that second, when they looked at each other, I could feel it. They *knew* stuff. After a while, she comes down the steps like a queen. Pop just stands there, and then he says — I swear this: I never forgot — he says, 'Neither party has so far precipitated an unmarried state.' I said 'What?' or something. Hell. I *still* don't know what that means. But he just shook his head and then he just waited for her. But his voice, and that poor hat rolling and rolling in his hands. Oh, was he scared. Listen, if I didn't enjoy the show so much, I think I'd have peed in my pants."

Jonas stood in the center of his big brother's countryside with a glass in his hand and dusk upon them, and he wept like a very young boy. He didn't speak of Jay's cruel relish in the telling of the story. And he didn't claim that Jay had dispossessed him of a portion of his past. He simply wept. And Jay stood a few paces from him, and then moved in to touch his brother's shoulder, hot beneath the dirty shirt. Each moved back at the contact. Jonas continued to cry, while he smiled and shook his head. Jay nodded, as if to agree with Jonas that it couldn't be helped.

Tuesday was usual, in that no new diseases were presented in the practice, and no fevers spiked so high in the ward that children's brains were damaged, and everyone was going to get better. He stopped the aspirin for a child with stomach irritation, though he thought that the real source of irritation was the parent who dispensed the aspirin. He prescribed a seasickness medicine for the young woman who kept falling down; although he explained it as an inner-ear infection that interfered with balance, he could not persuade the child's father that she didn't suffer epilepsy, and he therefore prescribed Valium for the father, but not out loud.

To make up for the work shunted to his partners the day before, he came to his clinic early and worked without a break, and he treated plantar's wart, and he gave children allergy shots, and he tested their urine, and he swabbed at crimson throats. He stared down over tongues and under uvulae to ferret where diseases hid. The kids looked up and he looked down and, while they gagged over his tongue depressor, he made gagging noises back at them so that they watered at the eyes and retched and giggled at once. He was happy all day.

Because he'd started early, he finished early — it was too bright and pretty a day for parents to make the trek to the clinic; on a nasty day, with nothing better to do, they'd show up, he knew — so Jay decided that it was time for a drive to Spruce Plains. He needed something to read, Jay decided. He knew a bookstore, and he went there. Outside, parked in his red car, in a day so brilliantly lighted that even afternoon felt more like a start than a finish, he listed to himself what he must do. A quick joke with Rachel, if she was there, and no protracted teasing: she grew sour under scrutiny or with attention — be avuncular, but also be quiet. Be reserved. Hold back. Make no more jokes with Nell about marriage. Say: Nell, you are a secret person. I know more about the hidden places inside children's throats than I know about you. I understand that you're hiding. I respect this. I hide too — look at my high hill, my dusty road, my house of many rooms, surrounded by so much forest and field. I don't presume to say you need my comfort or that I can give it.

"Hi, Rachel."

"Nellie! Jay's here! Hi, Jay."

"I thought you were calling her Mom from now on."

The girl with large eyes and pale skin and a curly permanent — she looked to Jay like a high-fashion dog with human features — shook her head with, probably, pity. It came off as bitchiness, and all at once he felt the fatigue of his day. "That was probably what *you* wanted," she said. "Mom and I have a different relationship. We try to communicate our feelings. I have this need to be her peer. I think it has to do with my father and everything."

Jay nodded. He wondered what it would be like to give this girl an allowance and smell her shampoo and watch her sneak off to beer parties. He wondered what it would be like to become Rachel's peer.

"Oh, yes," Rachel said, snapping her fingers theatrically enough for Jay to see — he was supposed to see — the posturing. "I forgot. Mom's at the market."

"Which one? I'll catch up with her," Jay said.

"The one in Millerton. You'd probably pass her on the road. Sorry I didn't remember, Jay."

"You're close to peerless, Rachel. Thank you for thinking of it finally."

"Would you like to buy a book, Jay? Or did you come to talk to Nellie? Or whatever you do to her, ha ha." She showed her long white teeth, and Jay decided that he'd been reminded of terriers, Scottish terriers. He turned a paperback rack around too loudly on his way out: another victory for the dogs.

Driving home, he had two thoughts that rotated in his head like the twin propellers on a pinwheel, around and around, so that neither went anyplace, and everything else got spun away. He thought that parents needn't be villains to make whacky kids, and then he wondered who ought to take the blame, and whether blame had purpose here. And then he thought that children never should be villains because their throats were so tender and, in infants, the thighs and forearms so innocent and made to be kissed; and yet they so often *were* villainous, he went on as the pinwheel spun, raping women in parking lots and running amok in subways in New York and sitting in someone's rural bookstore with twenty-one-year-old eyes and the face of a cunning small dog and the tongue of an asp. Around and around they went, and nothing came of Jay's unwisdoms, and soon he was home, and there — parent and child, villain and victim — was Jonas to greet him.

Jonas was beginning to smell bad. He was starting to rot, Jay thought. He wore no socks. He had left his scuffed loafers, wet from high grass, at the side door, and Jay could see that his feet were rimmed with dirt and had dark long nails. The anklebones showed dark patches too. His thoroughly wrinkled and matted seersucker pants carried staleness through the air, and his same blue oxford cloth shirt was stained under the arms and reminded Jay of what a high school gym locker had smelled like. Jonas had shaved on his first day there, but not today, and his dark jowls and bruised eyes, the slackness of the skin around his mouth, were challenged only by his great round heavy golden watch on its wide golden band: it proved that he wasn't a bum, that he was a prosperous man of business whose life had fallen down to stink and disarray.

They had drinks in the field again, because Jonas liked the sense of a lot of room around him, he said. This time, they carried a vacuum jug of vodka martinis, and as they strolled, like two old men in the neighborhood, they drank with the freedom of those who know there's more. Pollen blew around them, and seeds floated. The breeze that carried them carried also the smell of cows and the algae on still water and the lavender that was planted at the edge of the lawn behind the house — a combination of perfume and decay, like the merging of colors on the bushes themselves, the bright light purple in feathery clusters melting into dull brown mush. The wind took all the smells away, too, and sometimes they walked as if sheltered from the sensual world, although it lay about them, breathing.

"How was your day?" Jonas asked. But he didn't wait for Jay to tell him. He said, at once, "I feel like a housewife, asking that. Did you have a hard day at the office, dear?"

Jay nodded and sipped and kept walking. The ground was spongy here, and he wanted to get to a higher, firmer place.

Jonas also said nothing. They walked, and sometimes one or the other would sigh loudly and sniff, as if to tell his brother how fine the air felt going up the nose and past the hidden organs of taste and smell.

Finally, Jonas said, "I called home."

"Did you talk?"

"Yeah."

"Was she glad?"

"That I wasn't dead or anything. Yeah. And that I thought to call. You don't leave somebody worrying you're dead or something."

"Did you talk more, or is that the way it was?"

"We talked more."

"Good."

"Not good, Jay."

"You mean you talked tough. You told her all about the facts of life, is that what you mean?"

"I told her the truth," Jonas said. "I told her what I've come to believe. Hey: three strikes and you're out. I swung three times, she swung three times, so we're out. Everybody's out. I said that. Even Norma knows it's three swings and three misses and that's that. I took her to a Mets game once. She fell asleep in the sun."

"You instructed her about love," Jay said.

"Love, we got. That's what I told her. That's not — with us, that isn't the problem. I wanted her to know that. It's — *needs*, Jay. It's different needs, is all. Everything. But I wanted her, so she would remember it later, I wanted her to know the problem isn't love."

"So if love doesn't matter, how come you put so much time in, telling me and your wife and Christ knows who else that love isn't in short supply?"

Jonas stopped, wheeled, pointed a finger at Jay, who was panting behind him up the rise that enabled them to look at the meadow below, and then the forest surrounding the house and the clearing it hid within. "Hey, don't crow about it. Don't get swelled up like you're teachin' me something. Because I don't see *you* with twelve kids and a sweet little wife or nothin', anything. Anything. You know what I'm saying here, Jay? You're the one almost never was married, and our mother goes around saying she hopes you're not a fag."

"She does?"

"Well, she doesn't say it. She thinks it."

"Maybe you're the one who thinks it, Jonas."

"Maybe I am."

Jonas looked at his brother, and his brother looked back, and as it hadn't done when they were kids, and as he hadn't expected it now, at their age, or at this moment, Jay's stomach lurched and hot phlegm crawled in his gullet, an instant's awful taste that subsided, but that was part of a fact now. He had tasted it. And it was not because of what Jonas had said. Jonas lifted weights in health clubs. He played basketball several times a month with men who once were boys with him in the schoolyards of Flatbush. Jonas would worry about men who lived alone, and Jay had known that. But it was what he saw when he'd stared at his brother: the retreating but still heavy hairline, the broad nose that in profile was close to the face, the upper jaw's overbite, the configuration of whiskers, the size of the very dark eyes. What he looked at every morning in the mirror, early, humming to himself while the water sent up steam and the utter cleanliness of the daily shave made him glad to be awake — that was what he'd seen in Jonas. He had looked at himself. He had seen how far and proximate, and both at once, they might be.

Would he, Jay, maybe married and with kids, living, say, with a beautiful dark woman who had not gone home to a Southern city, and never mind the cultural problem and the racial garbage and the neighborhood bastards who might sit on his children's lives with deadweight buttocks — would *he* be gone from them by now? Would he have fled? Would he have traveled this far from them? And what if Nellie came there tonight and said to him: Yes. What if he then held his temper for enough years to permit Rachel to possibly grow tolerable? Would he, one day, be fleeing Nell as Nell had fled her former husband to come here and sell books to women with matching hats and gloves? Was everyone born to be separate? Was his baby brother here to tell him *that*?

He poured them each a drink, and they drank. They said nothing more. He poured them each a half of what was left in the jug. It was getting cold. It was dark. Jay said, "Cheers. Here's to what you want."

Jonas looked at Jay with Jay's face; Jay looked back with Jonas's. "To what I *need*," Jonas said.

"All right."

And then they went back down the hill, and over the meadow, through marsh and firm field, and over the fence, and along the yard and inside. Jay made an olive oil and garlic sauce for spiral noodles. He left the garlic peelings on the stove and fetched a bottle of Barolo that one of his partners had given him. They ate and drank in silence, except for Jonas's pronouncement that the food was good. They put the dishes in the sink, and Jay said that he might, at gunpoint, do them later.

In the livingroom, Jay played records — the Vaughan Williams London Symphony — and Jonas went upstairs, perhaps to telephone, Jay hoped. He didn't know why he hoped it. Surely, he wanted it for Norma and Joe and Joanne. He wanted it also, and maybe he wanted it mostly, for himself.

At the door a few minutes later was Nellie. He had been nearly asleep, slumped in the armless rocker, and he'd heard the crushing of gravel stones beneath wheels. Looking out the window, he'd seen her Jeep. So he was up and shaking himself awake and moving to the door as the knock sounded. It was constant, and Nellie didn't summon him that way. She knocked and knocked, was calling him for help, and he skipped along the floor in his stocking feet, wondering why she didn't simply walk inside. Then, opening the door, he saw why. She was holding Rachel. She was carrying her across her chest, and she had knocked with an arm under strain. Rachel's face was too white. Her eyes were open, the pupils dilated, and she looked almost shocky.

He held the door wide and Nellie staggered past, heading for the livingroom and its broad sofa. The bass of the big speaker was growling. Nell, panting, went to turn the record player off. Her eyes were huge when she came back, still gulping at the air, to stand above Rachel, who lay on the sofa with her knees curled up and her fist clenched, the right fist clenched, and dark spots on her cheek and forehead.

"Something happened," Nell said. "I was — something happened."

He turned on the lights at either end of the sofa and he kneeled to look at Rachel. He expected that Nellie would tell him what the matter was, and he waited, but she said nothing more. He smelled Rachel's breath, which was steamy and fetid, weak, and he touched her face very carefully at the sides, and then he started to feel at her bones. The face was abraded and scratched, puffy in spots where the vessels were bruised against the bone. He knew that her left arm was broken. He stood, went for scissors and a quick wash of his hands, then came back to see Nell covering her to the waist with a comforter. "There's nothing wrong with her legs?" he said. Nell shook her head. She kept blinking, he saw, and he was worried that she was going to faint. There was blood on Nell's white shirt. She looked like a meat cutter or a surgeon, there was something familiar about the white garment and about looking on it for spatters of blood. Then he bent forward and down to see what Nell had done to her daughter.

He cut Rachel's sleeve away. He wasn't talking in his easy chant — he sometimes had to use it for injured children who were frightened — because Rachel wasn't frightened. She wasn't there. She watched him from somewhere back behind her eyes, she winced as he got the sleeve off, but she was pretending not to be there. He saw that the fracture was simple, a clean green snap and nothing puncturing the skin or major blood vessels. He went for tape and some old lath he'd saved for kindling. He splinted her and then, with a flashlight, looked once more at the bruises and scrapes, looked inside her mouth and nostrils and eyes, peering down into her secrets but not finding Rachel, just her blood. He telephoned the hospital — Jonas wasn't on the line, he noted — to say that he'd need an orthopedist at the hospital in half an hour. He ordered the X-rays so there would be no delay. He got Rachel up. "We'll take the Alfa," he said. "It's faster. You can take the Jeep if you want to come. There's only room for two in the Alfa."

He heard himself pause because, he knew, what he said next would matter tonight, later on, and tomorrow, when it would be just him and Nell and what they needed to say, and what they ought to be doing. Then he saw his brother in his rotting clothes at the livingroom doorway. His brother Jonas was watching him, but with Jay's own face. Jonas looked at the battered child, but with Jay's face, except that Jonas was smiling now: a great wide smile had twitched over his mouth from right to left, like a carpet being unrolled. So Jay knew how pleased his brother was about being right.

And Jay, no better than anyone, turned his back to the cruel and frightening face that he recognized, and he said to Nell, "And I'm not sure that I give a good whether you get there finally or not."

Nell didn't answer. She was looking at his hands. They were balled into fists. He held them cocked across his chest. He realized that she expected him to punch her, just as she had punched and torn at her child. He wondered how much she wanted him to, and he wondered how far he'd be tempted to start in swiping at her frozen face. He banged his hands against his chest while his mouth made a shape he hadn't determined. Her face collapsed into its pallor, and she stiffened as if struck, hard, with a hard hand.

He saw her eyes and then he turned from her. Rachel was gray-white with pain. He put the blanket around her carefully and he leaned above her to shepherd her out, past Jonas's grin, to his car. He buckled her lap-belt carefully, and he settled the blanket about her as if she lay in bed. Nell watched them, and then she climbed up into the cab of the Jeep. Jay started the Alfa and put it in gear without waiting for the oil to heat, and they went down his road, Jay and the girl he detested.

He hadn't intended to stop his car, but he did. He said to Rachel, "A minute. Just a minute." He walked back to the Jeep that was idling with a high roar on the steep decline of his road. When he walked past the brilliance of her headlights, the air at the side of the cab seemed densely dark. He said to Nell, "Let me see your hand."

"What?"

"The hand you hit her with. Let me see your hand."

"The — what did you say?"

"I want to see if your hand's hurt. You can break bones, hitting someone like that. Your hand has twenty-seven bones. Most people don't get to meet most of their bones. Is it swollen? Does it hurt?"

"I didn't hit her," Nell said.

"You didn't?"

She looked down her headlights. They converged on the little red car, and the still shoulders and head of her daughter. "You think you know about this," she said. "You think you know all about it."

He said, "I'll see you there."

He went back to his car and when he sat behind the wheel, he saw that Rachel was crooked in the seat, her head along her own shoulder, her flesh gone clammy, her breath a kind of snuffle and wheeze. She looked like a broken stuffed dog. He drove very quickly down the rest of the hill, descending alone with what needed him, and when he raised his face to look in the rearview mirror, the great high sneering grille of the Jeep was close behind.

Time Is Money

Her father was a corresponding member of the Book of the Month Club, and I was a pale stale college poet who wrote the Ginsberg pastiche and wore black. I was a virgin, and I was scared, and she was not. On the floor of her parents' livingroom, I defended a dream of virtue and the fact of my fright by withholding, by denying, and by offering up a maiden's prayer. Not until we're married, I whispered to Laraine, whom I would know for eleven months, as I looked up at the walls while we loved with our hands, grim little master mechanics, under gold-framed pictures her father had cut from magazines. I remember "The Rape of the Sabine Women," whose rolling eyes justified the sacrifice of sexual pleasure, and there was "George Eliot at the Heights in Highgate Cemetery," an ugly woman in dark clothing who stood on a promontory of the north London graveyard and stared.

That was what I thought of as I signed the short-term lease for the flat — where else? — in Highgate, on the edge of Hampstead Heath. I was twice the age I'd been when I first had heard of the cemetery, and I was there to spend a large foundation's funds learning about Victorian crypts and sculpted headstones. Before I was settled in the flat, I had forgotten to think about early middle-age, about a girl who had fully populated my seventeenth year, about another woman in America who had peopled my thirty-second, and thirty-third, and thirty-fourth, and then had changed her ways, and mine, by settling in another man's life for what she described as the rest of her own. I had almost forgotten.

I thought instead about my budget, and TV rental, and readers' tickets at the British Museum and the V & A, about coming home through the Heath from Flask Walk in Hampstead, full of beer after closing time, and about how little I wanted to do my project but what a sizable amount of good I might derive from caring for my work. I gave myself a week for orientation, and then I gave myself another week. I slept late, began receiving mail, said hello to Bill, the porter of the apartment building, said goodbye in the morning to Sara, Bill's small wife, who washed down the hallways and scrubbed at the stoop. I rode on the Thames to see the Cutty Sark, ate in trattorias on Greek Street, walked one night from Covent Garden to Swiss Cottage before riding the last bus home.

Home was the narrow flat with flimsy imitation Danish furniture and a small kitchen smelling of enamel paint, a corridor opening into bedrooms, and me walking back and forth on the toes of my new Clarks' desert boots, wondering what to do with this new life: all that money in the bank, all that good work waiting, all those letters from all those American friends, and all the extra time I had — I figured out that the woman I would live away from was six hours earlier in her life than I was in mine.

I left a pub in Hampstead one evening at dusk, happy with whiskey but sad about going home. So I walked on Hampstead Heath, where children in the pale lavender light threw frisbees and kicked black-and-white soccer balls to their parents. I watched the young mothers as they ran to chase the balls. Their breasts moved contrapuntally to the happy pumping of their legs. I went home, past the men's bathing pond and the small brick and wood cottage at the bend of Hill's End Lane, and I saw Bill, the porter, standing at the short brick pillar where the apartment block's name was posted. He wore a hard twill suit and highly polished black shoes. His hands were clasped behind his back, as if he mounted watch, and in the streetlights his glasses glimmered, his hard face looked red. "Hallo, Jeremy," he crowed, "you're looking a little seedy tonight."

"Evening, Bill. Nice to see you."

I walked past, but Bill's hand held my arm. The hand was strong; its grip failed to differentiate between me and, say, the handle of a wrench or rake. "Jeremy, I'm happy to see you. On my word now, word of honor, I've had a few pots at the boozer. I went to see the police surgeon's people — did you know I was a copper twenty years? Not a bent minute, I swear to God. It was my stomach retired me." Bill's face rippled and a pain ran down it toward his gut, which he rubbed. He held my arm.

I decided that the next morning I would walk up to the cemetery and start to work. I said, as if I cared, "Bill, you all right? Everything all right?"

He dropped his hand, adjusted his stance to his drunk wobble, and said with too much matter-of-fact denial, "No, it isn't anything, Jeremy, I suppose. They don't actually *know*, in point of fact. It's these stomach tests they've been giving me."

"Bisodol," I said. "No: barium."

"That's it. They make you swallow it. You see, they don't know what I've got." Leaning in, gripping my arm again, speaking in a hoarse and confidential voice, he said, "They want to cut me open, don't they?"

"What does that mean, Bill? How bad is that?"

"Listen!" he said, falling back a few inches against the pillar. "Now, I've had a few pints, but I am not drunk. I swear to God, and you must promise me, word of honor, not to say a word to Sara. I'd not like her to know."

I said the sounds I could think of to say, including "Don't worry" and "Hardly cause for" and the coveted "Goodnight," and I was in my foyer, turning the lock, switching on the television set, heating the kitchen grill, staying inside for the night and as far inside as I could get.

I walked up to Highgate Cemetery next morning. The high iron gates beside the abandoned charnel house, which looked like medieval ruins, were locked. Inside the gates, standing near a small stone shed, an old man in a loud sportjacket and dark dirty pants hushed the small white dog that raged at me. I passed through the bars a letter from the president of the Hampstead and Highgate Historical Society, and the dog took it, shook it, and dropped it onto the mud and gravel. "Jeremy Selden," I shouted through the bars.

"Who's he?" the man called over his dog's barking.

"Me."

"What's the letter about, then?"

"Getting into the cemetery."

"It's closed."

"He said you'd open it for me."

"Who? Seldom?"

"No, I'm Seldom. I'm *Selden*."

"You wrote the letter?"

"No. Look, I don't remember his name, but he's the man who wrote the letter your dog is eating."

"And he said you could come in?"

"He said he'd talk to you."

"Nobody talked to *me*."

"Would you read the letter?"

"Oh, gladly."

The dog barked, the man read, we discussed my name, and then he said something to the dog, perhaps correcting *his* pronunciation of my name, and the dog stopped barking, and, while I was led to a wide rutted avenue of mud and stones. the dog went into the shed. "Been closed forever," he told me. "And they can't afford to keep it up. That one" — a stone sarcophagus with an eight-inch thick stone lid split down the middle — "it got hit by one of the V-bombs during the war and there it is. They'll never repair it. That one" — another sarcophagus lid, this one shoved aside by a slender tree — "the Australians sent us a gift of ash trees. Grew like kafirs, and no one to maintain 'em. Now they're taking over. The days here are numbered, I'm afraid."

Stones leaned, many were down, most were defaced by painted and sprayed initials and important youthful decisions: WOGS OUT and RANGERS RULE OK. The grass was high and yellow, the small tough ash trees were crowding out the older growth, and shiny green leaves reflected the light metallically, so that their brilliance, and the crowding ash trees, gave a sense of jungled darkness behind the stones. He showed me where George Eliot had strode. We walked up a muddy hill, into dense growth, to see the stones of Charles Dickens' parents. We walked down the slope around a curve, down cracked and mossy steps, into a small street that was bordered on both sides by what seemed to be broken walls. Then I saw that they were crypts, many of them opened, all of them defaced. NIGS OUT. The tombs gave off a coldness, and they blocked the light, and it was time to leave.

At his shed, he gave me a map and told me when I might come to do my work. He called me "Professor Seldom," and I tried to give him fifty pence. "Nice to know someone takes it seriously," he said as he refused. I shook his hand— the white dog shifted and made a throat-noise — and then I went past the charnel house, home. And because the necessary arrangements were made, and I could start in next morning doing some serious early work at the cemetery, I naturally got up late instead, and rode the bus to West Kensington and the V & A. We passed Harrods, where I had shopped once on a trip with the woman who no longer cared to live with me, and I got off at the next stop, walked back down the street, and browsed in the Harrods food halls, paying a good deal of attention to products I wouldn't buy. I sneered at some fellow-Americans, purchased a bottle of extremely good unblended malt whiskey, then went upstairs to the book department where I bought a new thriller, thought twice about my budget, took a taxi all the way back to Highgate, and stayed inside, drinking somewhat too much and watching a documentary on Midlands potteries.

The flushbox mounted on the wall kept filling too full, and the overflow pipe that led through the outside wall to the ground near the stoop kept running. I called Bill, and he arrived later to inspect. He told me that a Russian-born Jewish novelist who lived in the building had been making complaints about the spillage. I said I'd never read her. "Oh, no one hereabouts reads her," Bill said, "but she's very famous in the district nevertheless. Quite rich off the sales of her books, I'm told. Now, she's one of the reasons you may see me walking about of an evening with a spanner in one hand and a flashlight in the other. It's no emergency, and you needn't fear. But the building, you see, is fairly jumping with Jews. And London, even up here, has gone down to the dogs. With the Arabs buying the big house up at the top of Highgate West Hill Road, well, you never know, do you, who's planting explosives someplace. I'm to see they don't do it here. I was a copper once, remember."

I thought of the embattled Russian novelist, coping with fame and wealth and the PLO, and I did go back up the hill to the cemetery next morning. The old man showed me its other side, across the road, where Marx was buried. We discussed communism, labor unions, Arab oil embargoes and the price of real estate. He left me to work, and I didn't. I wandered among the stones, reading names I didn't know, looking out the fence at the mothers pushing prams and the patrons leaving the public library across the street. I wondered if any of them carried a book by a Russian-Jewish lady whose perimeters were patrolled each night by a metastasizing former cop.

And that night, Bill was there to clatter tools and unscrew nuts in the bathroom, clear his throat and grunt with his efforts. I stayed in the little livingroom and finished the thriller. When Bill was done, we stood together to watch the toilet triumphantly flush. I offered him two pounds. His eyes stayed fuzzy behind his strong glasses, but his face tightened, and he waved a hand. "No thanks," he said. "I was twenty years a copper and I never took tuppence. No thanks."

"But I'm not a crook," I said, wondering if the foundation would agree. "I wanted to thank you. No insult intended."

"None taken, my word of honor. No money either, though." Bill hung on the toilet chain again, and again it stammered and roared. Then he rubbed his hands together and smiled, said, "Even with villains, though, and surely you aren't one, though not a fountain of information about yourself either, I have been known to take a friendly drink."

So in the small sitting room with its aquamarine carpet and the half-glued furniture of a third-class hotel, we sipped malt whiskey and Bill talked about English crooks and early retirement, and the malefactors to be found near the Billingsgate fish markets, hard by Guy's Hospital, where there still stood a bar at which doctors drank with grave robbers who sold cadavers for medical students. He and Sara were Welsh, he said, "Which explains why that woman's so hard." He sat with his legs tightly crossed, elbows in his lap, chin down. Sometimes, as when he twisted his face to find a word, pain made a pattern on his lips, and they seemed to slowly flutter. There was gooseflesh on his arms in the overheated room. I looked, and made assumptions, and insisted to myself that I was young, and working at my job, and that solitude was rarely sickness.

"Oh, she's a proper bitch, that woman, you make *no* mistake," Bill said. He sipped and shuddered, clamped his legs upon himself, pushed his glasses back onto the bridge of his nose. "Jeremy — we're friends, I think. I swear to God, Jeremy, but she's tough. The youngest in a family of eight. What did you say your line of work was?"

I mentioned the history of Victorian art, then asked some questions about Wales, then screwed the cap back onto the whiskey. "Good old Jeremy," Bill said to the room. "He knows how to tell you to piss off without hurting your feelings all that badly. I beg your pardon. But I have had a drink."

It was the sheerest romanticism, and the people under those stones might have loved it: Jeremy Selden, dismal in his life, sitting over gravemeat and bones, writing notes about the decorations of the dead. But I worked there that next morning, and felt that I was coming to the point where I might start to really do some honest labor. So I rewarded myself by riding to the piers where I caught the boat to Kew Gardens. It was too early for the full display of tulips, but there was a lot of red and yellow to look at, and the fine arching glass building — someone under Highgate Cemetery had designed it, I was sure — in which breadfruit bloomed, and tropical mists rode the circular iron ladder to the high gallery. That night, I saw Alec Guinness on TV, a ship's captain who cavorted under similar trees on a myth-ical island, and I smiled because we were colleagues.

And then in the morning, a scraping sound at the kitchen window — Sara, on the stone stoop, smearing suds and spattering gray water. Her face was sealed. And then, in the later morning, just after closing time, Bill was at the door. He smiled and offered half a pint of Haig. "I beg your pardon, Jeremy," he said, "but I have had a drink. I've made so bold as to buy us a bottle at the boozer in the hopes you'll have the kindness to join me." I cleared the kitchen table of its coffee cup and half-full milk bottle. Seeing it, Bill grinned. "Stomach trouble?" he asked. "Ah, that's a killer, that one."

Trapped, I sipped small. Bill gulped, in the victory of the trapper. He crossed his legs, shuddered as the whiskey dropped, then delivered a monologue about a crook he'd caught who was a painter. Bill had purchased one of his canvases "for the cloud formation." He said, "I'm a sketcher, did you know that? I'm an artist. I know something about clouds, and that yobbo was good. He was a leatherer, mind you, I don't mean to say he had much of a soul. He'd leather you from behind with a great cosh and kill you, if it hap-pened that way, so he could lift your wallet, and that would be that. But he was a lad with some talent. I thought you'd like knowing that, you being a student of the arts and all."

I poured more whiskey for him, sipped at my own glass, nodded. Bill shuddered, flicked his cigarette ash onto the floor and seemed to wind his legs tighter as he smiled and then grimaced — the lips worked from one expression into the other with no interruption: his smile was of pain, his sign of suffering a pleasantry. He said, "Have you missed the cats?"

"What?"

"The big fuckin' howlers outside at the edge of the Heath, where the garden begins. Surely you've heard them, Jeremy. That big black fucker who screams like a little child?"

"No," I said. Then: "I heard that one, one night."

"How could you not?" Bill sipped, I poured more for each of us, and Bill made the face and hung his head, then sat up straighter, leaned forward, elbows on the table. "He was a particularly savage one, that bastard." Bill shook his head as if a small insect threatened his eye. "The tenants, you see, they're a proper lot of rich Jews. They've made their money. They don't like the smell of cat-pee on the garage walls. They don't like the sounds the brutes make. They don't *like*. And I'm out there on my Arab patrol, and you know what these people are? Yourself excepted, of course. They're a mob of fat, monied cowards." Spit popped onto Bill's lower lip and into the air. He shook his head again. "They couldn't do it themselves, don't you see. So they come cringing and whining to me, and I'll do it, I'll *do* it, all right, I'll kill the cats for 'em. You know how I killed the big black bastard with the little baby's cry at two in the morning when the Jews are asleep and the Arabs come out?"

He sat back in his chair and his chest swelled, his arm

rose over his shoulders and his nose lifted as if he addressed a threat: "I took ahold of him. I had my spanner, you see." His face was white with rage, his lips were compressed and they disappeared into the whiteness of the face. "I took him, and I hit him and hit him and hit him and hit him" — the scrawny arm rising and falling, rising and shuddering down to the tabletop — "and I said all right, you bastard, come on, you bastard, let's go, you bastard son of a bitch bastard son of a bitch." The voice that came through clenched teeth was thick with mucus and fury, the square face shook on its slender corded neck.

He lifted his glass, put it down, lifted it with two hands, and carefully drank. His breath hissed out, and he set his trembling hands in his lap, recrossing his legs. "I'm not necessarily a violent man," Bill said in a lower voice, almost hoarse. "I'm really not. But I was a tough copper. I know how to do the job. I swear to God. I've got cancer of the stomach, Jeremy. I had another verdict from the police surgeon's office. I beg your pardon. I'm a little boozed up. I've had a few drinks to drink. I am dying."

Bill's expression, his muscular tension, even his smell — a compound of talcum, alcohol, tobacco and old sweat — were unchanged. My back was suddenly wet, and perspiration tickled my sides. "They're sure?" I said.

Bill held up the arm which had just been killing cats, and he squeezed the broad forearm, which was much thicker than the pulpy-looking bicep, pulling at arteries that snaked just under the surface. "I'm losing weight, Jeremy. Look at this." He tore at the skin, as if to pluck it off. "Is this what a man looks like?"

"I had a friend who had polyps," I said, hating my voice.

"Cancer, Jeremy. I'm dying. They say they'd like to cut

into me and have a look because there's supposed to be some small doubt about these famous tests of theirs."

"Do it, Bill. Try it."

"Once they cut you, Jeremy, you're dead. The trick now is not to let them in. Word of honor, I'm dying and you mustn't say a word to Sara."

"All right. Word of honor."

"I haven't told her, you see, and I don't want her to know. She's tough, she'll be all right, she'll be fine. Believe me. Your word of honor?"

"Word of honor."

"Because I think I can do it. I think I can live it through to my regular — the scheduled end." Bill laughed at the whiskey he lifted toward his face. Then his face changed again, the tumbler struck the tabletop, and Bill was closer, then, to the black alley where he slaughtered cats: "I don't want her to *know*. I can live it out. But she mustn't be told."

"Word of honor," I said.

I had given that word before: to the woman with whom I had lived in recent years, to the State Department when I asked for passport renewal, to my banker when asking for loans, to the children of friends when I'd promised small certainties in their immediate future — gifts and snowfalls, the absence of ghosts — and withholding from a stranger's wife the manner of his dying seemed to me, alone in another country, only one more truth or one more lie to be told. I capped Bill's bottle and put it near his hand. Bill, always the diplomat, banged from chair to doorsill to foyer and out.

It rained the next morning, a gray hard London spring rain, and I felt for the first time the excitement of what's alien, heard with pleasure the whine of the electric milk truck, smelled with hunger the bacon in the doorway of the cafe across from the bus stop; harsh tobacco in the crowded bus made me want to smoke; the buildings' responsiveness to British demands for space and light made me smile as if in discovery. I read *The Guardian* through on my way to the V & A, and I noted with considerable pleasure that an advertisement was printed in Arabic, with English lettering condensed beneath the soft rippled foreign words. It was good to see that occasional men in the streets, though they carried black umbrellas, wore long white robes and were followed by women in darker robes. Selden of Arabia.

The manuscripts I sought were in the Forster Collection, given to Dickens' friend and executor by Alec Hughes, a devotee of Dickens who had traveled widely in Ireland and Wales, collecting grave rubbings and interviewing the men — and one woman, who lived outside Galway — who had created tombs and headstones. The books, wide as business ledgers and bound in red leather, were brought to me on a gray metal rubber-wheeled cart. I found many examples of the usual inscription — "As you are now/So once was I," etc. — and sketches of funerary sculpture that were ancient-looking, little more than Celtic crosses; but there were angels suckling infants such as I had not seen, and accounts of greengrocers who buried people as a sideline, and one story of a man in Oughterard who had tried to embalm his wife according to what he swore was an original Egyptian recipe. And while I had a lot of information after a day's reading and scribbling and drinking coffee in the dark cafeteria, I was pleased to decide that I still had to travel to Ireland if the job were to be properly done. Moving, it struck me, was an art.

Walking down the steps of the museum, I wandered into

a flock of schoolgirls in blue blazers and short plaid skirts; the teacher who herded them blew a silver whistle and they stood still, giggling, until I was out of their midst. Down the street, a tall broad American — his tan raincoat was stiff and new as a flag — was pointing his finger at a short blond woman in a stiff belted trenchcoat. Behind them was a broad man, shorter than the woman, wearing a burnoose and carrying a small red woman's umbrella that didn't prevent his powder-blue suit from turning dark with rain. The Arab wiped his mouth, with embarrassment, I guessed, or annoyance, as the tall American pointed his finger again and gave the sort of order that I often saw American businessmen in London give their wives. Though I usually had to guess, I was certain I was right: No, *you* make the reservations if we have to go to the   damn theater tonight. Or: You want to go shopping? So go *shop*ping, I came here to work. Or: I called him a fag because he's a fag. They're all fags here, aren't they?

What I wanted was what was different, what was away, the feeling of things as foreign to America as I felt then to me, and I stood too long with my briefcase full of monuments, I guess, or stared too hard with too much resentment. Because the woman felt me there. She looked up, squinted, reached into her bag for eyeglasses — his finger still hung in the air before her — and she called, in a voice I knew, "Selden? I don't believe this. Selden? Get down here!"

It is true that you meet much of your past in foreign capitals; a life isn't so unpopulated or escapable, I guess, as you might like to think. That banality is acceptable. If it *is* a small world, then I'm prepared to make accommodations, and to work a little harder at sidling into its corners. But — Highgate Cemetery, Book of the Month Club, coitus deferred and livingroom carpet — some coincidences are intolerable, and not so much because they occur, but because of their particularity. To meet your dentist in New Orleans — all right; to trip in a Brussels restaurant on the handbag of the only transvestite you met in New Hope, Pennsylvania — perhaps; but to stagger into business such as ours, so unfinished: that is to admit of certainties in a life. Because so much of my life was uncertain, then, and had to be dealt with as a slowly-forming emergency, minute-to-minute, and not in response to a past that dictated terms, I flapped my briefcase against my leg and walked away through the schoolgirls. The silver whistle blew again, and again they giggled and drifted in place, and she called, "Selden! Hey: it's me!"

Her footsteps made me slow my pace, her voice made me stop, blushing. The tall American and short Arab walked slowly after her, and I watched them, then looked down to see the oval face and slightly cleft chin, the long nose, blond hair. Her voice: wind over reeds, I had called it in twelve or thirteen awful poems, and I had, though awful, been right. There was a breathiness to any word she said that made the hearer want that word to mean far more than it could have. In the dark especially, her voice had been charged with sex, even if it said that the fuses were blown.

She was saying, "Are you still a poet?" when the men arrived, and we all stood in the rain for introductions. Barney Korn, her husband. Mr. Halabi, her husband's business associate. Jeremy Selden, an old friend. Mr. Halabi put on blue-tinted glasses and made some gestures across his chest. Barney Korn nodded and didn't shake hands. I shrugged my shoulders and told them hello. And though it still should not have been happening, I wanted to say to her, "I have been with women, and not always unsatisfactorily. I only was scared. Though you were a kid, I was more of one. I'm a *late bloomer*, Laraine." Korn and I made perfunctory passes at mentioning import-export trading, and the scholarship that always seems trivial compared to moving masses of tomato paste or wool across borders, and we stopped a cab and asked the driver to cross against traffic to take us to Harrod's for tea. I wanted to say, "You go to Fortnum and Mason's for tea," but I only smiled and sat curled on the jump seat to sneak looks at her legs while Mr. Halabi made uneasy faces and Barney Korn asked her, as if I weren't there, "Where did you know him from?"

He decided, before she answered, that we didn't want tea, did we, so Korn directed the driver to take us down the street to a pub he had heard of named The Bunch of Grapes. Whoever read *Gourmet* in the States had heard of it too, and most of the subscribers were there. Korn complained about warm beer and ordered scotch on ice. Laraine ordered brandy and I did too. Mr. Halabi ordered vermouth and drank it quickly, as if to sneak it down before I noticed that this Arab gentleman had swerved from the Koran's prohibitions. Barney Korn, leaning over the little table, said, "Mr. Halabi is a Christian Jordanian." Mr. Halabi smiled — it was the sort of smile that Bill might offer over drinks — and he cleaned his blue glasses by rubbing them against his wet suitcoat; they smeared, but he put them on. Laraine asked questions — was I married, was I divorced, where did I work, what kind of museum was that, and how long would I be in London, and did I know it well, and why didn't I show her around while Barney and Mr. Halabi conducted business?

Barney Korn was not only very tall, he was broad-shouldered and tough-looking. His hands were wide and short-fingered, his arms looked thick even in a business suit. His face, though smooth-shaven, looked rough with irritations. His nose had been broken once, and it was small and crooked. His hair was curly and tight. He made himself swell as he looked me over and nodded his agreement to Laraine's suggestion. He said again, "Where did you know each other?"

"In college," Laraine said.

"This guy — " He looked at me, then said, "You went to Vassar too?"

"No, when *I* was in college, Lafayette," I said. "Your wife was in high school."

"Couple of eager beavers," Korn said.

"What is that, please?" Mr. Halabi asked softly.

"Hey," Korn said, "you know what?" He smiled, and the coarseness of his skin smoothed out somehow, the nose looked only charming, not tough. He spoke in the lowest of voices, all the time, and that was the realest threat — you had to bend to hear him, and he surely knew that: he wanted you to obey. I thought of the teacher's whistle, and how innocent its shrillness was, compared to the murmur of a man who made you bend.

"Those are mammals, are they not?" Mr. Halabi asked.

"Listen," Korn said, as casually as if he offered a cigarette. He did, and Halabi, shrugging, took one. "I think I'm jealous, Jerry."

"Jeremy," she told him.

"Jeremy. I think I am. You know? It's peculiar that you knew my wife before I did."

"Somewhat like the English badger, I believe," Mr. Halabi said.

"Why don't we *all* see the sights together, then?" I said.

Mr. Halabi was looking, and listening, and drinking his second Vermouth. What I said knocked his glass to the table and his shoulders back against the chair, his neck moved forward, and he said, "Ah, business first, I fear, Mr. Selden. We are a people of business, you know. Have you noticed that London has changed? She is a trading city, now that we are here. You know this? We are traders." He whispered too, lower than Korn. I had no idea about his accent, and I had no sense of the Arab peoples either, except that they owned all the oil, and much of London, and were said to want to kill the Jews. Mr. Halabi smiled and said, "It is our way."

"Business," Korn said. "You two guys, go ahead. Get me some souvenirs for the girls in the office. She can tell me about it. Jerry — Jeremy, excuse me. You want to tell me about your research?"

"Not a lot," I said. "You want to hear about it?"

"Not really," he said, smiling that good smile. "Let's get going, okay? You two meet each other someplace tomorrow, how's that?"

Laraine said, "You decide, Selden."

"A ride on the Thames. That's where to start. Then from the piers, we go into the City. It's the original city of London."

"The banks are there," Halabi said.

"And then we see," I said.

"Hey," Korn said, wagging his thick finger at me as he'd shaken it earlier at her, "you guys watch that then-we-see stuff, huh?" He smiled his smile, his low voice disappeared, and then the smile did, but not because he hadn't meant it, I think, so much as because he and Mr. Halabi were moving, and then so was Laraine, and not without some pleasure taken by them all in the rigorous pace. I wondered if I ought to live in America anymore, and then I wondered where else I should live. I said to her, "Westminster Piers, you can take the underground."

"A cab," Korn said, buttoning his raincoat. "She'll be there at nine, ten o'clock, right? She'll take a cab."

Laraine turned to say, "I still don't believe it. We're here on business and what do we find? Unfinished business. And it's how old?"

"Never mind," Korn pretended to growl. He smiled again, waved his hand at me, and walked. Mr. Halabi made nervous gestures on the front of his suitcoat and followed.

Laraine bent toward the table and said, "Never *mind* never mind. You be there, Selden."

"I will," I said. "I will. Word of honor."

Which was what Bill heard from me, again, that night, when we sat in my kitchen under a blue-gray cloud of his smoke, surrounded by my late dinner he had come to watch me finish while he drank the navy rum he'd brought. "This is true, Jeremy," he said, "I'll tell you something. It's an interesting study in psychology. I haven't had sex with my wife for — yes, it's five years. Sara? My wife?"

Even to a man such as I, who had little ease with people at their best, much less in the darkness of their intimacies, this was familiar terrain. Everyone has been there before. There no longer are words to be spoken in reply because these are the sounds someone makes instead of killing animals at night.

"You've seen how smooth her face is? How tight her bust — Jesus God, her breasts stand straight up! That cost me nearly two thousand pounds over the years, and on a copper's pay this is, and with no money taken on the side, I swear to God. Two thousand sodding quid. If you look very close next time you see her, you can find the little white lines around the ears. That would be your tip-off. She's had her breasts made smaller and her face tightened up. It sounds like repairing some fuckin' car, doesn't it?

70

She's fifty-two, and now she thinks she looks twenty-two, and for her it's like when she was in the WACs at the end of the war. That's what she wanted, you see. She wanted everything the way it was.

"And you know who had to change the dressings? You know who had to peel those bandages off with their runny pus and put the fresh dressings on? You're looking at him. Of course. I do the dirty work around here, don't I? You just think of the cats you don't hear. Now, I did try to go to bed with her. I swear to God. It's important in this to be fair. I did try. I'd get into bed, after she was healed, and I'd put my hand on her breast, and I'd feel stitches. I'd feel these soft little rubbery bumps. Scars. I thought I would vomit onto her, the first time I tried it. Jesus God. Stitches, all the scars even after she'd healed. You see? Can you imagine it? I was going to bed with Frankenstein's monster. I was touching the monster, and her all moving about on the bed and thinking she was beautiful, you see, that's the part I hated as much as any other."

When Bill stopped and drank and poured more, lit a new cigarette, looked at me for response, I knew that nothing should be said because nothing would be heard. Bill was talking to me from the place where there really weren't words. "I'm an artist," he said, "a sketcher. If I made a sketch of her, the way she really looks, she couldn't stand it, could she? She wants to look the way she looked in 1948. But I'm an artist. I make things look the way things are. It's the only way a cop could see things. She couldn't stand it. My word of honor. Do you know a woman with five mirrors in her bedroom? No, thank you. I'll stay on the booze, thank you. And she can sleep alone. She's got what she wants, she's a tough little bitch, and she's welcome to it all. *I* don't know her. *I* don't know who she is. And that is why, now you have to listen to me: that is exactly why you're not to say a word about this thing to her. My little time bomb. You've promised me, remember. Your word of honor."

"Word of honor," I said.

I moved the rum bottle closer to Bill, but he dropped his cigarette onto the floor and stood, managed eventually to step on the butt, staggering. He said with great dignity, "Well, I'm off, then. You'll have to come and have a meal with us, Jeremy. You'll do that, I hope." He slowly turned, pulled the kitchen cupboard open, and walked into cooking oil and cornflakes. I took him to his flat with one hand tightly clamped around his biceps, letting him lean his little weight against me. To watching tenants, Russian novelists perhaps, I must have looked like a friendly policeman helping the neighborhood drunk along his way.

That night, I drank some of the rum Bill had left, and I wrote a letter to the woman who had recently left me. I wrote four letters to her. Addressed to the New York apartment she had kept, they all began with a chipper *Hey, here I am in London*, and then, like our discussions of marriage, our later talks about growing old in different places, our final conversations on the subject of knowing each other at all, the letters fell into staccato statements about need. My final letter said *You didn't need me. You were right. And I am exquisitely tired of needing you.* I was hardly drunk, and surely far from drunk enough to write across three thousand miles, and six hours, about need, when what really appalled me was how ill at ease I had grown with Jeremy Selden. He would have to apply for a passport to live even with me, I decided. I carried the letters to the toilet and burned them above the bowl. I pulled the chain and flushed them down. As I turned the TV set on to watch a cockney detective, I hoped that Bill's repairs had been inadequate, and that the Russian novelist would slip on spilled-over water and crack a small bone on the leaked solutions of a lover lost in London. "Tolstoy of Arabia," I told the guy on the screen.

I wore a tweed sportcoat over a sweater and therefore was dressed in too little for a chilly day. The idea, of course, was to leave my own tan raincoat home because I knew that Laraine would wear hers. She did, and she was warm on the deck of the *Queen Boadicea* as we cut away from the pier near the Houses of Parliament and sailed. Mist lay over the river, and I wanted to tell her that underneath it, rolling in the strong current, were drowned three-legged dogs, and sacks of garbage, and, beneath them, according to the Greater London Council, salmon good for eating and, lower still, phosphorescent with rot, the bodies of the dead. I pointed out handsome buildings designed by Christopher Wren, and then the pilot told us on his loudspeaker that we were passing Lime House, where the pirates once were hung in chains to be drowned by the tides. He told us everything else, and she stopped listening and so did I. Like kids, we held hands. Like kids, we watched each other from secret places and waited to be caught. When we got off and were sitting on the bus going to the City, we weren't talking about London or villains in their chains, but about her life with Barney Korn, the car he had offered on her thirty-first birthday, the death of her father, her mother's happy widowhood.

"Don't take this wrong," I said, "but I bet your father died of stomach cancer."

"Why?"

"Did he?"

"Heart. A heart attack."

"That's a relief, believe it or not."

"*Why?*"

"The story is just ridiculous, believe me, pal."

"You always called me nick-names," she said. "It made you feel older than me."

"I *was* older than you. I still am."

"No," she said. "I always was older than you. We're maybe the same age now." And, as ever, I delighted in the sound of her voice; she could have been telling me the weather, instead of the truth.

Barney was rich, he was older than she was and older than I, and she thought he did some peculiar kinds of business. "So why do you stay with him? If he's a crook."

"I don't know if he's a crook. He's my husband. He is wonderful in bed, Selden. You'd never know it, but he is absolutely insane, he's a genius at it. And he completely loves me."

"Is this the part where I ask if you love him?"

"Only if you're nasty."

Barney was on the board of a synagogue in Syosset, where they kept their magical bed and parked the cars he gave her, and Barney's great regret, she told me, was that they had no children he might raise — males, of course — to lead the community, or state, or world.

"Yeah," I said, "I was wondering about that. He's such a heartfelt Jew, how come he traffics with Arab mercenaries?"

"Mr. Kantibhai Patell?"

"Who?"

"Halabi. Don't you know anything about foreign people, Selden? Barney is a bigot just like everyone else. Hates the Arabs. Hates Brown's, where I made him get us rooms. Half of the suites were taken by Arabs. He can't stand them. They're going to burn us in our bed, he thinks."

"Whereas you and he are doing that all on your own."

"I'm sorry I told you that. I wanted you to get excited. No, he really does — but he figured, you're in London doing business these days, you better hang around with an Arab. You look like you have a lot of backing, you know? So he hired Mr. Kantibhai Patell, he works for Barney's bank here. He turned Mr. Kantibhai Patell into Halabi from Jordan. You believe it?"

"Barney is very creative," I said. Then I added, "As you've made clear."

Near St. Paul's, we entered the narrow door of the City Vaults, then walked down two flights to the huge high stone-walled cellar, where businessmen stood at the bar to drink wine, and couples sat at round tables to eat roast beef and ham. We sat too, and drank half a bottle of the house claret before the meal came, then finished the bottle and drank most of another. I ordered port for us, and while we waited for the waitress to bring us each a second glass, we finished the second half-bottle of wine. And by then, we were admitting how we used to walk across the Parade Grounds near Fort Hamilton Parkway in Brooklyn, kissing a lot on the way, and how we used to go to the movies where I would sit with my arm around her, my hand under her sweater, after she had opened her brassiere catch, and how, on the floor of her parents' apartment, we would writhe and gasp and speak our love and ejaculate our love and never *make* our love.

"You were so scared," she said, leaning at the wine bottle, then leaning back as the port came. "You know what I figured? You were chubby. I figured you were embarrassed to show your tush. I didn't want to say that in those days. I mean, I did, but I was afraid to. I wanted to tell you I liked your ass, and anyway we could have done it with your pants on."

I shifted and said, as calmly as I could, "You know, I never thought of that."

"Sure you did. You thought of everything."

"I kept thinking I was scared."

"Oh, well, you were. You were. I was too, but *I* was scared because I was such an easy lay."

"So you were glad we — didn't."

"I think so. Yes. But I also really wanted to. You're blushing."

Which made me blush more, and which made me order more port. If I could have, I would have started a small fire to divert her attention, and mine. Thinking about fire made me think about their mattress in Syosset, and the one at Brown's, and I said, in what must have been the voice I used at seventeen in that apartment — choked with humiliation at the distance between who I was and who I wanted me to be — "Better late than never, maybe. Do you think?"

"Oh," she said, "Selden, you *had* to be thinking that, back at the museum."

"Well," I said. "Were you?"

"I was thinking of your teen-age tush, yes. I was."

So it was required that I leave some money on the table, that we walk up the stairs, that we find a taxi and persuade the driver to ride all the way to Highgate.

In the cab, near Kentish Town, I said, "Does Barney follow you around?"

"You mean suspicious-husband following?"

"Or his hired hand. Because an Arab guy was on the street where we got the cab, and he got into one behind us. Look."

"Selden, how many black taxis are there in London?"

"With Arabs in them?"

"Even with Arabs. They probably own the cabs."

"Yeah."

"He trusts me."

"Why?"

She leaned over and kissed me under the ear, and I remembered — I smelled it, then — Old Spice after-shave lotion, which I always used to put there because she liked it. I remembered Johnny Mathis records on the stereo set in the apartment, and a song about getting misty when someone thought of someone else — presumably, in those days, me.

But I looked back, we were on the outskirts of Highgate, and I saw the cab, with perhaps a foreign headdress floating in the back, and I said to the driver, "Highgate Cemetery, please. Main gate."

"You're still showing me the sights?"

"If anyone asks."

The gates were locked. The dog was there, but not his master, so we walked along the black high iron fence, and I pointed to slanting stones in the yellow grass. Her only response was, "How far do you live from here?"

"Would you like to see where Marx is buried?"

"I'd rather see where Selden's buried."

"Oh, Jesus, Laraine."

"Big baby."

"Yes. It's just down the road."

Bill wasn't outside and neither was Sara, though I was certain that Mrs. Tolstoy was watching us and making notes. Laraine walked through the flat, told me I was a good housekeeper, went back up the hall to the bedroom I was using, and closed the café curtains. In the half-darkness of the room, she took her raincoat off, and her shoes, and then the tan silk blouse and brown tweed skirt. Her brassiere was blue, and so were her panties. So, in fact, were my boxer shorts, which she discovered when she loosened my belt and pulled my trousers down.

She sat in front of my feet, with her knees drawn up, her toes touching my heaped pants. "You have a perfectly sweet behind, Selden. It's nice to meet it after all these years." She pulled at the shorts, they went down, and she turned me by grasping my knees. When my back was to her, she rose and moved her lips up the back of my right leg until their warmth and little nibbles reached the buttock, where she nibbled harder, bit, then kissed me. I turned, we bumped all over, took the rest of her clothes off, and mine, and in the chilly room, in the artificial darkness where love is made in the daytime — it is the most far-away place, such a room — we resumed the unfinished business.

Except that I stopped. "*Did* you see anyone in the street behind us?" I begged.

She pulled my face down to her breasts again.

"You're a married woman, Laraine."

"I'm your teen-age girlfriend."

"I'm —"

Holding my face there, then pulling my hair, and very hard, she whispered, "You better not, Selden."

"No," I said. "Except there is an Arab assassin stalking us, who is an Indian bank clerk named Kantibhai Patell. And a husband who sent him after us who is four inches taller than me and probably a Golden Gloves champion, or maybe an all-Ivy tackle. And the fact that we are ... what we're doing —"

She twisted my hair. "Selden, don't you start in playing those too-late-all-American-boyhood-blues at me."

I nuzzled into her. I moaned, "I love this."

"You better."

"I love you."

"You better *not*." And then she twisted too hard, and I bit her, and she clubbed me on the side of the head, and pulled at me, and I pushed, and we conducted unfinished business. The initial conference was a short one. So then we discussed, in some detail, the conduct of business in the past. Our appetites were whetted for work, and we went back to it while the day outside lay hard and silver on the fibrous curtains, and there were motions, seconds, immediate action, delaying action, gestures of great generosity, instants of understandable profit-taking, and, because one of us specialized in research, there were deep delving, scrupulous examination, hard study, and happy results. We celebrated free enterprise. We consummated deals.

I wanted to say, "I did need this," and I think I did. Because she said, "Me too." I wanted to ask her why, since Barney was the marvel of the industry. But I didn't. I thought to say, "I need *you*." But I didn't.

And she must have known. For as we pulled the blankets up, she said, "Remember, Selden. We aren't seventeen, either of us. That's the only time you're allowed to pretend you can have what you want."

"I *feel* like I'm seventeen."

"Sure. But you only get that once."

"So I'm seventeen and thirty-four at the same time."

"Only for now. It goes away."

"Yeah. And you go away."

"I'll write you," she whispered. Her skin was warm, and it was so smooth that I didn't want to stop stroking it. "No more now," she said. "Sleep. Stop thinking." Then: "You never knew how to do that, did you?"

It was Halabi who woke me, from the small garden walk behind the bedroom windows, against the curtains of which the light was gold when I sat up. I mean, it was Kantibhai Patell, the undercover bank clerk, who woke me, calling, *"No!"*

"You know who you're dealing with?" Bill snarled. "Do you *know*, you fuckin' wog terrorist?"

We did what we could. We had done it seventeen years before, when her parents had surprised us by waking to call her name from their bedroom. We kissed a dry-lipped panicky goodbye. We gave each other addresses. I ran with her from the flat to the front courtyard to the corner at the bottom of the road — looking, always, for Barney and a machine-gun squad — where she would find a cab, with luck, and go to Brown's to tell lies. Or maybe she would tell the truth, I speculated: maybe the truths were what ignited Barney Korn. The last kiss was moister, her lips were warm, her tongue was cool, and I didn't want her to leave any more than I wanted her to stay.

I ran back up the hill to the apartment block, thinking of her voice, her tongue, the sounds we'd made, how far and how quickly I'd come from my boyhood to my early middle-age — three and a half hours, I calculated — and then I was around the back as dusk poured in, to find Mr. Halabi, Mr. Kantibhai Patell, dutiful *sub rosa* agent, behind the enemy's lines, stretched on his back and bleeding. I was panting too hard, and my legs felt too weak to hold me, so I didn't move toward Bill once I'd stopped, and I didn't speak. Halabi-Kantibhai-Patell's blue-tinted glasses were unbroken on the flagstones beside him. They caught the bright last orange of the sun and darkened it. His right knee trembled, and his fingers opened and closed. The blood on the bridge of his nose and on his forehead was dark and bright, and what looked like a string of curdled milk was at the corner of his mouth. His breath sounded as though it was bubbling up through water.

"Yes!" Bill called. In his dark-blue shirt that was buttoned to the neck, probably his dusk-patrol uniform, he looked like a cop. The stubby silver wrench he thumped against his left hand threw reflections. "Yes, my friend," he said. "I told you I had my suspicions, didn't I? I'm not dead yet, and there's no fuckin' Arab killers coming into *my* flats in the dark of night to blow the Jews up in *my* parish. I decided to do a little early patrol is all it was, Jeremy. Sara thought she saw someone around the back. Oh, she's a ferret, she is."

Kantibhai Patell moved his head. I expected him to ask if a ferret was like a badger, and I bent, then, to put my hand beneath his sweaty hair.

"But I knew they'd come some night," Bill said. "I came around back here from the garages, and there he was. Crouching at your window, he was. He was just waiting. I didn't know for sure you were a Jew, Jeremy, until just now."

"Bill, this man —"

"I've sent for a panda car, Jeremy. They'll come in a minute and take him off for a little conversation."

"Bill, you could have *killed* him. And he's an Indian."

"Oh, this is no Indian, old son. You see that headgear I knocked off of him? What they call it in his country —"

His country, Bill's country, my country, Laraine's, and the country of the woman with whom I had lived. But the police car's Klaxon called at the road in front of the building, and, ever the man of research, the man of diligence, I sat on the flagstones next to Kantibhai Patell and looked at Bill, who was poised on the edge of his death, chiseled by light, protecting us all. I worked at how I would answer the authorities. It was a professional matter, I would say. It was my business, I would have to say. It was because I was, like Kantibhai Patell, a trader. "Your word of honor," Bill reminded me, as Sara came running, and then the police.

The New Honesty

They lie in the black narrow roads because they are too stupid to run from cars. In death, they are like little men — mouth open in a parody of appetite, upper paws thrown back as if in song, hind legs stiff and elegant, composed for nothing. These are woodchucks, groundhogs, in the movies "varmints," brothers to the rat. Men there shoot them, their long brown fur, buck teeth, small heads, wide bottoms, because woodchucks are said to forage in gardens and to undermine the foundation-stones of homes. They steal your food and cause your house to fall, a shooter said to Somerset.

At a sign of danger, the woodchucks in meadows stand tall at the entrance to their home, a hole. The danger, if it is a man with a rifle, usually a .22 such as boys might have, stands tall and shoots. The woodchuck, doomed to peer, shivering, at his death, is dead. Sometimes the creature is stripped of his skin, and his pelt is sold to certain pet-food factories or buyers of hides. Sometimes his body is entirely disdained. But with or without its fur, his corpse is kicked back into his hole — a warning, perhaps, to his family: *Stay away from my garden*. Or possibly: *Greetings from the world*.

Dogs ferret the corpses. They fetch them home and lie

in the backyards, at the borders of defended gardens, and they eat the rotted meat away from the bones grown soft in the dark tunnels of the dead rodent's home. Somerset observed this process on his journey through central New York State, to him a backward place of rusted auto parts on stony lawns, and encephalitic children littering the steps of trailers propped shakily on stone blocks.

He stayed in a town named Steuben Falls. The locals referred to it as The Falls, perhaps because they knew that Steuben was a foreigner. To Somerset, they were ignorant and traditional: there were no falls, there hadn't been for twenty-five years, since a reservoir had been created two miles upstream of the town. Their principal industry was the manufacture, in a long, low, mostly-wooden, two-story factory, of cold cream. The white perfumed mucilage was sold to several firms which ladled and labeled and sold the goop as their own. In The Falls, once a town of mills and railroad stations and high commerce, the residue of nineteenth-century prosperity was the lard-like matter shipped on trucks, as well as a brown-green stain which ran from the factory into the wide slow river that came from no falls and went toward what seemed to be a large swamp. Boys fished in the river, and Somerset always ate meat when in or near The Falls.

His assignment was to drive in rented automobiles through various out-of-the-way corners of the northeastern United States, seeking possible locations for a film. Never mind the subject of the film: it never was made. Never mind the director of the film: he retired to northern California, where he raised butter and milk and died of neglect. Somerset had searched for locations in Rhode Island and Massachusetts and had found nothing: shorelines were crowded with motels and machinery and with the homes of people seeking surcease. He was driving, now, from Rome, New York, which shared an airport with Utica, New York, into the center of the state, said to be undeveloped. He was making up jokes comparing Rome, New York, to Rome, Italy, and he was even laughing.

On the outskirts of Steuben Falls, he found a rooming-house near a rough dirt road that, he later learned, ran parallel to the brown-green river where the boys caught varieties of fish he presumed to have been mutated through cold-cream poisoning. He drove twice through the town — two main streets that crossed, some side streets that seemed to be truck graveyards and squares of red dirt, shabby houses, trimmed lawns, fields behind the houses and outside of The Falls that seemed given over to cattle and large gardens, hard-looking men who tended to stare and who seemed to know that Somerset was from another land. He stayed at the boardinghouse at the edge of town because in general it is safer at the edge.

He could see the husband, to the rear and side of the house, away from the high roadside sign that said ROOMS. The man was slowly firing and reloading, firing and re-loading. As far as Somerset could tell, he was shooting into the side of a low hill which blocked the field behind the house. Somerset came to know him as Jack, his wife as Mill for Milly, both as the Hartleys. She and Somerset talked, she in her white head-rag over pink and yellow plastic hair curlers, her small body draped with a man's red and black wool jacket, her slacks of synthetic fiber showing just a teasing inch or so of white ankle above her black cracked ballet shoes. The husband drew nearer, his gun at port-arms, his mouth open to show that his teeth were the exact brown-green shade of his municipality's river, his short arms looking muscle-less where they poked from his ribbed white tee shirt, his legs in dark blue cotton workpants, his feet in ripple-soled ankle-high work shoes over white cotton socks. He was little, pasty, balding and bucktoothed. He looked ill, or prematurely old. He looked, with his dark brown hair that sprouted everywhere but on his head — back of his neck, undersides of his arms, insides of his ears — like a woodchuck turned into a man by a wicked witch. His eyes were blue, and the sockets were clear of lines and bags: he looked like an old man (or woodchuck) with a baby's eyes. His wife, with her low-slung chins and blue-veined bunches of neck, her pendulous arms and chubby legs, her white long teeth and thin lips, her simper, her gray-brown eyes which looked full of hatred in spite of her whine and her full nose — allergies, she said; poisoned water, Somerset speculated — looked to him like the witch who had changed poor Jack from a groundhog into a mismade man. They were happy to have him, they told Somerset. The sky, as they talked, was orange from sunset, with mackerel clouds foretelling high humidity and, no doubt, pollution from the cold-cream plant. Sky there smelled like a bureau in a distant dead aunt's bedroom entered for the first time; it was redolent of strange perfumes, exotic life, and was either frightening or boring soon thereafter.

Somerset ate with Jack and Mill and with Isaac, their faithful and stupid labrador retriever, who was bony on high legs, and who loved everyone he saw. There were potatoes in their jackets, over-roasted. There was a quart bottle of Coke (named, by Somerset, the *vin du pays*). There was a kind of chicken, roasted perhaps as long as the potatoes, which fell from the bone; it tasted like fowl, though not rosemary or garlic or lemon, or even freshly-ground pepper. Somerset ate as much as he thought he must. There was ice cream for dessert, and Somerset was certain that nothing resembling milk or cream had ever touched the soybean pulp that Mill scooped from the box into wide chipped coffee mugs. Isaac thumped his tail each time Somerset looked at him. His eyes showed white as if he expected to be whipped. "Good dog," Somerset crooned above his Strawberry Ripple pulpwood ice cream. Isaac's tail thumped and he looked at Somerset and cringed. "Good dog."

Mill put the dishes into the dishwasher. There was no machine associated with kitchens, at least none he had heard of, that Jack and Mill did not possess, save a French food processer. Christmas would take care of that, he felt sure. They had no apparent source of income except their house, with its wide creaking floorboards and thick furniture encrusted with carved pineapples, yet they owned washer, dryer, dishwasher, vacuum cleaner, blender, shaker, and two sorts of toaster. He learned that Jack was a disabled veteran and Mill the daughter of the town's dead plumber. They did not adjourn, the Hartleys for TV, as he'd been sure they would, and he for bed, as he had wished he might.

Their movements easy and smooth from habit, they stacked, racked, wiped and cleared, then set the Ouija board down and pounced upon it — fingers pressing on the spinner, backs hunched, eyes focused — and only then did Mill think to say, "We do the board every night after dinner."

Somerset thought not to ask, since he did not think the Hartleys ran to Hine, or *marc de Bourgogne*. "There's some schnapps in the cupboard under the sink," Jack said, reading Somerset's mind, and not for the last time. Next to the Spic 'n Span and Bon Ami was a quart bottle of something that actually said Schnapps. He tasted peppermint, raw alcohol and, perhaps, fingernail parings. He looked at the drink in the green goblet Jack had encouraged him to use.

"Depression glass," Jack said.

"I can see why."

"We like it. It's worth a lot nowadays. But we just like it."

"Exactly," Somerset said. "May I ask why you haven't asked me about the movie business?"

"Don't care," Jack said, spinning the pointer. "Unless you want to tell us about it. I suppose you will."

"We're making a film about living in the country. I'm looking for what they call locations."

"Well," Mill said, suddenly looking up. "There's an *awful* lot of country around here."

Jack smiled and nodded, dutiful woodchuck. Isaac thumped, good dog. Somerset drank the drink. They spun, crouched, hissed, wrote down in elegant old-fashioned script the letters their metal pointer directed them to, and Somerset dreamed through green Depression glass of hot California sun over ocean, and of a small hotel at sunny Nuits St. Georges where he had stayed to contemplate marriage to a woman who now sold the homes of the wealthy. He remembered a room in Aix where he and a different woman had embraced on a marble balcony three stories high. Now he drove rented American cars through cruel landscapes and missed each woman he had known. He wanted to stop wandering. He wanted to go home and be wealthy and do something well — make films about subjects more important than he was, perhaps. "No character," the woman in Aix, an American, had told him. "Interesting. Beautiful. No character. You're like a bad dog — you know, when the breed runs out? You're like a bad-hipped small-brained dog." He suspected that she was right. But he admired himself for not entirely believing her. He was a good driver, anyway, as he rode to look for locations. Isaac thumped his tail. "Good dog," Somerset said.

"NO CHILDREN," Jack said.

"That's right," Mill answered.

"No?" Somerset inquired.

"That's what the board said," Jack explained.

"And it's true. We never had kids," Mill said. "You can believe in it."

"Oh," Somerset said oilily, the unguented outlander, "I do."

He had sleep without actual dreams, on heavy ironed sheets that were cold to the skin and that made him huddle under comforters. Spring there was as chilly as autumn elsewhere. Though he didn't dream, he heard voices, one of them his, talking and talking. It was true: there was much he could have said about his life. Save it for the movies, he told himself. Not listening, and falling deeper into his sleep, he answered anyway. When he woke, he had forgotten what he'd said.

He hadn't the courage for breakfast in the local greasery, so he ate with Jack and Mill, reading the Utica newspaper — four pages for national and international news, twelve for sports and local deaths. Jack and Mill were excited because an antiques dealer from downstate was traveling through the towns, a circuit-rider antiquarian, visiting Steuben Falls and Deansboro, Oriskany and Madison, working house-to-house, cataloging, evaluating, making offers on whatever genuine antiques the houses held. Jack and Mill, going back a long ways as they said, were certain that their house held treasures. They were eager to be assessed.

Strolling the village, then, in mid-morning, squinting into the bright sun lighting the clouds of central New York in April, three hundred miles above Manhattan, smelling the lingering cold which came from the just-softening soil, seeing how sparse the vegetation was — gardens just planted with peas (so Jack said), no lilacs yet, the trees just unfurling the smaller soft leaves, everything clenched — Somerset was greeted, at the river, by maidens aiming their bosoms at him, giggling and looking away, shy and reluctant and nonetheless there: a Steuben Falls talent parade. Surely, Jack or Mill had got the word out — There's one of the *movie* people lookin' around, and it wouldn't hurt for him to see your girl some time tomorrow, if you know what I mean. Some of them had taken showers, Somerset observed. They wore their most provocative outfits — shorts rolled tight against the thighs which, because they were young, didn't wobble when they walked; sweaters too snug, shirts too small and made of cheap-looking, synthetic fibers; shoddy shoes on thick raised platforms; perfume that blew on the oleaginous winds coming over the river from the cold-cream factory. They walked in twos and threes, giggling, girls of twelve and girls of sixteen and a girl of possibly twenty-one. He smiled and made his eyes seem to be evaluating, but he couldn't remain, he retreated to the Hartleys' and prayed his car into starting and drove out into the countryside, to try to do his job, and to escape.

The truth was that Somerset was not awfully good at what he did. One can't be, really, he consoled himself. The producer would know about locations, and the director, and especially the head of photography, perhaps even the writers. But he? He had come from the Woodrow Wilson School at Princeton, where he was supposed to be training for diplomatic work and where, in fact, he was recruited, without success, for the CIA; he went, then, to Stanford, where he worked at being a poet. From there to Culver City was a small fall — everyone there, it struck him, was working at being something they were not: some novelists, some screenplay repairers, some homosexuals, some het-

erosexuals — and in Culver City he found work. He brought
coffee to his uncle's cousin. Then he brought coffee and
some wild ideas for films to his uncle's cousin's partner.
Later, he brought dialogue — coffee was brought in by
another tall young man — to his uncle's cousin's partner's
boss. And soon he was working in the movies. He was sent
out, once, to buy a book for Marlon Brando. By the time
he had found a store that sold such books, and a parking
place, and had helped the clerk to locate a copy of *Nostromo*,
Mr. Brando had returned to his home and the office had
begun to hum with dedication to a new project. They were
acquiring the rights to an essay by Graham Greene. It had
been Somerset's idea, really. They were to do a film about
a boy who played Russian Roulette. The project flopped,
and Somerset was sent by airplane and hired car, after an
expensive vacation in Europe at his uncle's cousin's expense,
to scout locations. He was not a traveling salesman, at least,
he thought. He was a traveling purchaser, seeking sky,
weather, water, earth and local lives that he might acquire
for the rendering of fantasies written by committees on
behalf of wealthy dentists and oil conglomerates. Ambrose
Bierce, Somerset liked to remind himself, called destiny a
tyrant's authority for crime and a fool's excuse for failure.
Bierce had disappeared in Mexico, and Somerset vowed
never, at least, to do the same.

There were ridges to ride along, the two-lane roads nearly
paved, and one could look down along the valley in which
Steuben Falls squatted. The winds blew harshly up there,
and again Somerset doubted that it was spring. There were
few houses and they, unimaginatively, occurred only at
crossroads. Sometimes a tractor trudged along, but rarely;
once in a while, boys drove a truck past too quickly. Descending from the ridge, past falling wooden silos, and one

topless brown ceramic silo from which an entire tree was growing, past swaybacked gray barns and blistered houses that leaned away from the wind, past cannibalized truck cabs and abandoned tires and plastic bags of trash and scrawny children who stared at his car because there was nothing else they cared about, Somerset was thinking: To have a good life here, you must be a fool with no expectations. Or you must be a religious fanatic — a fundamentalist who thinks there *is* a Lord, and that He wants you to suffer. Or you needed to be someone whose life held, or manufactured, much beauty. The green was good, Somerset thought. It would glow with moisture under the right lighting.

Back in The Falls, when he returned, Mill was reading tea leaves. She was staring into the bottom of a white china cup with a delicate handle, and she was whirling the remaining liquid of the nearly-empty cup as though rotating a kaleidoscope. Apparently the picture clarified. She held still, then she peered, and then she whispered, "That's peculiar." Somerset nodded to Jack, who pointed at Mill and raised his furry brows over baby's eyes. Somerset nodded in return and went upstairs to nap.

When he descended, there was a new smell. Jack was drunk or crazy just then, because he weaved toward Somerset from the darkness of the livingroom they hadn't yet invited him into, and he said, as though he'd heard Somerset thinking of a question, "That's why she was reading the leaves. In case of it was a sign." Jack pointed down the hall that went from the foyer through the kitchen and out the back door to the garden and the hillside that rose to seal it from heaven. Somerset peeked, stared — he saw only hard western light, a pearl-shimmer that made him blink — and he walked down into it, blind, through the large kitchen and out into the yard. There was Isaac, alleging their long history of friendship, wagging at Somerset from ten feet away. Somerset thought that his tail made the earth resound like a child's rubber drum. Between Isaac's paws was something pink, about the size of a small animal's head. It was, of course, a small animal's head, a woodchuck's. Blue ropey projections at the bottom, he saw, were what Isaac had torn to get the head away from the neck. And those must be the little Disney-teeth at the other end, he thought, and the pinkish-grayness must be the meat's corruption, and the stench, he thought, must be of death and decay, the earth doing its famous work. Somerset started to cough. He knew the cough would become gag, and that he would shortly humiliate himself. So he breathed through his mouth, shrugged Gallically, and went inside, with Jack following, to meet Mill at the far end of the kitchen. She had probably been looking for him. For she held in her hand Exhibit B, a robin, it appeared to be, with one wing distended and with its chest eaten away, its bloody little organs on display. She dangled it from the wing. It bounced.

"Dogs don't eat birds, you know. Too slow to catch 'em. So a cat must've brought this by. We don't have cats, you know. I will not have a cat." Somerset had thought that all witches had cats, but wisely didn't say so. "And what I'm wonderin' is this — why did Isaac drag it into the house from off of the door stoop or wherever the golblasted cat dropped it off?"

In such situations, there is little to say. Somerset said it: "Is everything there?"

Mill flushed. She cried, "*No!* How'd you know to ask that? Jack? You hear what he said? No! Everythin' is there except the *heart!*" She looked at him with her wicked eyes set into her ancient face as though each of them had divined a central truth.

Somerset raised his eyebrows and said the only other thing he'd thought to say: "If you'll excuse me, now —" The knocker on the oak front door sounded. The third omen appeared.

Mill seemed to forget the reek of woodchuck, and the heartless robin redbreast, when she shrieked over her shoulder to them, "It's the *antiques* man!" Jack was several feet to the rear, on his knees at the kitchen sink, his shoulders and head shielded from them. Somerset thought he heard the pumping of bubbles in the bottle of peppermint schnapps.

The antiques man was about five feet tall. His upper arms, sticking out of a tee shirt labeled ROLLING STONES ON TOUR, were perhaps the size of a child's bony arms. He was the smallest, thinnest apparently normal man that Somerset had ever seen. He wore striped railroad engineer's overalls and workshoes. His eyes were surrounded by exhausted-looking dead brown skin. Speaking or smiling seemed to hurt him. He pushed his gold-rimmed glasses onto his small nose, rubbed his cleanshaven face, removed his engineer's cap to reveal baldness and age. He was close to forty, maybe over forty, the last of the hippies come to central New York. He smelled of marijuana and sweet aftershave lotion. Somerset was reminded by the smell of embarrassing evenings, in Bronxville, New York, with girls named Merri and Denise. The man's voice was deep, his locution as expected: "Now, folks, I won't take too long, because I am like wiped out tonight."

As he began his patter, Milly's hand began to wave wildly. Somerset, backing away, watched her other hand, containing the robin, wings furled, begin to wave as well. She was pointing with fierce delight at her wooden end tables, her Victorian love seat, her colonial kitchen chairs and, of course, her green Depression-glass goblets. She laughed her pleasure, a witch's cry, the sound of chains in an iron pot, shaken. Somerset left them to it, walking past the dealer's — what else? — orange Volkswagen van, on his way to drive thirty miles to a country inn whose advertisements were on the small state highway, announcing elegant dining in a rustic milieu. He knew that he would not order fish or fowl.

And when he returned from a meal of undercooked pork *rôti*, a bottle of Soft Mountain Red (like his childhood grapeade, only sweeter), the taste of tinned *petits pois* still high on the roof of his mouth, the whole awash in his after-dinner Tawny Hill Old Brandy, Somerset found a new, stronger smell of woodchuck chez Hartley, and a hostess in mourning.

First the smell: Isaac — cringe of white in eyes, thump of snaky tail, pink grin of gums, Good Dog! — had brought home what was probably the hind end of the decapitated woodchuck with which he'd greeted them earlier. It was grayer than the head, it had appendages which flopped, with the loose body, into grim puddings. It had a stench of hot old cheese. The smell lingered in the sinus chambers over the eyebrows and next to the nose. Isaac, happy old friend, good dog, stood guard above his trophy. Then, in the brownish light slanting from the kitchen, he aimed his thick-boned head at the varmint's corpse, and then he dove onto it — first hitting it with his brainless head, then scraping his thick neck and chest over it, wriggling finally with at least half his rib-cage and sometimes part of his flanks, until he had no doubt acquired some of the effluvium of dead rodent, which he guarded, tail wagging, when he didn't dive and roll upon it again.

Isaac repeated his trick. Jack sat, legs crossed at the ankle before him, in the wet dark grass. He drank peppermint schnapps — the bottle was before him and between his legs — in what seemed to be a green Depression-glass gob-let. He was composed mostly of shadows, but as he moved the brown light ran weakly across his little woodchuck's face. He was looking past Isaac at Mill, who was wearing a bright scarf of shimmering material over her still-wet, but uncurlered, hair. She wore pants of some sort, and a sweater that looked pilled from as far away as Somerset was stand-ing. In her eyes — they shimmered as the scarf did, even in the back-light (a professional term) — were thick tears. In her hand, dangling like a talisman, or evidence, was the heartless robin or one just like it.

"There were signs," she said softly, her voice unpleas-antly high.

"Well, we saw all of 'em," Jack said.

"We saw the head of the woodchuck."

"We did," he said.

"We saw the body of the bird with his heart ate out."

"Yes, we did."

"And then I told you what the leaves told us: no day of gain."

"*I* heard you."

"And the board told us: no children."

"Which is for damned sure right."

"And more death in the garden."

"We can see it. Hell, Mill, we can *smell* the bugger."

"Is there bad news?" Somerset asked.

"Oh, there is," Mill said.

"We're worthless," Jack said. "We're just about worth-less."

"Shall I pay you something in advance?" Somerset said, remembering a woman in a foreign city: no character. Bad dog. "Is there an emergency, I mean?"

"We been counting on the assay." She said *ass*-ay.

"Assay."

"From the antiques man?" Jack reminded him.

"The troll," Somerset said.

"Ain't he the littlest damned man you ever come upon," Jack said in all his smallness.

"He come in," Mill said, waving the chestless robin. "He walked around every room in my house. He walked into my closet and poked my lingerie" — *lahnge-uh-ree* — "and he even climbed up into the attic-way."

Jack said, correcting her, "We don't really have no attic. There's one of them little trapdoors into the crawl space up there."

"He felt of the bed," Mill said. "He slid the drawers in and out on what I *know* is a genuine cherrywood slabsided dresser. He looked under the hutch in the kitchen and he bounced on the four-poster bed."

"A remarkably comfortable house," Somerset said.

"Not to the antiques man," Mill shouted.

"Little puppet," Jack snorted, pouring more schnapps. "I kept looking, you understand, to find the *real*-size person who done his talkin' for him. By throwin' his voice?"

"Eight hundred dollars for everythin' in the house," Mill announced. "Eight hundred." She took a breath. "Why —" The robin bounced. "Why, you can't live on that."

"You can't *live*," Jack amended.

"Darlin' Jack is a drunk and a woodchuck killer," Mill said to Somerset. "I'm the poor daughter of a plumber who wasted all his money on his second wife. Now, we *can* live. If you mean breathe and walk around and not smell bad without refrigeration. We can live. But I mean *live*, don't I?"

Somerset was offended by Mill's assumption that he

understood her life so intimately. And he was attracted by how untouched Jack seemed to him. Jack had a gift for not receiving offense from a world intent on giving it to him. Jack was offended not so much by the dealer's estimate, Somerset realized, as he was upset on Mill's behalf. Give Jack some peppermint schnapps, a cringing retriever, and a little rifle with lots of ammunition, and he could live contentedly by killing little simulacra of himself and kicking them down into holes, watching his shovel-headed dog retrieve the corpses and roll all over the stench of their bodies, then bring the smell inside for the night. Somerset wanted to applaud.

"Now the door's a different matter," Mill said.

Jack, speaking through him as if Somerset were hardly there, were the ghost of the long-departed short-term tenant, said, "He says our door's mismatched. Says the house is pure not-much. Says the door's genuine Victorian off of some 1850s house near Albany or Renssalaer. The little window's bubble glass. He says it's almost green. Looks clear to me, but then he's supposed to know. I guess folks nowadays like all them curlicues in the wood and all. But he says we near to ruined it with paint. Figures there's all them coats of paint to get off of the front and back, strip it down to the buff, so to speak. Says he can sell it for a lot, but he'll have to have a fifty-fifty split of the proceeds. Now, you got to ask yourself: half and *half*?"

The bird whirled, spun, bounced, drifted in her grasp as Mill said, speaking to Somerset, he presumed, but seeming to speak through him back to Jack: "What kind of *life* is this supposed to be when everything precious we ever held onto adds up to eight hundred dollars worth of old junk? And the front door's worth as much as everything else put together? Just what you go past to get in and out!

And he tells us it's mis-matched? How can you live in a house without a *door*?"

Mill sat down in the back doorway. Jack, as if signaled, stood up, though very carefully. Isaac stood too, wagged his tail, then dived onto his pink-gray piece of corpse. Mill cried with evidence in her hand. Jack walked toward her with determination: a husband was coming to tend to his wife.

Somerset walked, on garden and gravel, around the side of the house, until he had passed his car and was turning into the front doooryard. At the unremarkable-seeming front door, lit by a little bulb enclosed by a wrought-iron holder, he stopped to run his hands over generations of paint that hid what was most worthwhile in the Hartleys' house from the world. Then he went in and up in the smell of Isaac and his triumph — it had spread to everything by then, was on the shabby carpet and in the soft chalky wallpaper of his room — and he went to sleep as quickly as if he had worked a full day.

When he woke, he felt like one of those portly traveling salesmen in motels at which, in Somerset's line of work, one sometimes stays. They try to sit at the bar after dinner, and they do for a while, drinking quickly and watching on the television set above the bar precisely what their pre-adolescents at home are watching, the family jaw slack, the family lips apart, the family eyes timid and unalert. Then they pull themselves from the stupor of the bar and walk droopily toward their room. One can almost hear them, as they set the alarm for dawn, compose the family features for sleep, say their prayer: "I got to get home." Since "home" was a rented stucco cabin in West L. A., Somerset really didn't have to get there. Nevertheless, he felt an urgency, on waking in the chill of early spring in Steuben Falls.

The stink he had slept in was subsiding. Jack, shooting in the far field this morning — his little gun went crack instead of making a movie-bang — would soon set the cycle of smells in motion again, killing a woodchuck and kicking his corpse down a hole for Isaac to find, once rot had set in, and fetch home to wag above, cringing, and then begin to dive onto.

He risked the small diner. It was clean, more spacious than he'd thought, and not very crowded. To his left, along the counter, sat men and a woman who had finished staring at him. In their dungarees or blue work pants and boots (the woman wore sneakers and white anklets) they sat now with their backs toward him, perhaps discussing the Hollywood mogul who had spurned the village daughters.

The little antiquarian approach from the back of the diner, speaking, over the Muzak, a mouthful of orange-yellow scrambled eggs and the time-honored "Mind if I join you?" which people say as you fail to think of ways of escape. He slid a plate of eggs and a cup of coffee to the table and went away to return with silverware and a glass of juice. The slowly defrosting music was the theme of one of, or all of, the James Bond films. He said, chewing, showing his perfect teeth, small but symmetrical and marred only by a marbling of egg, "Those people's house I met you in?"

"Jack and Mill."

"Jack and Jill?"

"Mill."

"Oh, yeah. They your parents?"

"*No.*"

"Fine, that's cool. But listen," he said, pushing the egg from his teeth with toast, closing his eyes. Little muscles rippled under the Rolling Stones shirt each time he moved. He prodded his tongue at his teeth. Finally, while Somerset was at last brought coffee and an English muffin, butter ostensibly on the side, and no napkin, he said, "They were very, very bummed out, Jack and Jill. Your friends. They friends of yours?"

"Mill. My landlords. I'm staying there temporarily. I'm here on business, I don't live here."

"Yeah. This part of the country, did you notice? You know anything about antiquities? This part of the country is loaded with dynamite material. And the locals here, most of them don't know what they *own*. They think they do. They can tell you how they remember when you could buy citrate of magnesia when you find an old bottle in the cellar for them. What they *don't* know, it's worth maybe sixteen, eighteen bucks when you sell it to the right people. All you got to do is pay, say, five-six bucks, and they think you're doing them this huge favor, you know? So this is a very high-profitability low-risk area. Buy pretty cheap, offer the goods like a small investment via cleaning materials and labor, then bide your time and sell at a significant margin of profit. So listen." He prodded his teeth with another piece of toast, cleaning specks of egg away, then chewing with relish. He said, "You can call me Smith if you want to."

"Smith."

"Yeah. It's really my name."

"Smith?"

"Incredible, huh? Probably, half your life you hear about guys on the run signing Smith into hotel registers, right? Because it's such a common name, right? And you never met anyone named Smith so how come in the movies it's supposed to be so common? So, how do you do. I'm a genuine Smith, just like my father." He smiled modestly, adjusted his overall straps, then pulled a pouch of tobacco from his breast pocket. Somerset watched as he poured tobacco into a paper, rolled and twisted, then lighted the cigarette with a wooden match he struck on the wall. "Bull Durham," he said. "Just like in the movies. You ever see a guy —"

"No."

"Couple of first times for you, right?"

"Mr. Smith."

"Right. Business. You're in a hurry, I'm in a hurry. The world's business cannot rest while those who tire too easily beg for a time to reflect."

"Benjamin Franklin?"

"Jim Smith. You ready to listen to me?"

"Mr. Smith, I'm only renting a room with the Hartleys."

"Jack and Jill?"

"Mill. I'm not an intimate of theirs, nor should I be privy to their business. I wanted only coffee and a muffin this morning. Did you see her smear it with butter when I asked for butter on the side?"

Smith shrugged his small shoulders. "It's like business," he said. "Risk and gain. The name of the game is venture. Nothing —"

"I have heard that one before. I'm trying to explain my relationship to the Hartleys."

"No problem," Smith said, closing his eyes against his smoke and stubbing his cigarette out. "No problem at all. That's why I'm here talking to you. Dig it: their house is worth shit. Understand what I'm telling you? It's all this veneer junk used to be made in Michigan for Montgomery Ward in 1925. Pure junk. Nobody wants that except for the local antique stores, maybe they can unload it on the tourists going through. Not me, pal. I pull a big rig to fairs all the hell over. I do good ones, you dig? I do Rhinebeck

in Duchess County, I do Westchester, I do Manhattan twice
a year. I do good work on good stuff and I sell it for like a
shitload of money very commonly. So I am not *about* to
acquire crap and purvey it as decent goods. I'm talking
reputation. Jim Smith is not a name I intend anybody taking
lightly. So these people of yours, they insult my intelligence
with a household full of, I don't know, strap it on a dinghy
and sell it to the boatpeople, understand, Jack?"

"That's *his* name. The man —"

"Sorry. Right. So I could see it right away. Still. They're
old people. They're ugly old people. They are obviously
high on antique-dreams. You know, biff, you score off of
the big-money dealers and retire. So I gave them half a rush
by doing half a lookaround. Zip. Montgomery Ward City.
Maybe one candlestand upstairs. But who needs it? Nobody's into candlestands anymore, they look too phony for
people's apartments now. What people want, they're into
hand-made quilts that have like mildew in the fibers and
they're falling apart. They're into these honest-looking old
Hoosier cabinets, especially if they're all-oak, with the flour
bin and the old glass doors and the canisters? It's the new
honesty, Jack. Rugged, simple, functional, but still handsome. You know. Bullshit, in other words. But that's the
times. I'm serving up what people want, what can I say?
Your people, they got *rien de nissy-vous*, they got zero."

John Wayne would have smiled, Somerset reflected, in
something like *Rio Lobo*, and he would have punched the
little man without standing up. In *One-Eyed Jacks*, Marlon
Brando would have called him a scum-sucking pig while
turning the table over on him and then killing him with a
sawed-off shotgun. Clint Eastwood, a happy medium, would,
in *For a Few Dollars More*, have shot him with a long-bar-
relled pistol, without either speaking to him or touching

him. Of the three, he was the only one who would have lit a cigar directly afterwards. Somerset sat where he was, regarding cold coffee.

"I felt really bummed out for them," Smith said. "This is not being patronizing. I'm a businessman, and it's bad business to feel sorry for people like that. But these are old ugly people and they are just about out of space. Where are they gonna go to have a dream? They're losers. Their breed is like extinguished. So I offer them a few yards for a few things. I can make it back over a few months. Still. Believe me, advancing money is bad business. You tired of hearing about cash-flow? Listen, you're not half as tired as I am. It's like a *disease*. Still, what the hell. Then I see this door. This is a decent door. I can sell it, no problem, and not for a little. Not for a lot, by the way, but not for such a little. But I was thinking about it last night, after I told them what was what. What was almost what." He smiled his perfect teeth at Somerset, who kept hoping that Mill had cast a delayed-action spell that, any moment now, would turn Smith into a hair on an ingenue's brush. "What I'm thinking is this. I can get into the door, bringing it back very nicely. That's rewarding work. But I have to confess, I *am* regretting my previous offer which, if it isn't charity, comes uncomfortably close to being a free pop for Jack and Jill. And I am wondering how good you could be, on a commission basis if you like, at lowering their expectations for the door and the household junk and everything else. You understand me?"

Somerset poured his coffee on the small man's head. Somerset mashed his muffin, butter patently not on the side, directly into the small, astonished features. It was a good moment, for Smith was very much smaller than Somerset, who felt quite safe. But he had forgotten a salient fact: Smith was in The Falls to spend money during hard times. The diners at the counter turned to study what Somerset was — he saw himself revealed, in their uncomprehending terms, to be — a bully, a victimizer of a man who had brought with him *cash*, a man who was flattering their family households on the strength of his ass-ay, a man who might purchase for them that week's meat and Coca-Cola. A diner with a bulbous bright nose, and glasses which looked just like the granny glasses Somerset had smeared with butter, pushed him back by the shoulders. A lean nasty man with a pointed hat and a pointed nose took Somerset's own long nose and twisted it in his cold fingers. The woman in sneakers said, "Just about damned time someone did that." Somerset wasn't sure who had won her approval, and for what, but it didn't matter. One more chap, young and strong, his face buried in a black beard, joined the fray. Somerset flailed, the others flailed, things shuddered and danced, and then Somerset had fled the beanery, was running while panting and bleeding a bit from the nose and upper lip. They didn't pursue him too far, probably because they were tending to Smith. He ran, however, until he came to the broad part of the river in the center of The Falls, where cars passed on the road leading to the highway, and where the cold-cream factory poured its refuse into the river which had no falls.

Two of them stood at the grassy verge above the river, just off the road. Today they wore blouses and skirts, perhaps thinking to represent the new honesty. They were pretty, Somerset thought. He hadn't time to tell that their prettiness was probably a function of being young; that they should look at their mothers, who once had been as pretty as they and now were wearing out; that being pretty and even seeming talented would never be enough; that not even possessing actual talent was enough; that neither the old delicacy nor the new honesty could ever be enough; that they should wash the makeup from their eye sockets and relish being children. He pretended to smile. He dodged around them and started once more to run.

In the yard again, where Jack was at the far end, staring, it seemed, directly into the hill, his rifle in the crook of his arm and Isaac for once out of sight, Mill was seated on the back sill, reading aloud from a folded-up newspaper: "I just turned to it and there it is. It says, 'It is urgent you handle budget problems. Put family security first or it undermines your peace of mind. New talents emerge when you spend time with *creative people*.' Isn't that you? Do you think? It surely is all about *us*, and it's pure Gemini. I say this tells us to sell that man the door, that little antiques fella."

Somerset breathed shallowly so that his panting would be less apparent. He pretended, then, to yawn. But they weren't looking at him. Mill was staring up toward him from the sill, but she was really staring, Somerset thought, through him and into her future. Jack still looked into the hill. It occurred to Somerset that he might take travelers' checks from his wallet, sign several, then leave. Suddenly, Mill focused on him. "Hey. You cut your face? You been in a *fight*?"

Tears leaked from his eyes. He nodded his confession.

"At your age," Mill said.

He nodded.

Isaac returned from over the hill. He was carrying a very old one, for they all smelled it just as they noticed his great shoulders in silhouette. It was long and pulpy, irregular in shape. Somerset thought that it might be a head, but it seemed too soft for anything containing bones. Yet it seemed too small to be a chest and hindquarters. It was like blared

brass in the strength of its stench. Somerset retreated. Mill
sat upright, as though prodded, and Jack, from the bottom
cried, "Why that's *all*, by Jesus!" Somerset was at the side
and turning the corner, making for the front door, when
he realized what would happen. He was holding the door-
knob when he heard the first one, soft as never in the films,
and he was pushing the door open, had its paint-covered,
handworked harsh weight in, when he heard the second,
and then the third, and then the fourth. Shutting the door
from within, he heard the fifth cracking against the hill that
sealed the house in.

Isaac hadn't made a sound. Good dog. Jack was holding
his fire, and then Somerset wondered if anyone was left.
Inside, the smell, despite Jack's shooting, was gathered and
dense. Somerset began to weep.

But Isaac barked a long, triumphant volley, then. And
Mill shouted, "You may be a fool, Jack, but you never
missed *nothin'* that bad. You old fool. Of *course* you still love
him. Now, you tell him so. Pat his head, you fool."

Somerset, wiping his eyes and sniffing, thought he heard
Jack make his reply. By then, upstairs, he was packing his
overnight bag. He signed traveler's checks and left them on
the Montgomery Ward bureau. He tugged at corners and
folded taut so that the bed he made up was so smooth and
so flat, it looked as if no one had sweated between its sheets.
He was calmer, by then. He smiled, in fact, when Mill
laughed, chains someone shook in a pot. This is almost a
happy ending, Somerset thought.

Critics

I used to say to my father, "Are you famous?"

And he used to smile his slow almost-frown — I understand now that he enjoyed the question, admired his own struggle for proportion — and he would answer, "Maybe a little. But not with the critics." Then he would finish with what I learned early and by heart: "And just about everybody's a critic, pal."

When I was ten, we rented a house on the coast of Maine, as far northeast as you could drive without entering Canada. It was a cottage, really, small and dark and cold, but a picture window in my parents' bedroom opened on the Atlantic, which, in fog or bright sun, made my father stretch and wriggle with delight. He was a sedentary man, wiry and pale, with bright red hair that looks to me now, in the colored photographs I don't often examine, like a cheap synthetic wig. He made little motions, that summer in Maine, which were new to me — in the openness with which he flopped shirtless on rocks near the water; in the smallness he suggested by bowing his head to stare at kelp on the tide; in the happiness with which he heard my mother sigh at the sight of diving cormorants; in his willingness to do no work, to only read green-spined Penguin thrillers and scribble postcards and broil fresh fish over driftwood fires on the beach.

My mother seemed taller than he, though I think they were both the same size, average height. She was beautiful and blond and angry. She was married to a writer of nearly-successful novels; she herself wrote essays for the glossy magazines and she practiced patience with his moods — the dreaming energy he drifted upon when he was working, the anxious chatter of his fright when he couldn't produce — and surely she loved him as I did, though neither of us found it easy to do when he snarled and yapped between the end of one book and the start of another. When they were published, and he moaned over *Kirkus* reports, crowed for *Book World*, stammered with rage at his publisher's refusal to pay for ads, she listened without answering; there was nothing safe to say. And it was her silences that provoked his anger, the *disloyalty*, he called it, of her failure to respond. Then they would fight. It once went so far as her packing bags for herself and me and demanding that he drive us to the airport. And then he would sulk, and then repent, and then apologize, and then we all would wait for the next time.

The summer in Maine was paid for with my mother's check from *The Atlantic* for a two-part article on a family of migrant grape-pickers as they traveled from California to New York State. It was my father's idea, though — to go to someplace new, where he would give us vacancy: no expression at all of the usual needs. When he thought I wasn't listening, he said to her, "This is for you." Gesturing at the ocean, the black and purple rocks, high tamarack: "This is for you."

Naturally, I was bored. There was the rowboat in the tide pools, the fishing from high rocks, the building of forts on the beach, the riding up and down our country road on my bike, occasional trips to a sand beach, the rainy afternoons — soaked dog fur reminds me of their smell — spent mooching up and down the aisles of small-town pharmacies and hardware stores. But there was, I complained one rainy afternoon after a day of sitting around while rain hung over us in a cold suspended mist, nothing to do.

"Nothing to do," my mother said. She was reading a magazine in the small living room, her feet tucked up on the sofa. My father was playing with his fire in the Franklin stove. "Nothing to do?"

I was biting my nails again, which was a pleasure I had pretty well learned to renounce except when my parents fought, and when we traveled. On his knees, face red from blowing at the dying coals of driftwood I had hauled from the beach, my father said, "Terry, this is the last stronghold of pirates and smugglers, and you're telling me you're bored here?"

He was skilled at that — dropping in a little detail I could *almost* count on his having made up, luring me from the privacy of a mood and into his constructions. I dutifully said, "Pirates?"

"Well, smugglers, anyway. You know Dennis's Point?"

"No. And there aren't any smugglers anymore, Dad."

"No? Look: Dennis's Point — well, you can't see it in this weather. It's the spit of land you can just make out across the bay, when the sun shines. It's almost in Canada. But it isn't." He was in an Indian squat, and he was in control. "That's the point, it's kind of a border. Well, if you get your heroin and cocaine — drugs."

"I know about drugs."

"Oh, yeah?"

"They're bad for you. You go crazy and you die."

"Exactly. Well, there are these ships, they come from France and Singapore, places like that, druggy places. And somebody on one of those boats has a deal with somebody who lives in a house that *looks* deserted, but isn't, over on Dennis's Point. Well, the sailor on the big ship drops this waterproof bag filled with drugs over into the ocean, close to the Point. It floats, see. And then the guys from the hideout across the bay take off in a very powerful boat, probably forty feet at least, probably run by a couple of big Ford engines, and they pick up the bag. They pull it in, go back to the hideout, and then some family-looking people, you know, a father and a mother and a kid, say, a boy — they just steam up to the house like a bunch of tourists on vacation, and they put the bag inside, oh, maybe a dark-blue sleeping bag" — like the one I slept in up-stairs — "and then they go home with a million other tour-ists. Nobody looks in the back of their station wagon" — like the dark blue wagon we'd driven to Maine — "and *boom*: all the drug addicts in the city of New York are crazy and joyful again, and very very sick, because the Jones Man came."

My mother, listening along with me, and doubtless in spite of her wish to read every page of *Family Circle*, said, "Jones?"

My father smiled the silly grin and said, "Cop-talk for junk. Addicts' talk. Drugs. I think, specifically, heroin."

"Well-researched," my mother said.

"Thank you, Caroline."

"You're telling me there are crooks doing that out *here*, Dad?"

"Ask Mom. There was a big article in the Eastport papers. The FBI arrested half a dozen of them."

"Right over there?"

"Ask Mom."

I looked at her, but she was reading the magazine again. "I think he made it up," she said.

I looked at my father, who was staring at her. So I tried. I said, "Everybody's a critic."

My mother put the magazine down a little harder than I'd have wanted her to, but before she could speak, the door thumped, as if someone had struck it with the side of a fist and not knuckles.

"It's the landlord," my New York mother said.

"It might be the cops," my father hissed. "Terry, get rid of the Jones!"

"Terry," my mother said, "please answer the door very politely."

Standing in the mist, with weak sun behind him, the man at the door had a kind of rainbow shine on his shoulders. His wire-rimmed glasses were wet, and his hair was slick on his head. He wore a navy-blue tee shirt soaked black, and jeans over heavy boots, and the tight straps of his knapsack made the muscles of his shoulders and upper arms look very large. He peered past me to say, "Mister Philip Maslow? Is he staying here?"

My mother said, "Phil." I said, "Yes." My father said, "Coming. Coming."

"Mister *Maslow*," the man said, pushing his arm past me to shake my father's hand. My father stood behind me, moving his free hand through my hair. "Mister Maslow, I heard you were here this summer. I'm Philip Hansen. We have the same first name."

"Hey," I said.

"Mister Maslow, I read your novel."

"Oh. Great — which one?" I heard my mother blow her breath out in an ugly noise.

"I only know the one, sir. *Morning Glory*. I think it's a wonderful book. I'm a real fan of yours. So when I heard you were renting here, I walked out from town to say hello. You've written more books, then?"

Without turning, I knew that my father smiled the way he did when I asked him about fame. "I've written a number of novels," he said.

"Well, gee," Hansen said. "It's a standout pleasure to meet you. *Morning Glory*'s one of my favorite books. I'll have to read the others."

"You walked a long way," my father said.

"Oh, no problem. I do a lot of walking. I collect mineral specimens, and I help take the census on the osprey. I walk down here a great deal."

"Well, I'd sure hate to turn you out in the rain," my father said. "Especially after a walk like that —"

"We're in the middle of *dinner*," my mother called from the livingroom.

"No problem," Hansen said. "I'll get down here again sometime. I do a great deal of walking."

My mother had come to stand behind us. I felt my father shift as she arrived. "He'll probably be writing," she said very loudly.

"I wouldn't want to disturb you," Hansen said.

My mother said, "But it's nice of you to call."

My father said, "Well. Hey — thanks a lot, eh?"

"No problem," Hansen said, looking through his spotted glasses as I looked through the little shimmer of red around his head and knapsack straps. "Just wanted to express my admiration."

"Really nice of you," my father said.

"Sorry about the dinner and all," my mother said.

"No problem," Hansen told them both.

And then we were in the livingroom, where I looked out the window to see Philip Hansen walking. When I looked in, and saw mother fall back to the sofa, and my father crouch at his fire and ferociously blow, and when I saw their faces, I started on my fingernails again.

My father said, "You know how many times anyone ever walked someplace in the rain to talk to me about something I wrote?"

"Very flattering," my mother said. "But he was weird. Did you see his eyes? He's weird, Phil, and I don't want him around here, at the end of a dirt road in the middle of no-place — you know what happens out here?"

"No," he snapped. "Do you?"

"I know what *could* happen out here. But I don't think Terry has to worry about it, do you?"

"His eyes, huh? That was what made you chase him? Those baleful glittering eyes you could see through my back from the livingroom sofa that made you tell him a little story about dinnertime?"

"Everybody tells stories," she said. "I thought telling stories was an acceptable practice around here. I seem to recall a perfectly *fraught* little tale about Oriental smugglers and the dreaded Jones Man."

"That happened to be *true*, Caroline. And that wasn't the same as what you did, and I think maybe my motives for telling it were slightly different from yours. You think so? You think that's a possibility?"

"We're out here to *not* worry about what some people write and what other people think about it. I mean, that's the story you told me during three days of hot driving. That's what I remember. Maybe I didn't understand that one?"

"Maybe I *do* understand it. Isn't it the one about making

sure I don't engulf you and the other victims with my omnivorous needs?"

She hiccupped a small laugh. "We're talking about the same story, all right."

"Yeah, well what if he came out to see *you?*"

"Philip: I don't need him to."

"And I do?"

That was when I went to the hook near the door for my yellow slicker, and I called out, "Going down to the beach. I'll see if there's any dry driftwood left. No more fighting, okay?" I got out before I could be cautioned to mind my business, or manners, or to be careful of the nameless dangers they thought resided only outside.

The path to the beach was slippery, and the low-hanging spruce branches dripped. I stopped to watch the moisture run down the trunks and needles of the trees as I had seen water run off buildings in New York. Then I moved on to the beach, which was all dark stones, some of them enormous; and in the center there was a great green-gray mass of some different kind of stone that was an island I often stood upon as the tide came in. I went past shattered pieces of telephone pole and rough timber, thrown up, my father said, by winter storms. I climbed down along the boulders, then up to the green-gray rock, and I stood there, frowning in imitation of my father, looking into mist and the fog that had begun.

The tide was out, so there wasn't much sea-sound, and I could hear the evergreens dripping. The fog poured swiftly, and I grew frightened; I always did. The fog sealed me up, it hid me from home. But I stayed where I was, nibbling at my fingers. "Hello," someone said, and I knew that it was Philip Hansen.

He was down on one knee just a few feet behind me,

looking at the knapsack mouth in which his hand moved. I wondered whether he could carry drugs from Dennis's Point in a knapsack, and whether he might try to convince me to sneak them back to New York in our station wagon, wrapped in my dark-blue sleeping bag.

"Finish your dinner already?"

Another story, I remember saying to myself. "Oh, sure. We eat really fast. We're — fast eaters," I said.

"Want to see something — what was it — Terry? You want to see something I found?"

"I don't know. What?"

He came closer, and I backed toward the edge of the green-gray rock. Then he extended his hand and opened it, showing me a small and many-faceted purple shining stone, a crystal of some sort. "I dug it out of the rocks up there, where the beach bends." He smiled so simply, though with invisible eyes, as if he wanted only that I smile in return. I tried to. But I was also trying to remember whether they made drugs out of any varieties of stone.

"It's pretty," I said. "I have to go back for dinner. I think my Mom's making dinner now."

"I thought you folks already bolted that," he said.

"What? Oh: *dessert*, I mean. We always take a walk before dessert. My Dad likes us to do that because of blood pressure and everything. Mom and Dad are walking back now and I have to catch up with them, okay? We're ready for dessert now."

He was closer to me, and his wet glasses tilted down as his fingers opened and closed on the stone. "Well, fine," he said. "No problem. I wish you'd tell your father how much I enjoyed meeting him."

"Oh, I will. Sure will. Thanks for letting me see your rock."

"No problem. Don't get lost in the fog."

"No, sir," I said.

"You can really get fog around the Point."

"Yes, sir," I said. I slipped on the rock as I started to run, but I kept running, over the pebbles and larger stones, up the slithery trail, under fingery branches and along the meadow floating in mist. I slammed the front door, locked it behind me, dropped my slicker on the floor, and went into the livingroom to find them sipping wine and looking at the fire.

"All clear," my mother said.

I sat, panting, and they waited for me to speak. But there was nothing to tell them that was true except my strange and nameless feelings, and I suspected — now I'm guessing — that they were as much of a story as anything else had been, that long day of vacation. The silence went on, and then my father said — I know it now as an offering to her — "He was some weird guy, that whatshisname, Hansen."

I gave my father one of his smiles back and reached for something to say. "He's probably the Jones Man, Daddy."

"Nah," he said. "That was just a story, pal."

And the way he took it back — desertion of me, gift to my mother, one more tale chipped out and extended and then withdrawn — sent my fingers to my mouth, then me from my chair, toward the stairs.

"Terry," my mother called.

"What's wrong?" my father asked.

She called again, but I was in my room and closing the door. I looked out my window toward the beach. I wanted to see Philip Hansen. I wanted no one who loved me to call again from the rented sofa or walk up the stairs to say a single word.

The News

Half an hour after the radio station in Monticello warned of problems in upstate New York, the sky over Route 17 disappeared, and a depthless glow lay on everything. It didn't make light, but it threatened massing energy. Harry felt it through his fingertips on the steering wheel.

Opening the window, sniffing the night for snow, he was soaked by something slimy, and then his windshield started going opaque, and his car began to drift toward the shoulder of the two-lane road. Freezing rain fell through cold air onto a colder road and the high-banked fields off the highway grew a crust that shone blue in his lights; the road went dirty gray and cold light from underneath made the macadam shine. And suddenly there were buses stopped, and a truck standing still in the passing lane, and cars off the road, their lights pointing up like the snouts of great dead animals.

He slowed, but he drove ahead, yanking his seat belt across his waist and lighting more cigarettes, but still going. There was no reason to stop — no-one in the apartment, because he was here, not there; and no one expecting him at work, because Harry had quit and now had no editor, and no Metro staff and no features to write on sick, dead, orphaned or abandoned children.

He turned to avoid the station wagon that seemed to be aiming at him, but the wheels didn't respond, he felt as though the car were floating, and he said, "Thank you," either to the force that botched killing him or the luck of the dumb, which took him and his inertia three or four centimeters to the left of the other skidding car, and then past it in a more or less straight line in the outside lane.

On the other side of the highway, a State Police car, with all its lights blinking, was broadcasting GET OFF THE ROAD CONDITIONS ARE HAZARDOUS THE ROAD IS CLOSED. The police car was bang-on with its nose against the metal roadside divider and looked as though it would be there all night. I am running on the luck of the dumb, he told himself, as his car remained on the road, as his hot windows kept the ice off while the windshield wipers kicked back and forth with the idiot energy of cheerleaders at a college basketball game, and as the radio downshifted, for an instant's nostalgia, into "It's a Sin to Tell a Lie." He sang the song with Oscar Peterson's piano and Joe Pass's guitar, and he was warbling "If you break/My heart/I'll die" before he knew that he knew the words. They made him think of the woman who lived in the house toward which he was driving, but he didn't know why, nor whose heart was in danger, nor who might die in what manner. But he had his suspicions.

He was off 17 and going, sometimes sideways and sometimes forward, always very slowly, though too quickly for the road conditions, and always smoking and coughing and sighing about broken hearts and death — what else should radio songs be about? — as he made his way from Route 11 north through the backroads he had found on a detailed map in the *Daily News* library: behind Guilford, behind Oxford, around Norwich on a small winding ice-slick called the East River Road, and then out to the final leg, the run north on Route 12 through Sherburne and then Earlville, each of which had one stoplight that, coated with ice, danced in the wind. He ignored the lights and drove through, cutting eastward, onto another country road, and then he was in gradual hills, going no more than fifteen miles per hour, and often less, sometimes drifting with his foot off the gas pedal, content to be in motion and this close to her house and still alive. But he was sweating now, with an apprehension that made him cough as much as the cigarettes he chainsmoked.

On the last toe of the final leg, coming past immense banks of snow frozen over with a glassy crust, driving under the bare brown branches of trees surrounded by thick but transparent sheathes of ice, dancing toward her in the dark, Harry started to pump the brakes. He skidded anyway, but safely, and he came to rest beside the other car. It was in the middle of the ice-covered country road, made narrower by mounded snow at the shoulders. Its interior light shone on the seats, but its headlights were off. He was going to open his door and walk to it, but he was afraid that he would fall and break his ankle and die of exposure before he saw her, or end up in some country hospital, with frostbite and in traction pulleys, suffering her impatience with common pain and standard diseases while her kids grew bored and he became afraid to tell her that his shattered kneecap and splintered ankles *hurt*. So Harry settled for sidling, skidding, inching and being lucky, and he drove close enough to look inside.

It was a horribly built car, this derelict, with a rear end too high and fat, the front a bit low, yet nothing about it streamlined. It was the color of meat streaks in cheap bacon, or the awful rust-colored pimples of pork that are found in fatty breakfast sausage. It was covered with ice, the windshield reflected his lights, but he was fairly certain that no one was in it. There was something familiar about it. He didn't know what. He smiled for his own car-pride, at which Katherine would have sneered, because he, a resident of Manhattan and a prisoner of public transportation, had purchased a Peugeot for $10,000 when he barely made that much in a year writing about dead babies for the *News*.

But the car sat in the road, and he sat beside it in his own car, thinking about abandoned ships and the Sargassos Sea and the Bermuda Triangle and upstate New York and the woman who, several years before, had turned him gently, devastatingly, away from her house, her children, their questions about Dell their father, Harry's fumbling answers about divorce and how much he cared for their mother. He knew why she had sent him on the long bus ride from where she lived then, in southern Vermont, back to his apartment in New York — because she felt that he, a fat man in those days but now a leaner one thanks to cigarettes and pride and loneliness, was devouring her just after she had swept her children into her strong arms and had leapt with them from her former husband's plate. A card had come from Katherine recently, and after he had told himself to continue abandoning hope, he had tasted a crumb of it anyway. And he'd grown miserable again, with as fine a misery, as cruel a need, as unsatisfied an entire *network* of appetites, as he had ever suspected could ruin someone. He had asked for leave and had been denied it. He'd whined — he had read about it in a James Bond book — for compassionate leave, and he'd been laughed at. So he'd quit, and Harry had turned happy, and here he was, leaving the abandoned car, fishtailing away from its smoked-orange color, which the storm soon curtained off, and he was heading for Katherine in her new house.

She'd nearly as good as called for him, hadn't she? It was a very old souvenir postal card, its colors as phony as those tinted photos of kids you still might find on someone's piano top or breakfast table — often, the dead kids he'd written about were survived by such pictures — and it said *Grave of Buffalo Bill.* On the back, beneath a lot of stuff about Cody and his wife Louisa, was Katherine's block printing: "Guess who's moving into your state? I'm on a new job. Kids are terrific. Hope all's well. K." And then she'd given her address. And that was as good as a trail of fairy-tale bread crumbs, he told himself as he swept down a hill too quickly and came to what might be her home. Bread crumbs made him think of breaded pork chops. He lit another cigarette. His tongue jumped to the tune of the windshield wipers. And Harry sang to Katherine, before he found her house, that if she broke his heart he would die.

EX BOYFRIEND SKATES ON THIN ICE, they might say back at the paper. They loved their headlines. JUDGE TABLES TENNIS MATCH. And here he was, in the center of New York State, a few hundred miles above Manhattan, and not that far from Canada, parking the Peugeot next to a rusty, ice-covered small car, and sitting for a minute so as to feel what not being humiliated was like, since he was probably about to depart from that station.

He recalled the *News*'s headline when President Ford sniffed publicly at fiscal aid for the city of New York: DROP DEAD the giant letters had said. DROP DEAD. She wasn't awake. No window lighted up for him in the two-story farmhouse identified by her name on the mailbox beside the long icy drive. The houses on her road were far apart from one another, surrounded by bare black trees, each of them alike in that each was squat enough to fight the winds and therefore ugly as a bowlegged wrestler in his crouch. Half a dozen of them, he thought, had been victimized by the same salesman, fifty years before, who had sold the owners imitation-brick siding, which seemed to be made of brown or yellow asbestos, that would bleed black tar in the summer and that in winter looked ersatz, ineffectual against the blowing ice and rain, and as bare of spirit as the people must be who bought and sold it. And no window lit up in her house, neither on the second floor nor down here at the side porch before which he sat in his car as the windshield crusted over and the engine grew cold.

After four years, you do not throw gravel at the beloved's window. Harry estimated that you could throw gravel or twiglets or even sizable lawn clods up to the twenty-fourth month; after that, you write or phone. If, after receiving a postal card that is clearly a come-on or maybe a come-on, an act of undeniable or maybe undeniable provocation, you drive to the beloved's home, and if you do so within, say, thirty months of having seen the beloved, then you might hurl objects at the beloved's window. But not after four years; after four years, you call.

Harry got out of the car and hunched against the wind and the eyes of neighbors. Looking around, seeing no neighbors, he relaxed and stood erect and fell on the ice that lay over everything. Before he was on his feet again, his lightweight parka was covered with frozen rain. He looked at his iced arm, and he thought of the abandoned car. His glasses, by then, were as opaque as the windows of the car, and he had to stow them in his pocket and squint into the darkness and rain. He saw nothing. It was a nothing similar to the one he'd seen when, four years ago, Katherine's former husband Dell, an angry man, had visited while Harry was visiting too. Dell had knocked Harry down and shattered his glasses. Dell had left in shame. Harry had soon afterwards left in blindness and without Katherine, and he hadn't come back until now. Once you see a nothing, all nothings look the same, Harry thought. BOYFRIEND BLINKS AT TRUTH. And, after four years, you don't just show up. You call.

On her ice-covered side lawn, Harry called. "Katherine!" he called. "Katherine! Kath!"

No dogs barked. No cows bellowed. No big trucks spreading sand and rocksalt passed. And no windows lighted up.

"Kath-er-*ine*!"

He felt her wake up. He heard nothing, and he saw nothing, but he felt her waken.

"Kath!"

And then a light upstairs on the other side of the house went on. Looking through a downstairs window, he saw to the other of the first floor and out, and there was a glow on the ice near that window, and it must have come from the upstairs bedroom. Katherine. He didn't call again.

Then there was light downstairs, on the inside, and then the side porch light came on, and then Katherine was at the storm door and then at the side door. He wondered if she might say, "Oh, Jesus." He had prepared for that, turning onto the driveway. He had decided that he would say, "Second-best." But she opened the door a little and she said, "Come on."

By the time he had slipped on the steps and made his way up and in, shivering now, turning to see that he'd left his lights on and must remember to go back down soon and turn them off, Katherine was in another room. He stayed where he was, looking at her record player, and the records, some of which they'd bought together — not as many as he would have thought — and the small black-and-white TV set they had bought together, and the low bookcase containing paperback science fiction and books about popular debilitating psychological conditions, and novels from presses like Red Dust and North Point. There was an old sofa, chocolate brown and fuzzy-looking, that he wanted to lie on. He had lain on it before. But he stood and shook ice from his shoes and water from his coat and sneezed and fumbled for his glasses to smear them nearly dry against his shirt so that he could see without squinting.

Katherine came in. It was as if she had waited around the corner, where he assumed the livingroom was, and had taken a deep breath and then had turned the corner, making her entrance. She was not quite that poised, but she nearly was. It was only because he knew where she blushed, far back on the chin, near the ears and up on the temples, rarely at the front of her face, that he knew how disturbed she was. She wore a flannel nightgown with small blue figures on a cream-colored ground, and over it she wore a white crewneck Irish sweater that he hadn't seen before. Her feet were in ankle-high slippers lined with fleece, new also, and in her hand she carried the tissue she usually kept in the left-hand pocket of her bathrobe.

So Harry said, after four years, "Where's your robe?"

And after four years, Katherine knew what he meant, because she waved the tissue and smiled. "Upstairs," she said. "I came down in a hurry, so I grabbed this off a hook in the kitchen."

"Hell of a woodstove," Harry said, moving forward to look around her at the Danish stove with its arched heating chamber.

"We really burn a lot less oil."

"Yeah, I'll bet. I'll bet. Remind me to tell you about this family in the Bronx, they didn't have any heat for six months, no hot water for six months. We did a story on them. I did. It smelled horrible in there. Terrific little children with big brown eyes, and this awful smell — codfish, it was some kind of fish. Everything smelled like old fish. Except, it was *them*. FAMILY THAT MAKES ITS OWN WARMTH was the story. We ran it on a Sunday because it was all about love. Of course, the kids are finished. We didn't do that aspect of it. How are the boys?"

"You're crazy, aren't you?" Katherine said. "You know, I really don't need this, Harry. I have to get to a job every morning. I have to drive all the way to Cooperstown."

"It's Saturday, isn't it?"

"An hour and a half, and in this weather it's much longer. I have to go over the mountains. I'm working at the historical association. They have a museum, and I'm sort of in charge of the photographs. They have a wonderful collection of nineteenth-century photographs."

"And you don't need this dropping-in-at-all-hours stuff. I can sympathize with that. I would hang my head in shame, as a matter of fact" — hard-hitting, clue-gathering newsman confronts them with the evidence — "except for this postcard I received." He took it from his pocket. It was folded and wet, and it was lightly crusted with tobacco crumbs and lint. He held it before her as if it were credentials. "Remember?"

"I shouldn't have sent it. I thought this place was closer to New York City."

"Closer would have been all right?"

"Never mind. I'm not making sense. But that's okay,

because you're crazy, Harry. Driving on a night like this. Coming here at — what time is it?"

"I don't know. My watch stopped. Katherine, I don't care. I admit it. I don't care, I wanted to come here. That's all. I wanted to come here."

"All that time on the newspaper didn't teach you not to be such a romantic?"

"All that time didn't teach me very much at all. And I quit. Oh: I learned how to type really excellently. I did do that."

"You quit your job. When did you quit your job?"

"Last night. Well, in the afternoon. Yesterday, really, I suppose."

"And then you came here?"

"Yes."

"Do you know why?"

"No."

"Well, at least you're still acting rationally. Would you like breakfast, an early breakfast? Harry! You're *skinny*!"

"Skinni*er*. Can I smoke?"

"Until the kids get up. In school, they show them movies about lungs with black stuff all over them. Then the kids go home and talk propaganda to their parents. I think they get a star if they inform on you. It's the Hitler system of education — send a parent to a coughers' camp and the State makes you a hero. Sure. Light 'em up. You didn't used to smoke."

"I used to just eat."

"Well, you look pretty, Harry."

"Katherine, so do you."

She turned some valves on the stove, and then she told him to take his shoes off and sit in the rocker in the kitchen while she took scrapple from the freezer, cut it with a little coping saw, and put it in a pan to slowly fry. He didn't know which to look at first, Katherine or her kitchen, because she announced herself, always, through her rooms. But as she worked he watched only her. Her face was gaunter, or had somehow reshaped itself; or perhaps he hadn't wanted to remember that she was two years older than he, who was thirty-five, and had always been leaner, and still of course was an inch taller. Her face was hardening into a single face, he thought, whereas she had offered many to him and to the world when he'd known her before. It was a benevolent face, the forehead wrinkled because her eyes seemed wide under lifted brows, as if she were surprised but didn't object to whatever surprised her. He knew her blue eyes well, and the nature of her forehead in repose, and he decided that he preferred some of the other expressions he had seen her fold into. As if her face were a creature that knew how to survive in a world of staring people, it had grown the benign expression, he guessed, to counter the one that lived, from Katherine's nose down, on its own: deep parentheses, curving the triangle from her nostrils to the corners of her mouth; a slight lag at the right-hand corner of her mouth, as if the lips themselves would make the face unhappy if they lived there on their own. It was a handsome face, it was a pretty woman's face, and it was surrounded by nearly-blond hair cut short and growing thick and shiny around the face, and yet it was the face of a woman who seemed to be in danger of disintegrating. She gave you a choice with that face, Harry thought, sitting by Katherine's oak kitchen cabinet and slowly rocking in and out of his smoke. You could choose to squint, and tell a little lie, and announce that she was gorgeous. Or you could look very hard and want to hug her and then go to Sears,

Roebuck with her to shop for maybe tools and finishing nails and a soda, and then come home and make something sturdy so that she could store trivial objects in it.

He woke in the chair. The kitchen lights were out, and wooden shutters were over all the windows but one. Someone had taken his cigarette, and the scrapple wasn't cooking. He thought of congealed fat and soggy meat and then he recalled the Aguilar children, with large eyes and pilled, soiled synthetic-fiber sweaters on their thin bodies, who drank cold water in the cold apartment on East 139th Street. "You got to feel fulled with something," Mrs. Aguilar had told him, gesturing at her children and watching him write it all down. Knowing that she was on the public record, she wept. Harry had done enough stories like hers — the intrepid journalist, stooping to sordid nasty-landlord articles — to understand that her tears didn't belie her real distress: she was, simply, a person who knew when to do it out loud, and that leads us to this upstate New York adventure, Harry thought, and this house and the people herein.

His legs ached from holding him steady in the rocker as he slept, and from the clutching he had done — third to second, third to second — on the ice-covered roads. His eyes inside the streaky lenses of his glasses were sore from staring at the ice. And, of course, he was frightened, and more than he'd been when his long day's motion had swept him along to the driveway and then the rooms of her house. *Now* he saw Katherine standing in her baggy white sweater over her cream-colored nightgown. *Now* he imagined her toes splayed inside the slippers as she held to the doorframe and watched him slide up and down her icy steps. And *now* he had to meet her, as if for the first time in years, and wonder whom she really saw when she looked upon him, and what she thought of this man, and what her children would say.

He used to depend on her younger son, Bobby, for distractions at tense times. Little children were good to watch, almost always rewarding, and you had to be Oedipus the King not to find some obvious irony or even a belly-laugh in what they did. But Bobby would be too large now to play the useful role of lapdog or clown. And Randy, thirteen by Harry's estimate, probably stayed in his room all day and masturbated to those rock groups that specialized in burning guitars and eating one another's socks. He was temporizing, he decided. He was trying not to think of Katherine thinking of him, arriving in the darkness of an ice-storm to make her life bulge exactly where she'd been smoothing it.

The steps creaked, and then the landing, and Bobby came in. Harry lit a cigarette that, when he inhaled the smoke, bit him in the lungs. Bobby was a tall eight- or nine-year-old, nine he thought, with long legs and slim hips, very broad shoulders, long arms, and enormous brown eyes — they reminded Harry of the eyes of the Aguilar children in The Bronx. His pajama bottoms were dark blue and they clung to hips and a bottom that must have tempted Katherine, constantly, to swat and hold. His tops were a baseball shirt that said Yankees. On his right wrist was a sweatband. Harry called, "Bobby, you're a *jock*!" The boy's rosy face turned crimson. "I'm sorry, Bob," Harry said.

Bobby nodded, held onto the tin counter top of the kitchen cabinet, and looked at his green woolen slippersocks that said Eagles.

Harry tried again. "Hi. I used to play with you when you were little. I took you sledding at the hill near the high school, in Vermont? When you used to live there? We went sledding together. How do you like New York?"

Bobby said, "Fine, thank you. Excuse me?"

"Nice to see you, Bobby," Harry called, as the boy went around the corner and up the stairs.

Harry wondered if she were sending them down one by one in a series of tests he had to work through. Would she be the final test? Children were people, he assured himself, only with fewer patent deficiencies. He told himself to stop worrying about Randy, who surely was on his way. Question Two is coming and he's an adolescent boy, and just barely, and I'm scared. Wily old journalist like you, he chided himself.

And Randy did appear, skinny and long-limbed, sporting an actual pimple, grinning big yellow teeth, wide of mouth and glad of expression, and holding a bottle in his hand. He strode to Harry and, a kid who had been taught all his life to kiss his parents' friends hello and goodbye, and whose adolescence hadn't yet driven such formal tenderness away, he leaned in to kiss Harry on the cheek, and to receive Harry's awkward hug and pat on the back, and to proudly display the bottle. He said, "Good to *see* you, Harry. Can you stay a while?"

"Hot damn, Randy. I'm glad to see *you*. Thank you for that greeting. You made me feel at home."

"Well, you are, sort of. You sure used to be at home with us in the other house."

"I missed you. I really missed you. I did. You look okay."

"I am — hey, Harry: you remember we used to dig for fossils and Indian artifacts?"

"I haven't been digging since we all stopped visiting each other."

"When you and Mom broke up."

"Well, yes, really."

"Are you going together again?"

"Just visiting, Randy."

Randy smiled a wide and knowing smile. "You never can tell, though, right, Harry?"

Harry waggled his eyebrows. The Sanitation Department press aide used to do that with his brows when he meant to signify No Comment. So Harry did it again.

Randy went on to the main subject — himself. "I dig in dumps now," he said. "I look for bottles."

"Any kind of bottles?"

"Old bottles. Very old bottles. I'm a collector."

"You always were a collector."

"This is one of my favorites. I'm very proud of it —aqua, blob-top with porcelain stopper intact. Watertown, New York — a medicine bottle. It's from the early eighteen-hundreds. It's not rare, but it's worth, oh, thirty-five dollars. And it's beautiful. This is a personal favorite. The factory burned down, so these weren't sold after 1880. Isn't it nice? You see that roundness on the top? That's the blob-top. This little mark here is from the pontil. They used the pontil to shape it. See?"

"Good morning," Katherine said. She was in jeans and her slippers and a tee shirt. She still looked good in a long-sleeved tee shirt because her arms and hands were sturdy and capable-looking, and because her chest — the ribs and cartilage and muscle under the breasts — was heavy and broad and as good to watch as it was, he remembered, to stroke. "Please get dressed, Randy. I *know* you're dressed, but you don't have socks on, and sweatpants aren't 'dressed,' and the shirt you're wearing smells a little gamey."

"Ma," Randy moaned.

"Dressed, please."

Randy made a persecuted face, said, "See you later, Harry. You're staying a while, aren't you? Is he staying, Ma?"

Harry said, "Thank you, Randy," avoiding the answer for them all. "See you later on, okay?"

Randy went around the corner and upstairs while Katherine opened shutters and filled a kettle for coffee. "Do you feel better?" she said.

"I guess I really fell asleep, didn't I?"

"You went down like the Hindenburg. What'd you do, Harry, drive all night?"

"I did."

"Just to get here?"

"The only way to get here was to drive here, Kath."

"To see me."

"Yes. That's a pretty soppy thing to do, isn't it?"

"It's ridiculous. It's irrational. In a storm like that, it's dangerous. I'm flattered. I'm trying not to be, because it wasn't my idea and it was your trip, so it's your problem, Harry. But it's a very keen way of complimenting a person."

"You sent the card to me."

"A month ago."

"I couldn't come up here until I quit my job."

"*Why?* You're crazy, Harry. And things don't change like that. You're nuts."

"Well," he said, "not entirely. I did have to quit the job. I was aimed in that direction for some time. And people do change, Kath. Sometimes what they change to, after a very long time of being the same thing, is what they were meant to be all along."

The coffee water was boiling and she poured it through ground beans. The smell was right. It belonged in a kitchen like Katherine's, filled as it was with wood — dark dining table with stocky legs, the light oak of the Hoosier cabinet, the counter of wood stripped down and oiled, and the book-case next to the refrigerator, as well as the narrow tongue-in-groove with which she had lined the walls halfway up. The floor was wide boards, and light coming through the unshuttered windows was bright and hard, but with some sun as well as glints of ice and snow on it. The smell of coffee belonged there, and so did Katherine. "So do I."

"What?"

"I didn't say anything."

"You didn't?"

"I was thinking."

"Keep it up," she said. "We're going to need some of that. The scrapple's done, I'm sure. Would you like me to heat it up?"

"No, thanks," he said. "I'll have coffee and cigarettes, no meals, thanks. Tell me about your job, Kath. And the boys. And Dell, who will probably appear to beat on me again." His stomach was jumping — not the digestive organ, but the layer of muscle under the skin. His muscles were shuddering, contracting and releasing so quickly that he felt as if he were shivering. This, he told himself, is what it means to be excited by a woman. Anybody can get goggle-eyed over somebody's tits. This is what's *supposed* to happen, though.

She said, "I'm an assistant curator. They know all about museum procedure at Cooperstown, restoration, preservation. I'm learning that as an underpaid assistant, an advanced apprentice, really. I even get a degree, eventually. I'm gouging Dell, which I didn't want to do, and I borrowed from my parents, who can hardly afford that. I'll hit *you* up for a few bucks if you're not careful. I'm handling it all right with the boys, except I'm not home from work when they get home from school, and that bothers me. But I'm learning something, and I'm doing my best in the finance department, and I like the way I live."

"Cooperstown," he said. "That's where the baseball Hall of Fame is, right? You ever go there?"

"Would you believe it, I never did. I'm too busy during the week, and of course the kids have school, and on the weekends we have ice skating in town during the winter — there's a little rink there — and the kids want to play with their friends. There are a lot of kids in a couple of houses down the road, there's sort of a little hamlet about half a mile away. The kids walk down there. No. We never went."

"I'll take them. I'll take you all. Would you like to go?"

She poured more coffee for herself. He'd forgotten to drink his. He did, and then he lit another cigarette.

"Clarify your motives, Harry."

"I don't know —"

"And don't smoke so much."

"Keeps me skinny," he said. "Keeps me less fat. And my motives are, we were living together, nearly, a few years ago because we loved each other."

"And?"

"Say it's true," he said.

"It's true," she told her coffee. Then she drank it. The words went down with the coffee.

"So I want it again. I wanted it before, but you told me you wanted to be on your own. 'Stop *eating* on me,' you said."

"Well, Jesus, Harry," she said, whispering and turning red at the back of each cheek, "you happened to be nibbling all over my body under the covers at the time, if you remember. Don't make me out to be such an insensitive monster."

"No," he said, "the trouble with being food is that you

do get eaten. And I was treating you like that. No. I understand that. I was talking nourishment in those days. You weren't in the mood to be supplies."

"And now?"

"I don't eat a lot," he said, exhaling smoke.

"But you came up here."

He clacked his teeth, showing them in what felt like a sort of snarl. "Now," he said, "I'm here for scavenging." He felt his lips come down, he felt his entire face sag as if the weight of his heavy head were on the skin of his brow and nose and mouth. "I take what I can get these days." He closed his eyes. He was too embarrassed to open them right away.

He heard her move, and he felt the kiss beside his nose. Her lips were cold and coarse, chapped, he supposed. He didn't want to complain. "That's just a chaste hello," she said. "You didn't need to say that. You shouldn't be willing to feel that. And it's not so terrible to see you again."

They drank more coffee, and then against his judgment and with huge relief he ate some scrapple with ketchup and bread with jam, thinking that he'd regret breakfast before very long. She forced him to drink his orange juice, though he said he'd rather smoke, and when she triumphed he was very grateful.

The boys were putting on coats and mufflers and knitted hats, and Harry realized that he and Katherine no longer had to zip or buckle anyone into their clothes — they had grown that old, each of them. He had a cigarette in his mouth and was lighting it when Bobby said, "Did you ever — Harry, did you ever hear a thing about when you smoke I smoke?"

136

He said, the cigarette on his lower lip and bobbing, "I never did. I can guess, though."

"They showed us pictures in school of this black stuff all over this lung. It's kind of like tar, like they put down in the road? Except it isn't that hot. But it's *hot*. But you can get it from other people smoking."

He took the cigarette from his mouth and walked to the kitchen sink. The coal sizzled in tap water, and he pinched it and then dropped it into the trash pail.

"Good," Randy said.

"You don't like them either?" Harry asked.

"No, it's that you live longer, Harry. I don't want you to die."

"Thank you, Randy."

Randy looked away, and they all went out. It was in the thirties, not warm enough for the ice to melt, not cold enough to keep it solid. So there was water everywhere, and an iron-gray to the sky that promised more moisture and sufficient cold to make the moisture into snow. They slid on slushy ice to Harry's car, salt-sprayed and sandy from the highways, dripping icicles at the exhaust pipe, foggy of window, dirty brown of color, and dead as the woman they found on the lower West Side in New York who had lived in a large cardboard refrigerator carton. HER HOME WAS HER COFFIN, his story had been headlined. And Harry had left the lights on last night, and they were all sitting in the smell of his cigarettes and sweat and the litter of his long drive, and they were going nowhere. The starter-motor wouldn't even whine. It clicked repeatedly, then made single clicks each time he turned the key, and then it said nothing. That was what he said and that was what Katherine said too.

Randy, in a bluff voice that Harry thought must come from an old-fogey TV character, chortled and said, "I guess we might think of walking."

Bobby said, "It's four miles. I'm not walking."

Harry lit a cigarette. Katherine opened her window. Bobby started to say, "When you —" but Harry had remembered by then, and he leaned across Katherine to shove the cigarette out her window. As his face passed hers, she patted his cheek with woolen fingers.

"I think I left the lights on last night, Kath."

"Would you like to call a tow truck? I think I have a number for one."

"Nah. Let me be stranded."

"Oh, you're stranded, all right. Let's take our car, if *that* starts, and then we can do a little shopping and come home and — let's let Harry treat us to pizza, take-home pizza, okay?" The boys murmured small cheers. So they moved from the Peugeot to some timelessly ugly small colorless car with no room for the boys' legs in back and barely enough for theirs up front. Katherine made it start at once, and they backed over the ice as if it were dry road, and in they went to the small town she lived near. Harry told each of them, using different expressions, that this shopping trip was the happiest of his life. Each looked at him as if he were febrile or hysterical, but each knew enough to be flattered and each liked him enough to want to be flattered, and each smiled back the precise replica of the others' wide-mouthed, large-toothed, fond, fast grin. Katherine managed, while really smiling, to look worried. They stopped at a Pizza Hut and Harry went in to buy too much pizza with too much of everything on top of it, and then he went back for sodas and a small pizza with nothing on top of it except cheese because he suspected that Bobby would not

enjoy anchovies and pepperoni and canned mushrooms —
"Complete," Harry announced as he slithered back into the
car bearing favors to trade for their affection, "with botu-
lism, spirochetes, liver larvae and smarm."

"It's the smarm," Katherine said.

"That's my charm."

"False alarm."

And Randy finished for them: "Causes harm."

Bobby said, "That's a *poem*!"

"Let's go ho-em," Harry said.

Katherine said, "Burma-Shave." It took the remainder of
the ride for Harry to explain that to the boys, and by the
time they were inside, stoking the fire up and laying out
plates and pizza, Harry was happy enough to drift about
the house and end up in the wide parlor he'd entered last
night, where he leaned against the wall of tongue-in-groove
boards painted white and he yawned and yawned, like a
dog made nervous, until he calmed down enough to join
them all in the kitchen. He sat with them and nibbled a
small piece of pizza but didn't finish it. He pulled a cigarette
out and lit it and, in nearly the same motion, excused himself from the table and went to the sink to drown the fire
and return, smiling still, but awfully hungry and uncomfortable.

Katherine, her mouth full of crust, said, "You seem to
have to give an awful lot up just to sit around here with
us."

Harry shrugged. He thought she was possibly right.

The late afternoon was taken up with whiskey over ice
in the livingroom near the woodstove, while the kids buckled and zipped and strapped themselves in and out of layers
of rubber, nylon, insulation of various sorts, and mis-
matched gloves. They went in and they went out, shov-

eling, throwing ice, breaking the skin of one another's face
with iceballs, slushballs, chipped-away ice and long shafts
of icicle. Mostly, they were around the house with friends,
making high noises of great anguish that meant they were
having fun. Sometimes, Harry looked from a window to
see them. Most often, he took their well-being on faith and
listened to Katherine tell more about her job. Then he told
her about why he quit covering ugly stories that called forth
what he considered inordinate amounts of emotion, whether
happy or sad. The emotions came from him, he explained
to her, but they didn't have to do with him. They came
from him but were for strangers. "It seemed to me, I was
always crying, after a while," he said. "I was always getting
too emotional. It got so I'd see an ad on TV, a kid with a
parent, and I'd cry. Just as sincerely as I would when I'd
be *with* a kid and a parent who were in trouble. Or who
weren't, for that matter. Or a husband and a wife. Or lovers.
Or dogs. Station wagons, barbecues in the park, tenement
fires, you name it. Name it. Name it," he said, walking
across the room. "Name it." He looked outside at the branches
of evergreens around the house and down at the roadside
as the wind whipped them back and forth. The children
had felt the wind, because one of the taller playmates was
directing Bobby and Randy to pull the woolen face-shields
of their balaclavas down. One of the others pulled his cap,
with no eye or nose holes, down in front of his face. The
skin that Harry saw seemed to glow red. And then, as Harry
was marveling that they looked like creatures from another
planet, or deep-sea divers, or even bank robbers, something
frighteningly different, he realized what they were doing
as they stood with their legs apart and held sticks and plastic
guns at the ready, waist-high. They were terrorists, he
thought. They were skyjackers, they were PLO gunmen,

they were Red September and Black December, they were in Beirut or Teheran or Munich, standing over prisoners they might kill. They were terror figures swiped from television screens, and he said, "Name it."

Katherine poured more bourbon for them and they sat in her livingroom while he smoked a lot. Then it was her turn to tell him some more about the pictures kept from acid-laden old paper, and from light, and finally from invisibility. She pointed at one, across the room, on the back wall near the door that went through to the kitchen. He was afraid to look, but there wasn't a window on that wall, so, while the kids outside were killing one another on another world, or, worse, on this one and in disguise or camouflage, he went to see where Katherine pointed. In the picture there was a great Victorian house atop a hill in winter. Grim-faced grownups in thick clothing stood, away like gods, to watch dozens of children as they slid downhill, on thick sleds, over very little snow, to disperse as they reached the bottom. The photograph caught them as they fled in their several directions on their sleds. All of them smiled or shouted or laughed, or tried to. All of them were going to climb back up toward what Katherine told him was the Cooperstown Orphanage. They were all getting on toward adolescence, all ready to be smelly and bristly and hard with muscle and need. They all were laughing, though they were going, after one slide down or another, to climb back up to the orphanage and have to stay there, because they were too old to be adopted. No one would have them, Harry knew, because they weren't puppies anymore. They were too old to slide down the ice and snow and into someone's home. Harry looked at the orphans, laughing on their sleds, as Katherine told him about where the photographic plates had been found and how they were displayed, once

developed, and how prints were sold to people from all over
the country, and how she felt that she was preserving something from being permanently lost. "That's a little gran-
diose," she said, "but only a little. I tell myself, that's one
something-or-other that won't get forgotten."

"Yes," he said, his back to the photograph now, his eyes
on her, on the old sofa, at right angles to the woodstove.
She had tucked her legs beneath her and she sipped her
drink. He watched her, and then, each time the kids outside
were framed in the bright window, he looked at them until
they moved on.

"You came here because *you* didn't want to be forgotten,"
Katherine said.

He nodded and said, "That must be some of it, Kath."

"I didn't forget you."

"I didn't know that."

"I sent you the card."

"Being not forgotten is not the same as being — as being
distinctly *remembered* in specific ways."

"Oh, Harry, you're talking about love again. I'm a divorced woman. Dell and I are divorced people. I don't want
to get married anymore. Or live with anyone. You're the
only man I ever lived with except Dell. That could count
for something when you're adding up the score."

"Thank you. But I *was* meaning love. Living conditions
aside, I was talking —"

"Yes. About love. Yes. I have to tell you, I think I mostly
love me. The boys, of course. Absolutely. And me. I think
so. What's that, when there are certain words you just can't
read?"

"Anorexic," he said.

"No!" She laughed, and it was a happy laugh. "No. It's,
it's — *dyslexic*."

"Exic," he said, making his excuse.

"True," she said. "But that's what it is for me. I was trying to tell you: the kind of love you're talking about, the kind of relationship you're talking about, I think it isn't in the picture for me now."

"On the page. If you mean dyslexic."

"Fair enough. That hurts your pride?"

"Pride? It hurts my *heart*. I feel like I'm Lady Brett and you're Jake, and I keep crawling all over you and you can't do it."

"I don't think I want to do it. I don't *think* so. If we're talking about Lady Brett and Jake. So it's really different." Her face was breaking. It fell into several expressions. They competed for his attention. None of them was happy, and each was sad on his behalf; but none mourned for her, he could see. And she sat quite still, except for the hand that moved with the glass. "Anyway, you must have a lot of friends in New York. You're not the kind of man that women ignore."

"I don't know," he said, demanding of himself that he at least not whine. "I'm really not the kind of man that a lot of woman live with. Marry. Get old with. Die next to."

"You know what, Harry? I think you're feeling something like a spinster these days. Would you be insulted if I said it has something to do with the age you're closing in on? The terrible tumble into forty?"

"Kath, I will not be alibied by natural cycles and psychological cycles and premenstrual tension and hitting forty and doing sixty-five in a fifty-five mile per hour zone and allergies to radium and *any* of it. That's baloney. Wow. Kath: I'm —"

"Are you guys having a fight?" Randy called from the kitchen.

"No," Katherine called. "No sweat."

"Good deal," Randy said. "You want to see my bottles, Harry?"

He didn't. He went upstairs and he saw them. Randy filled the air with round bottles, ancient cola bottles, high-shouldered bottles, square ones, something ugly and brown that Randy assured him had to do with bitters and was worth a hundred dollars at *least*, and Harry stood in the litter of underpants and twisted socks, bottles on book-shelves and tabletops, half-read paperback books and al-bums from rock groups he had never heard of, and he nodded and made the faces he thought that Randy should see. In that boy-debris, among Randy's obsessions, and across the hall, he knew, from Katherine's bedroom — where she slept with whom she wished and, somehow even worse now, where she slept by herself — Harry was overtaken by the lust that had apparently been following him along the ice-covered roads. But this wasn't icy. This was brain-less and cruel and slick with sweat. The penis makes a man into a compass, he told himself, and with it he can navigate instead of wander. He replied: a penis is the naked man's gun, it can be that. Harry nodded at Randy's display of something that looked like every other milk bottle he had seen. This family's life together was seamless, and Harry searched along the surface of their lives with his sense and his memories and — as downstairs — with his words. But he could find no entrance. He saw himself as tiny and hairy and dark, crawling over her long, wide, white body, as his small dark car had crawled along the ice of the enormous countryside within which Katherine lived a life away from his. He was ridiculous, he thought. He seemed to have no hope. The steam behind his sexual desire flushed away throughout his body, and he only felt uncomfortably warm.

So why, then, had she sent the postcard? If it wasn't an invitation — and it seemed now that it surely wasn't — then it could only have been a cry of delight at her own new condition. And she must have known few people to whom such a cry could be called. She had relied upon his affection, and his patience, and you shouldn't do that with people you don't love, he thought. Unless you think the world's a decent place, and unless you feel that you don't have to give yourself away in order to celebrate yourself, but that people, certain people — he — would permit you such a pleasure without demanding payment in return.

"Thank you," he said to Randy, who seemed to understand that he was boring. Randy's face showed his embarrassment, or hurt, and Harry could no longer hug him in apology, it had been too many years, so he said, "I'm sorry, old pal, I really am." And he was, though not so sorry as he felt for himself. When he went downstairs and into the kitchen, Katherine was listening to the radio and chopping onions on the counter near the back window.

"It all has to do with the postcard," he said, lighting a cigarette as he stopped to lean against the refrigerator. "It has to do with what you meant by sending the postcard." She was listening to something, but it wasn't he and it wasn't on the radio. Her face was raised as though she sniffed at something. "Kath?"

Bobby came into the kitchen through the back door and called, "The truck's here, guys. The tow truck's here!" Harry hid the cigarette in his cupped hand. Bobby went back out, presumably to watch what Harry now understood Katherine had been listening to. She had sent for it some time during what Harry had thought of as the finest day of his life. She had called for a wrecker to come and charge his battery so he could leave. She was doing everything but lacing on his wet shoes and zipping shut his parka so that, with a few shots of bourbon in him, he could drive the long drive home, as dusk closed down, and in the cold, and probably in hail or slippery snow. She was watching his face now. He was watching her fingers. All the while, she pushed the peeled and halved onions into the blade of the knife, and she chopped, shedding no blood, living in the habits of her family's full nights. Still looking at Harry, she called, "Rand? Randy? Set the table, please."

From upstairs: "It's Bobby's job."

"He's helping the tow truck man. Set the table, please."

"So what does Bobby do?"

"Table, please."

Harry stayed where he was, leaning back, as Katherine dumped the onions into a hot black pan, then grated parmesan cheese into an egg mixture she had in a mixing bowl. Randy, his head sunk neckless into his shoulders in protest — he looked like a parody of raging boyhood — stalked around the table on his long legs, slapping down plates and slamming silverware. Katherine seemed not to notice. From the refrigerator, not touching Harry as she signaled him to move from it, she took three old baked potatoes and sliced them open, crumbling them skinless over the frying onions. In a minute, she poured the eggy stuff onto the onions and potatoes, turned the flame nearly off, told Harry that they could make the salad later, and gestured toward the frying pan: "Frittata. Twenty minutes. Thank you!" That was for the man, presumably from the wrecker, who had stomped onto the porch, waved, then walked off. Harry, at the window, saw that his car was throbbing in place in the driveway, a plume of white exhaust smoke rising to be dispersed by steady winds. "We have time for another drink if you'd like," Katherine said, very casually. Her voice was nearly not natural. It was Harry's first sign of hope. He offered up, to unspecified gods, a promise that he would never touch her if they let him stay. He would renounce her flesh as he had given up food and as he was, almost, at least inside this house, giving up cigarettes. He would sit in his car when they didn't want him, and listen to chatter about bottles when they did, and he would not disturb their lives. By the time he was in the livingroom, he was disgusted with himself — not because he wished to crawl if that was the way to get to them, but because he didn't believe that he loved her enough to yield his enormous pleasure at her flesh in order to be closer to it.

Before he sat down on the couch, he went back into the kitchen and studied the table. Four places were set. He went upstairs, though he wasn't invited, and he knocked at Randy's door. The boy was sitting at his desk, hunched in a shape that spoke of the enduring of inequities. He kissed Randy's hair, which smelled like Harry's memory of the mossy underside of an old porch, and he went out before Randy could ask him a question or talk about glass. He went along the corridor, past Katherine's door, to Bobby's room. Bobby was still outside, probably guarding the un-occupied car as it charged itself. All of Bobby's bookshelves were taken up by trophies and ribbons — third place in a relay race, fifth place in a football throw, first place in a basketball tournament. Harry nodded his approval.

He went downstairs and into the livingroom. Katherine watched him. She knew him, for she said, "Don't get cocky." He was certain that she knew him. "Don't go counting chickens," she said.

Harry sat on the coffee table that would have been be-tween them. Bobby slammed the back door and threw boots about and thumped upstairs. Harry picked up her wrist so

147

that he could kiss her hand. He therefore spilled the drink she was holding and made his trousers cold and wet. She laughed and covered her mouth with her other hand, her hand so broad that it covered the bottom part of her confused, confusing face. She reminded him a little of the kids outside, acting either like a child wise against the weather, or a sneaky sort of menace. But she was smiling inside her hand.

The lifted wrist was still attached to fingers that held an empty glass, but he kissed the knuckles of the hand nevertheless, what the hell, and he said, "I think you sent me the card because you wanted somebody to send up a cheer for you, and you figured I might come across."

Katherine moved her free hand away from her mouth, and it went to the top of her face, hiding her eyes. Her lips turned in on one another. She leaned back against the sofa, and Harry, encouraged by some passivity — Give me some *weak*ness, he prayed — leaned in to kiss her sexless knuckles again. Harry went on: "Now, that's fine with me. No, it isn't. But it's not *that* bad. What I would like to know is that you really sent the postcard because you wanted to get me up here some way, and that was the way you chose. Knowing me, you'd know that one syllable of encouragement was all I'd need to get me moving. Knowing me, you'd know that I would accept four years away from you as four years of indignity, which is what they were, but that I would accept them, once that very pragmatic postcard arrived. Because you figured, knowing me, that I would love you that much. Kath, do you think I could sneak a cigarette even if they're in the house now?"

"Where do you intend to go tonight?" She moved her hand away. Her eyes were red, as if with the strain of too much reading, but she hadn't grown ugly yet with long crying.

"Where would you advise?"

She said, "Here."

"Done."

"Then you can't smoke. I gave it up on account of them and you have to do it too if you stay here."

"For how long would that be?"

"Frittata!" she cried, sniffing at overdone egg and moving quickly past him and into the kitchen. He wished for a cigarette.

Following her, then, into the kitchen, grouchily lumbering, he said, "We were talking about — Kath? Katherine. Am I being *tested*?"

She looked up from the stove, her eyes wide and innocent, her forehead matching her mouth. "Of course," she said. "Since you got the card. But you knew that."

Tough old newspaper man like me, Harry said to himself. Wily old streetwise journalist like me. ACE REPORTER ACED. He nodded at Katherine as she called the boys. They clattered on the stairs, Bobby shouting that Harry had better not forget to turn his car off, and Randy declaiming his need for food. They descended like the orphans at Cooperstown as Harry wished, suddenly, that he might be a part of that photograph, seen from the back, as he stood at the bottom of the hill to welcome the sledders down. And then he admitted that it was he who slid on the long icy run, and it was he being greeted as he slid, wildly crying, toward a family's late meal. He turned toward Katherine's boys, looking back over his shoulder once, veteran coper with fast-breaking news events, to tell her, "Sure."

A History of Small Ideas

There was no way not to know how difficult the trip was for Sidney. He was careful not to talk about his father, and that was the first sign. He was careless about his driving, and that was the second. Third was what Laurel called his Theoretical Condition. When he was obsessed with something that seemed to her to have little bearing on his immediate life or hers, or on any of Victor's fifteen years, and when he talked and talked about it, not really expecting her to listen or reply, then she knew to look for something wrong. In Sid's theoretical state, his voice seemed to come from higher in his throat than usual. His breathing was harder for him to catch up to; his parts didn't work together.

It was like that, driving up to see Sid's parents, who lived a few hundred miles from Manhattan, and who were not divorced because their dissatisfaction, along with his father's small medical practice, gave them what matrix they could find for their lives. Victor was asleep in the back seat, his long flanks and legs taking most of it. He slept because he hated riding in cars and because he didn't want to go visiting his new father's family. Laurel was sitting in silence because Sid was still talking about a suspected Black Hole at the center of the Milky Way, into which stars and who knows

what other cosmic stuff — irradiated dust? the flakes of
shattered moons? spores bearing life? — were possibly
sucked, irresistibly, into the high density of the tiny dead
sun, the Black Hole. It was all about gravity, she gathered.
She was wrong. "Maybe the entire rhythm of life of the
universe comes from that," Sid told her, high in his throat.
"Maybe what falls into that, and then a billion years later
blows up again, maybe that's the systole-diastole of the
whole universe. Maybe that's the source of all the life-death,
yes-no, rhythms in creation. Maybe computers do that,
binary numbers, one or two, one or two. But it's the same
thing. It could be."

He looked at her. She was looking out the window, at
the same lay-by on the road not two miles from his parents'
house. They had sat there for twenty minutes now, while
Sid sipped at the coffee from their jug, a drink of which
had been absolutely necessary, he'd said. So Laurel finally
said what he'd known when he had pulled over: "Big stall."

He nodded right away.

"You're afraid to see him," she said.

"What else is new?"

"That possibly you aren't acting your age?"

"No, that's only old, not new. But I did mean that, about
the Black Hole. Do you see anything in that?"

"You know this by now," she said very patiently. "I don't
do Black Holes, changes in foreign governments, national
ethics or anything to do with the economy. I do little ideas."

"I don't have any of those," he said.

"That's how you get out of full-time living," she said.
"It's very irresponsible of you, only worrying about Freud
and the creation of the universe and foreign aid. When you
worry about body lice on the kids three doors down from
us —"

"No!"

"There was a mild scare, a false alarm. You have to pay attention, I told you that. I tell you all the time. Lice. Fleas. Dogs that have them. People attached to the dog by a leash. Every one of them, one at a time. That's the ticket, Sid. It's the secret of life. When you're senile or insane or you've left for Tahiti with a much thinner nurse who does it for doctors in the laundry room, I am going to write a very short *History of Small Ideas*. No Black Holes will be in it. It'll be about the difference between malt and hops, and how come the Yankees sell you tickets by mail but they don't refund by mail. Take a deep breath, just one."

"What?"

"Take a breath."

He did. She took his coffee cup and closed the Thermos and punched him lightly on the arm. "I'll write down how Thermoses work too. Now. Drive."

The two-lane road went over gradual hills and a lot of flatland. It was already early spring near Manhattan and in the suburb where they lived, and she felt uncomfortable with all the degrees of several seasons she would have to manage, newly married to a man who had entanglements in two climates, at least — New York City, and this peculiar place five hours north and west of it — and several states of mind she was going, soon, to learn more about. She wondered if history were as difficult to study or write as her husband's history made her suspect; she wouldn't ask him, though, for fear that he might answer and not stop, since he was in a state of high Theory. Snow had shrunk back from the shoulders of the road, and it left a long and strangely even dark brown strip of cinder, sand, roadbed and blown junk. The snow itself, in shoulders as high as the middle of her car window, was also brown, although farther back in the fields it was a handsome bony white that made her squint. The houses were shabby, weather-worn, many of them gray and paintless and even leaning crazily. Parts of machines littered lawns, sometimes, and garbage, strewn perhaps by dogs, lay designless on the bone-white snow. "They admit their poverty here," she said. "They've given up. In New England, they would never let you know this much about them."

"In the spring," he said, then stopped speaking and frowned into sun-dazzles and the dark wet road. Then: "In the spring, but not early enough, never — it was always around now. Early March. It would be supposed to be spring, but it wouldn't be yet. And he always had to have his way. He'd decide we had to drive up into the state's lands — you can't see them yet, they'll be across the fields behind their house, and then a good way up the hills behind the fields. The state owns thousands and thousands of acres there. Forests, meadows, there are houses there, and horse trails nobody uses. And a lot of dirt roads, mostly for logging. They license logging up there. And he'd get me and my mother into the car and we'd go up to look for deer. Because if you're lucky, you can find them coming down from where they've wintered in the thickest woods. They come down to the higher farms, and they eat at the corn stubble. Except, of course, as you can see, there's too much snow for the deer, and there was always too much snow for us. Each time. Every damned time. It was like now. Early March. And half the country would be having spring, but he wouldn't, so he'd get mad as hell. Denied again, understand? He'd put us in the car, and up we'd go. Up the dry roads, and onto the muddy roads, some of the mud would still be frozen. And then we'd see snow and have to turn back, and he'd be madder. And — I remember this one time, we went up into the woods, and it was something out of Hansel and Gretel. The woods were very dark. It was late in the day to be starting out. And we got up there, and we hooked a left. Bloop. Stuck in a foot of snow. My god, he was angry. He almost had a heart attack digging us out. And he didn't. We had to walk down. It took us hours. Nobody talked. It was like Hansel and Gretel coming home. I actually —"

"You would."

"What?"

"Think they were trying to leave you there."

He looked at her and then back at the road. They were descending a steep and curved hill where the road ran parallel to a narrow bright stream. Forest crowded in on the road. He said, "You know a lot, don't you?"

"No," she said, "but you're not *pure* puzzle, you know."

"I don't want to be."

"I know you don't."

They stopped clumsily at the foot of the hill and turned right, onto a street of little white houses. Every house was white, with the exception of a gray crumbling wreck, apparently abandoned, and a small maroon house that was surrounded with barrel-shaped rounds of tree trunk that might be split into firewood. "This is it," he said, from up in his throat.

"It's a Whitman Sampler box," she said. "All these perfect little white houses."

"With all these perfect little white people," he said.

"Racist," Victor said from the back seat. He loomed behind them, pushing their seat forward with his knees, leaning his elbows between them, breathing his gluey sleeper's breath around them. Victor was Laurel's, and his breath, early in his life, and in hers, and in that of her first marriage, had smelled of fresh cold apple juice, no matter what he had eaten or drunk. Now, at fifteen, he was taller than she, almost taller than Sid, and his soft face, with his father's round Irishness and small merry eyes, had become longer, and bonier, had seemingly shrunk in on the frame of his skull, so that it looked hard to her, and scarred — it has once been soft, rosy and unblemished — by acne that erupted sporadically, with a gouging effect. His voice was a hoarse, braying mixture of loud and soft, boy and man, high and low; it seemed incapable of carrying kind notes. She often didn't like him, especially now, when he was trying to keep Sid away from them in spite of the marriage, while she was trying to anneal Sid further into their lives. Sid often bit his lower lip and held his mouth closed with a jaw that grew stern lines, and she knew that he was trying to show Victor that Victor's voice mattered. We are one big happy family, she thought, going to see another real domestic winner. Grant us, she said in tones of prayer, *do* grant us an absolutely *stunningly* swift weekend, please.

"That's me," Sidney said in reply to Victor. To Laurel, it sounded as if he were telling them about the house he had stopped alongside. It was a white frame house, like the others, except that a porch with carved Victorian ornamentation ran far out onto the lawn, rather more elegant in line than that of many of the little utilitarian farmhouses that squatted on the road while behind them fields ran out to the river she thought she could see — he had described it to her — over the large stones and dry soil (under all that snow) which made farming a hard way of life. Where the river probably was, she made out a long and graceful line of leafless black elms. Elms, she knew, stood up like hands, fingers originating at the basic split of the trunk. Some day, there wouldn't be elms again, she thought, and she grew impatiently sympathetic for Sid.

And here came Hank, out the porch door and down the steps in all the awkwardness that Sid had trained himself to overcome. He was stocky, sturdy, soft and wrinkled at the throat and on the backs of his hands, but muscular in his movements, for all the skidding he did on the snowy steps and in spite of his nearly pushing the door into her as she moved out to greet him. He wore thick glasses with black plastic rims, and he had a lot of hair that wasn't white or gray. In a deep voice, hearty and phony as what they knew here as spring, he called, "Here she is! Here she is!"

"Oh, Jesus," Victor said in the back of the car.

Sidney, standing at the other side of the car from his father, and perhaps hiding there, was pale and quiet.

"Who said that?" cried Hank. "Who moaned about me?" He jiggered to the rear window of their car and looked in, making himself more like a monkey and less like a man. "I'm you're Grandpa, son. I'm your new grandfather." He straightened, flushed and unhappy-looking. "If you want," he said, smiling with intelligence at Laurel, then looking around for Edna.

Wrapped in an old sweater that must have been Hank's, she walked slowly and carefully down the steps. In dungarees and the dark turtleneck under her cardigan, she looked just-fifty, instead of over sixty. Her face was even less lined than Hank's, and her throat was tauter. At this distance, pressed in as it was on her windpipe, it looked like a spine. I'm seeing backwards, Laurel thought.

Edna walked straight to her, looking at her face and her eyes. Edna might have looked into them, but Laurel looked away: she was unprepared for that sort of intimacy now.

They hugged and cooed. They patted one another's back as if each were a sick child. When Victor arose in adolescent hauteur from the back seat, Edna knew to treat his sense of majesty with a reflection of it. She stepped back, offered up a stiff forearm with a handshake at the end, and said, "How do you do?" Victor, who couldn't cope with graciousness, blushed and didn't speak.

And then Hank was at the other side of the car, wearing sneakers in the snow, hugging his son and saying congratulations, and then Edna was there too, but not congratulating him. She said only, and over and over again, "Thank goodness. Thank goodness."

The males pulled luggage from the car. The females carried a bottle of wine and a bundt cake that Laurel, lying, claimed she had made. In fact, one of her nurses had made it for her on a cost-plus overrun basis. Edna talked about weather, and Laurel marveled at its extremities. Victor carried all their bags by himself, slipping on the steps as Hank had done, but managing as well to drop two bags into the snow. Sid and Hank came to help him, and they mounted the porch in step with one another, talking also of the weather and its wonders. Laurel acknowledged her own practicality, but she didn't feel guilty, as she figured that in twenty-eight hours they might be going home.

Laurel was shown the house, and she was as interested in the small bedroom upstairs that had become Hank's study as she was in Sid's old bedroom, which was on the other end of the upstairs hall. The second floor smelled of old linoleum and damp wallpaper, a mixture of the lightest vanilla and the sweet oils once sniffed in the corridors of dark public schools. Sid's was what was left of a boy's room that had become a guest room and storage chamber. There was a very old blue and yellow cowboy decal on the wooden bedstead; it must have been made in the thirties, saved for the forties, when it was applied, and it seemed sturdy enough to outlast them all, with its little cowboy on his little horse, each curled in a boneless flex that matched the attitude of the cowboy's little lariat as it hung on the maple headboard over perhaps the same pillow Sid had set his head upon at night. She felt so far in time and experience from that small Sid, and this small house and its history — she was thirty-eight and Sid was forty-one — that she smiled affectionately, as one might smile for someone else's adorable baby; but she felt none of the strikes at her heart and solar plexus, the terrible sense of loss a vanished childhood can cause, that she had expected to feel. And she was relieved. She grew happier. She might still remain herself in all this tide of others' emotions.

Victor, having offered what he interpreted as the requisite politeness — he had almost smiled at his new father's mother; he had nodded when his new father's father had talked to him of school — went into the livingroom and turned on the television set and watched a college basketball tournament that he, who had said Shakespeare sucked because all they did in his plays was talk, claimed was more dramatic than Shakespeare.

In Hank's room, Edna pointed at the walls and the big cluttered desk and all the books on every surface, many of them very good books, Laurel thought, and not the sort you'd expect a country doctor — any doctor — to be reading. Edna asked about what Laurel read, and Laurel explained that her schedule as an ER head nurse gave her little time to read — "I never get to finish anything. I'm always either falling asleep or getting a call because someone on the roster's gotten married or sick or dead" — so she read mostly short stories. She was reading John O'Hara, Laurel explained. "They're true," she said. "His stories feel true. And they end, but the characters 'keep going. I keep hoping I get to read about them again, the good ones."

Hank came in, then, with Sid in his wake. He puffed with pride about his study, as he kept calling it, and he asked Laurel whose stories she had been talking about. When she told him, he agreed. "One of the finest, least pretentious writers, at his best, mind you, that this country ever produced. He was a doctor's kid, like you," he told Sid. "Like your son, Victor, as a matter of fact. What's the practice showing you these days?"

And Sidney, who specialized in internal medicine at Montefiore Hospital, talked about outbreaks of strep and the new penicillin-resistant venereal diseases making the rounds of hotels used by prostitutes and bars used by male homosexuals for casual pick-ups. They went downstairs, single-file, on the narrow staircase, and in a wide room off the kitchen they sat at a square old table and drank coffee while Edna sneaked back and forth from Victor's open-mouthed concentration before the television set — Laurel, of course, had spied upon her former baby and present shame — bearing him turkey sandwiches and sodas, fruit, and the lightest of strokes across the shoulder, at the temple, on top of the curly head, as if she must touch him to know him. You should spend a day with him when he is aimed toward self-interest like a homing pigeon, Laurel thought — *then*, you'd really know him.

Hank said, "We had a lot of burn cases this winter. You'd expect that around here, especially with people worrying about being broke and paying for fuel. The fools have been heating their   ned trailers with kerosene and paraffin and Christ knows what-all else. One after another, of course, they blow up. Even the ones who burn wood seem to burn it too hot, or they let the creosote build up in the pipe, and there they go, boom, kids with third-degree burns on forty percent of the body, drunk parents dead in their beds and these maimed kids are orphans while they're still unconscious. It's a hell of a stupid place to practice medicine."

Sidney nodded. Laurel saw him decide to stay quiet and she filled the silence he wouldn't. "Do you have any trouble with the soluble dressing you've been using on the burns, Dad?"

The word made him shift in his chair to hide his pleasure. She had guessed that it might. He seemed actually rosy, a merry fellow, this man who so frightened his son. He shook his head, cleared his throat, said, "Not that I know of, dear." And she pretended that the "dear" hadn't made him blush or dive at his cup.

"At Bellevue," Laurel said, "they've been finding a high incidence of kidney damage — now, these are people burned over fifty percent of the body or more, probably going to die anyway, maybe kidney-damaged to begin with. In *deep* shock. It's not a scientific conclusion, just an observation so far. But they've been finding kidney damage associated only with the soluble dressing. We changed brands about a year ago, probably the purchasing staff got flown to Tahiti for a week by a new manufacturer, so we changed suppliers. It's worth a thought, though."

Sidney nodded. Across the table, in the cold sunlight that came through the window behind her and shone on the table and on Sidney, he was sending her thanks. She received them, and she was going to name the brand of dressing when Hank said to Edna, who had rejoined them, "You get a good nurse —"

"And you got yourself a goldmine. Invaluable, those

women." Edna had deepened her voice to imitate his, and
Laurel saw that she was a good deal brighter than Hank,
and knew him well enough to probably love him more than
Sidney thought. Past the first dozen years or so, smart
women do not stay with bad men. Unless they need to,
Laurel corrected herself.

"Well, hell, it's true," Hank said. "They know more about
the patients than the doctors do. Jesus, look: I go into the
hospital a couple of hours a day. I see the patients at this
clinic in town, Laurel, it's a family health-care clinic, cheap
and almost efficient, and the administrators, *they* make out
all right. But I don't really see the patient a great deal. It's
the floor nurse, the — hell, the damned candy-stripers bearing chocolates and magazines, *they* see them as much as I
do. And they got bigger tits."

"Stop it, Hank!" Edna said.

"I apologize," Hank said. And Laurel saw the triumph
in his eyes. He had sneaked out the sexual signal he'd been
wanting to express, possibly before he had seen her, tits
and all. He was competing with his son, she understood,
for at least the idea of the new wife's body. She thought of
the cowboy with his drooping rope on the headboard upstairs, and she began to feel something of Sidney's need to
stay away rather than come home. "I do," Hank said, "I
do. Laurel: I apologize."

She smiled politely. And Sidney said, "Are they paying
their bills, Dad?" Which was enough to launch Hank on
the tirade Laurel was certain that Sid knew would follow —
the one about cheats and blackguards and villains, and how
he worked late and early and in-between, even with his cut-
back schedule, and still they felt that they could call him
at dawn for a sore throat or boil they should have seen to
days ago, while they never, *never* felt that they should pay

within a month or two, the way Hank paid *his* ~~own~~ ~~damned~~
bills.

Edna yawned loudly. Hank shut up. Laurel and Edna
went into the kitchen to be women at the range, while the
menfolk sat in the dining room, with its hint of warmth —
at least the light was brighter there — and drank lukewarm
coffee and talked about medicine and accountants and mal-
practice insurance. Laurel could hear Sidney's deep rumble,
which meant that he wasn't piping a high, breathless theory
about the universe, which meant, in turn, that he wasn't
as nervous as he'd been; and she was amused, at long distance anyway, by the darting, high, more energetic snarls
that Hank threw into the conversation. Edna went to the
radio, on a shelf above the sink, and turned on sad country
songs so that they would not have to talk if they didn't want
to. Laurel smiled at the woman who came up to her shoulder, and she hugged her as, at the complex of emergency
rooms where she worked, she might hug a co-worker who
had responded to a demanding moment with sure, unspec-
tacular grace.

Edna disguised herself as the livingroom with its polished
softwood floor that glowed like honey in the parchment
tones of the lampshades. She camouflaged herself as sandwiches. She managed, *sub rosa*, to become, alternately, the
fat sofa with crushed cushions, and the red leather chair
with its matching ottoman, and even the dark wicker basket
with its weeks of newspapers cupped in its shell; and she
was the Dutch colonial hutch on the shelves of which Edna
kept jugs and pitchers and pots, fired in the last century —
this is almost the new last century, Laurel thought — and
painted with blue flowers. She dropped away from the slow
conversation in the livingroom, which skipped from how

much Hank had sweated while he ate dinner to how high his blood pressure might go to how he still liked splitting wood to how much a face cord cost — thirty-five dollars — delivered and thrown off the back of a pickup truck by savages who escaped with your check before you saw how little you got for your money. With her eyes drooping as if she feigned sleep, Edna moved in on whatever was there to be harvested in her new grandson. Laurel watched her, wishing Edna the best of luck, and wishing too that she, his mother, might wish to have such designs on him these days. What she prayed for now was no drugs, no *hard* drugs, no violence, no formation of a rock 'n' roll band so that he had an excuse to seek his fortune along the West Coast, no gang rape, no motor-vehicle accidents. She looked forward to a time when he would not be fifteen and full of rage about his first father and his second, and his mother's infidelity to first father and present son and every kind of holy ghost of the dead marriage that the boy could, when he was angry, which was often, conjure. So she looked toward his being twenty-five and liking her again. In her daydreams of them, Victor never appeared to be younger. Now, and in the immediate future, she depended on herself, and probably on Sid, but not this boy.

In a short while, Victor was explaining things to Edna — the rolling pick, which apparently wasn't legal, but which was used by larger men on each team to shield the smaller men from defensive players so that they could shoot the ball; he called the big men forwards and he showed, his finger thick against the lean grace of the figures on the screen, which of the players were guards; when a referee put his hand on the back of his neck and waggled the elbow on that arm, he indicated charging, Victor said, and he explained how, if a defensive player had established and maintained his position, the man who ran into him was guilty of a foul; a player might commit six such fouls before he was removed from the game — and Edna didn't make grandmotherly noises, she didn't twist her intelligent pretty face into expressions of stunned delight; she just talked basketball with Victor, asking nothing more of him than that she be permitted to pay attention to those things he said were important.

Well, Edna could, Laurel thought. She was smart, and she had nothing except this silly old physician whose dominance over his son — so Sid had always described it — seemed (and about time) to be fading. And Edna was bright. She had written children's books once, during *her* youthful first marriage, before she and Hank together had manufactured Sidney and this life. She could do what all grandparents do: pluck what was fun, and leave the bitter stuff, the grandchildren's failures and inattentions and assaults, to the parents, who probably deserved a good part of them anyway.

Victor was enjoying the old girl, Laurel saw, so that he didn't notice when the halftime intermission of the umpteenth game of the day and night was over, and the second half of play had begun. He still nodded and actually smiled with pleasure, as he had before the onset of adolescence and the marriage's certified death, talking now about girls in school, and embarrassment in general, and the showers in the boys' locker room. He looked back at the screen only when Edna rubbed his arm and reminded him that the University of Virginia was on the floor again.

"*Again!*" Hank cried, from the window, his chubby rump and short back protruding through the curtains while his head and shoulders were on the other side. "It's snowing! Again!"

Sidney, whose long limbs must have come from Edna's side of the family, stretched his legs on the ottoman and sighed. His smile was happy. His hands were folded on his belly. He looked content. He said to Laurel, who sat in the rocker to his right, "We always have the same surprising snow at the same time every year. And we are always staggered by it. What does *that* tell you?"

"I'm not sure," she said, "because, as you're aware, I don't make major inferences on a broad scale. I'm not sure what it means. But it does seem like there's a bitch of a lot of snow up here. And that you people are slow learners."

Hank whirled in the blue and white fabric of the drapes, which adhered for a moment to his head. Then he emerged, bright and red and with light winking off the lenses of his eyeglasses, his teeth a prominent white in the gentle livingroom light. He snickered his pleasure at Laurel's wit. He clapped his hands and nodded, several times, with great energy. "We are," he said. "We are. Except maybe for Edna. But the rest of us? Listen: what we are is the synecdoche for the rest of the race. Understand?"

"I don't know that word," Laurel said.

Sidney shook his head to show that he didn't know it either.

"I got it reading poems, reading *about* them," Hank said. "Robert Frost. Shakespeare. Ezra Pound, a little, the old economist. Wallace Stevens: now there's a man who made some mouth-music, though I have to confess I don't understand a great deal of what he wrote. William Carlos Williams, he was a doctor like Sid and me. I studied them. I studied the art. Synecdoche. That's the secret, I believe. The great ones did it. The lesser ones? Sweet sounds, but not so you'd know it a hundred years later, I suspect. I think I would like to drink some George Dickel poured over ice. Laurel? Sid?" In a lower voice, he said, not quite whispering, "I think I probably shouldn't offer any to Victor, eh? As for Edna — I think she's in love."

Laurel said, "I envy her. And I'll have a little something, thank you."

They three had a little something. Laurel felt, from the first smell of it, the start of the first sip, that she wouldn't be able to sustain the assault of the whiskey. No: it wasn't that the liquor attacked her, it was that she realized now how she had been waiting for a long time, perhaps six or seven years, to *not* be on her guard. That was all. She had been waiting through the death of a marriage and the breeding of malice in a boy who had been beautiful, and the twisting of her life from a simple straight line between her present and her future into a corkscrew shape, and shapes even less predictable for staggering through — shapes like that of the IUD, like those of the serrated edges of the key to a young couple's apartment. She had been waiting, or her body had been waiting, or her secretest mind. And now, in spite of all the aspirins, and occasional tranquilizers, and the Bloody Marys with lunch for one bad month, and in spite of the possibility, once in a while, during sex, of not being wholly oneself, or of not remembering to have to be exclusively alone with oneself, and in spite of good work, and patients helped, and stupidity and illness contended with, and in spite of the presence of Sid, who was a considerable fact, and sometimes even fun when he wasn't sitting near his father, it was *now*, only *now*, in this house in March during a false spring when it had just begun to snow, that the extra rigidity, to which she had nearly grown accustomed, went away. She was deflating. She felt weak. She felt ill, endangered, loose at the joints. She was losing something, and whether she had needed it or not, its accustomed presence was vanishing, and she was very uneasy about the loss.

There were seven minutes to go in the game, and Victor had to explain to his grandmother, who by now was as flushed and galvanized as a girl about to be seduced, that Virginia's opponents were going into a four-corner stall, passing the ball from man to man in a shape like a square, so as to let the time remaining in the game pass away; because the opponents led, they didn't need to score; and if they scored, then Virginia would take possession of the ball, and probably score, and anything could happen. They were eliminating randomness from the contest. And Edna was arguing, "That isn't ball-playing, Victor. That's *politics*!"

Victor said, "It really sucks, Grandma."

Laurel turned her jealous eyes to Hank and Sidney, who were making another drink so soon. Five minutes to go, and I'm numb over half my body, and I don't want to be. In bed with someone. In bed with Sidney. Alone. In the tub. At the supermarket, even. But not now, Laurel told herself. Hank was saying, "Like a confession. An admission of sorts."

"Listen, Dad. I went into medicine because of you."

Hank looked down at his glass. He shook his ice and watched it drift.

"But you tell me," Sidney said. "You tell me anything." Laurel sensed that the whiskey had cut something loose in him too. Well, no wonder: the tension when we drove up was so — it was like ice. It was *hard*. And this isn't the worst family in the world, she thought. Henry's all right. Old Hank. So's Sid. They're just — stuffy, maybe. Needful. Well, why shouldn't someone *need*? I've spent a good deal of my life practicing to do just that, she told herself.

Old Edna over there, old Edna, she declaimed, finishing her drink but not feeling the liquor on her tongue, you have given me a new hero to emulate — you. I can't decide whether to hate you for it or love you. Except, I'm tired of loving people. Do you know about that?

She crunched the ice cube and listened to Hank's voice — his admission — come over the breaking noises in her mouth. "I've been waiting for something to happen to you," Hank said. "To your girl friends, now to your wife. To, ah, Victor over there, say. But mainly to you. And I'd find out, and I'd get into the act somehow. And I'd be able to help. I've been waiting for that, and I've been waiting to admit it to you."

"Dad, you needn't be ashamed about something like that. It's flattering, don't you know that? It's very —"

"I've been waiting for it. Nothing big, mind, nothing necessarily exciting, even. Just something I'd have picked up in my hick practice out here in the boonies that the guys with CAT-scanners and living liquid dyes and European beta-suppressors wouldn't know about. Something to do with the hands. Putting your hands on the patient's skin and feeling something and knowing what to do." Laurel saw that his hands were around his drink and that he didn't take them away from the glass.

"That's a synecdoche," Sid murmured.

"I thought you'd know that word."

"I don't."

Hank shook his head and rattled the ice in his glass. "And I'd know what to do, and you'd be all right, or whoever you loved would be all right, and you'd thank me."

"Yes, I would," Sid said.

"And you know what? I would take your thanks. This

is like a kid having Superman daydreams. You remember
those? You dream about rescuing the pretty girl from the
runaway car or something, and she loves you for it? *My
hero*, she says. I'd take them."

"I'm sorry it didn't happen."

"No, don't say that."

"I am, though. So I could say them."

"The thanks?" Hank asked.

Sid nodded his head.

"You're a nice boy," Hank said, looking at the ice in his
glass.

Two minutes to go, Victor called from across the room,
and then he told his grandmother that Virginia had to foul
someone and hope they missed the penalty shot and turned
the ball over to Virginia. One minute and fifty-seven seconds. "Call a time-out!" Edna shouted. Victor said, "Right
on." Laurel noticed the game clock, whose digital numbers
were now shown on the television screen, and she noticed
the paralysis in which Hank and Sidney sat, having said
something to one another and now not knowing what they
ought to do with the statement. She noticed Edna's proximity to Victor, and how the room seemed to darken, though
not totally. Virginia was down by a field goal and the other
team refused, in what struck her as manifest unfairness, to
relinquish the ball.

Laurel cried out, "Foul!"

Edna looked up.

Victor said, "They have to. You're right, Ma."

"Foul him!" Laurel cried. "*Hit* the son of a bitch!"

Edna looked at her and started to laugh. Laurel laughed
back. Hank and Sidney stared at her, but she kept watching
Victor and his new grandmother as the game clock's num-

bers ran, and as Edna hooted at the ball's slow, predictable path over the wooden floor, and as a slump of easiness broke the harsh horizontal lines of Victor's tensed shoulders.

The seconds ran, and Victor sighed. He said to his grandmother, one old person on a sofa to another, "It's like life, you know? The way this kind of game ends up?"

Sidney turned around where he stood and he seemed to shine with delight. "That's not your mother's field," he said. "She wouldn't know." He said, "Try — what was it? Fleas. The dogs that have them. People on leashes. Something like that."

Laurel said, "He wasn't talking to me." She tried not to sound relieved.

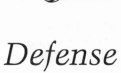

Defense

D r. Sarah Hartley, late-Renaissance, often less than demonstrative, and now showing only lines of strain above the nose in Wolfies Restaurant, around the corner from Brooklyn College, while prodding french-fried onion rings: "The whole *idea* of family is due for revision, don't you think? It is, according to the kids."

My possible replies, which number three. I am lacking such a family; help me, please, revise myself. Or: your long and sunburned nose should be the subject of a poem. Or: all else failing, and all else is, the New York Giants' first-round draft selection is a party named Rocky Thompson who, each time he walks, falls down and damages himself.

Sarah Hartley receives this information, comments that she doesn't care for football and she has to get back, and so we leave. As we approach Bedford Avenue, she says, "You're very healthy, aren't you?"

"You mean, as in not sick?"

"As in liking things that boys like. Games."

"Oh. You mean, as in not mature."

"Or maybe just not old. We'll have to see."

Which I accept, in silence, when I leave her for the long walk to the BMT and the ride to Manhattan, as nearly a promise — surely more than I'd hoped for, though less than I'd wished, from this tall, clenched woman on whom, in the name of business, I pay more calls than I should.

She is one in a succession of proud-nosed women whom I trace to Cousin Beatrice, who was hooked of nose, fourteen when I was ten, possessed of breasts and secrets, and disdainful of the eight-millimeter cartoons which her father, my Uncle Jake, showed in his Queens apartment when we visited them. The films were to keep me occupied, and they did; I watched them while the grown-ups drank in the livingroom, with Cousin Beatrice unwillingly seated behind me in the master bedroom, on guard for projector problems. Cousin Robbie, Beatrice's twelve-year-old brother, played touch football with tough guys while I watched Mickey Mouse. Beatrice married when she was nineteen, and Aunt Rhoda wept for a week, I was told. Cousin Robbie went to Hofstra on a football scholarship, and when Hofstra scrimmaged us in the hills of Pennsylvania, I stood on the cinders of the track with other freshmen to watch Cousin Robbie, a slow senior guard, lead a sweep and break his leg. I believe that's why at the last minute I went out for freshman football, though I'd barely played for my high school team, and I believe that's why I made the squad as a substitute defensive back and went on to play a total of forty minutes during the year. I loved the practices, and I got to wear a maroon cardigan embossed with the name of the team, and I went out in my sophomore year to make the varsity squad. I played back-up safety for the next three years and graduated with a letter. Cousin Beatrice and her passionate nose had much to do with my defensive career, and, though I haven't seen her since I was small, I recall her often.

Four years, thousands paid out by my parents, a heart

that broke and healed five times (not counting its weekly, sometimes daily, insults and injuries), the usual failures in the classroom, a handsome quantity of successes, two fist-fights, and a separated shoulder in senior year: not a bad total, considering that I emerged alive, employable, whole of heart, glad of mind, and possessed of the defensive man's ability to run backwards.

When they put a fast receiver on the line of scrimmage, and unless you're red-dogging the quarterback or are sig-nalled, riskily, to cut around the linebacker to pinch the corner on a possible run, you start to drop back as the ball's snapped; you run backwards until your man posts, and then you make for him, unless he runs directly into your face, in which case you follow, trying to see his eyes as they seek out the ball which, nine times out of ten, is already beyond you. It was that initial backward run I loved, its different-ness from the patterns of the other men on the field, the vantage it offered: I could see what the offensive players only heard. And of course, I was risking, on every pass-play, a public failure the threat of which I found exhila-rating. I was a very healthy kid.

I met my wife while I was backpedalling on a beach in Massachusetts, reaching for a football thrown to Wilbur, my friend and former roommate. It was the usual hypno-sis — shoulders squared to the imagined line of scrimmage, thighs pumping, the Achilles tendons happily stretched as I dropped back to step between Wilbur and the ball. I bumped into a young woman whose nose, while not Cousin Beatrice's, was nothing, in its proud arc, to disdain. When we were married, two years after I'd left college for what a backfield coach had always called laterlife, Wilbur's wife baked a cake in nearly a football shape. When I was di-vorced, six years after that, Wilbur came over to present me with a deflated football and a bottle of single-malt whiskey. Some hours after his arrival, in the midnight streets of Cambridge, Massachusetts, I was detained by large policemen while I was backpedalling under streetlamps in pursuit of the ball, which Wilbur and I had inflated with a bicycle pump. I recall trying to explain that a defensive back has rights equal to those of a receiver while the ball is in the air. One of the policemen, enjoying himself a good deal, reminded me that there was no one around to compete with, and that I was therefore liable for drunk and disorderly conduct. In an unrelated decision, I was sent that week to work in New York.

Selling books as a traveler for a textbook house, I was one of two representatives for the metropolitan area, and I was rather good. We were early to offer a line of fiction and poetry by black authors in the mid-sixties, and I became something of a resource to local schools. We served each other well, the house and I, and when I brought in professors' manuscripts they received attention from the college department, and two were published. I lived in a pleasant, characterless apartment house on Bedford Street in Greenwich Village, tossed a football with local kids, sent free books to professors who wanted to add to the unread texts on their shelves, corresponded with my former wife, with Wilbur, and with Wilbur's former wife, and I became a thirty-year-old man.

Sarah Hartley, assistant professor of English at Brooklyn College, gave a party in the autumn of my thirtieth year. She invited me to attend as an overnight guest in the Ossining home she commuted from, and I traveled the New York Central on the designated Saturday because of Sarah's grand, but not great, nose. She picked me up at the station and drove us, in her cream-colored Volkswagen beetle, without saying more than "Hi." It was hot for October, and her face was bright, slightly filmed above her upper lip; I thought, as we drove across the Taconic Parkway, that I could feel the heat radiating from her denim skirt and loose white blouse, the sleeves of which she wore rolled above the elbow. I wanted to kiss the taut tanned flesh of her arm.

"I never talk while I drive," she said, pushing the little car down a country road past large white houses and more dense forest than I'd seen in years.

I nodded and watched her wipe her lip with the back of her hand. I wanted to kiss the hand. I also wanted to kiss the space above her lip, and then the lip as well, and both lips, surely, and the long full cheeks, and the ears, surprisingly small, which were bared by the loose piling-up of thick hair that, each time we banged over ruts, I watched, hoping it would fall.

She said, "It's just an old habit. You don't mind."

I nodded again, studying the white metal of the dashboard on which, with a dark felt-tip pen, she had written notes to herself, presumably while driving to Brooklyn each day, judging from their scrawl: MILTON THE PROPHET, one said; another said QUIZ; another said COFFEE.

"I just get nervous if I don't concentrate on the road," she told me, staring ahead. "You don't mind if we don't talk."

We went past a stretch of fir trees, and then she slowed and turned up a driveway that took us to a large Colonial house with a long porch, all in white paint which needed a scraping and another coat. She parked in front of a two-story stone-foundation barn, also painted white, and as she pulled the parking brake up, I noticed the absence of cars.

"There," she said.

"Did everyone come by train?" I asked her. It had occurred to me that Sarah loved me, that I was to be her only
guest, that I'd been lured to the forests of Westchester for
seduction. "You know — the other cars? I mean, there *are*
no other cars."

"Oh, they'll be here. You took an early train. They'll be
here." And I didn't like her tone: she knew what I'd been
hoping.

"Great," I said, pulling my overnight bag from the back
seat. "Nice afternoon for a party, Sarah."

"I'm happy you could come. I think you'll like these
people. Well, some of them. I hope so. Oh!"

The exclamation was for a blue van which pulled in beside
her car. My disappointment at its arrival reminded me how
proprietary I'd become of a woman to whom I had only
talked about textbooks a few times, though for longer
salescalls than were necessary. We had eaten lunch at Wolfies, near the college, and we'd even stood, once, to watch
the children across the streeet, at P.S. 152, punching pink
rubber balls at one another in the schoolyard, on the other
side of a high mesh fence. I couldn't hope for a dirty weekend, or even an interesting one.

So: defense. I absolutely bounded to the van, pulled the
driver's door open, quite nearly shouted my name and my
greetings, stuck my hand into the poor man's face. He
looked as though I'd asked him for a loan, then he recovered,
reached for my vibrating fingers, told me that he was Milton
Gold — obviously, MILTON THE PROPHET — and
then he emerged from the van as I stepped backwards, then
backwards again, to let him stand to be hugged hello by
Sarah.

I thought of the clacking projector, Cousin Beatrice behind me in the darkened room, as Mickey Mouse jumped.

Sarah's nose seemed merely long, and that moment it was hidden in Milton Gold's collar as he pulled her head toward his shirt and squeezed her. I stepped backwards again, a long growling foreign car drove up, and soon there were greetings, introductions, two more cars, embraces and exclamations, gin-and-tonics, a pitcher of martinis; and Sarah's party, lit for me by reflections of autumn sunlight from Milton's hairless head and heavy glasses, was terribly under way.

Brit-something, Margaret-something, Les-and-Debby-something, the Something-somethings, and Milton Gold, the young distinguished Ed.D. from N.Y.U., who at thirty-two was Dean of Students at Bronx Community College, and who had something to announce. "Family," he told me. "But not the old nuclear family. We're talking about an end to the *loco parentis* idea of campus administration, aren't we?"

Sarah, standing next to him, shaking ice cubes in an empty glass, said, "You don't mind."

I had wit enough to say, "Huh?"

Milton was saying, "It's simply a new time. The old time's over, we're dealing with new people in a new time — the race business, two hundred years of bloody oppression and humiliation. The War. I mean, pure colonialist thought, and they're taking these kids and killing them. And what *they* perceive, *they* see it as an extension of the whole old family stuff, it's a total violation of trust. So what I'm saying, if you want these young people, and I don't mean that in a patronizing way, you want them to be productive for themselves, you're finished with *loco parentis*, period. It's over. We're talking about a revised notion of family, a completely new sense of trust. That's what I mean by *new* family."

"Terrific idea," I said, nodding so that Sarah would smile at me. She did. I nodded again.

She walked away, to the black piano against the wall of her pine-floored livingroom, and while Milton and I colluded, by nodding, to usher in the new age of on-campus trust, she returned with a pebbled black spring binder. "You don't mind, do you," she told me.

It was, of course, Milton's manuscript. And before she spoke, as I held it in one hand while I drank off my second martini on ice, Milton said, "Sarah thought you wouldn't mind kind of looking at it? Is this an imposition? I mean, I hope not. Because I'm thinking, this isn't just a book. This is a message. Maybe it's a *little* message, but I honestly think if somebody puts it out and people pay some attention to the, well, you know — it's *medicine*, is how I see it. Our campuses are sick and maybe this can help us get well. Do you mind?"

"I don't mind," I said. It was like telling my corporal at Fort Leonard Wood that I didn't mind calisthenics at dawn.

Margaret-something prodded Brit-something with her elbow as we spoke, and he looked me over and turned to her and smiled. Debby-something brought me a fresh martini and took away my empty glass.

"Sarah," I said.

She smiled her quick nervous smile.

"Sarah, I mind. I have to confess. I'm being severe and square and unreceptive. But I mind it, Sarah. What I came here for was to win your heart and mind. I came for your *body*, I came to nibble on your earlobes and your throat. Milton the Prophet — you know what Milton is?"

He said, very gently, "Now, stay loose."

"I was afraid you'd be offended," she said.

"I'm not offended. I'm in love. That's worse. And you stand around with this campus quack, and I *despise* myself because I continue to lust for your neck and your ears. Your nose. That's the worst part."

I held the binder at my shoulder's height, but couldn't decide what to do with it. I'd been with too many books to adore them anymore, but a rough respect was habit, so I lowered the book, passed it over to Milton as if it were a football and he were a back taking it in his gut on a plunge. He received the binder with both hands, dropping his glass, which shattered. That was signal enough of imminent violence: Brit-something, in his light brown tweeds, took my arm and pulled. I pulled back, I stepped back, I announced that I was walking to the station and that anyone who wanted to fight could meet me on the road. And then I left, walking out of the house and off the porch and across the hilly lawn, leaving my suitcase behind, I realized after I'd strutted twenty yards or so, and carrying, with carefully cocked elbow, a squat cold glass of gin and vermouth on ice.

It was a sweaty trip home — the long walk to a busy road, the search for a service station with a telephone, the imploring by phone for cabs, and then the ride to the station, the wait for the train, the crowded journey into Grand Central, shuttle to the IRT, the bumpy ride to the Village. That night, I walked my apartment in underwear, watched movies on television, and then telephoned Wilbur, who with his second wife lived in Maryland. I bored him and hung up before he could intimate that he'd better things to do than talk with me about loneliness in the Big City.

On Sunday morning, I went out for the papers, read the book section because of my business, then made a second pot of coffee for the reading of the sports section. According to a reporter who didn't like the Giants (none of *The Times*' sports writers liked the Giants), Spider Lockhart, the legendary defensive back, was getting too old to play much longer. I reread the article and closed my eyes and argued with it, concluding that even if he'd lost a step, the Spider could still sting the receiver so hard, there was a good chance he'd drop the ball he had outrun Spider to catch. Early lunch, the pre-game program, and then the game: Giants vs. Bears, a couple of losers contesting for the loss, but much to-ing and fro-ing on the field a good prospect.

Each time I thought of Sarah — of my boyish expectations, of Milton Gold's familiarity with her home, of the little speech I had made and for which I wished to publish on the front page of *The Times* a retraction — my face burned as it had burned in Uncle Jake's and Aunt Rhoda's apartment in Queens while Mickey Mouse swaggered and Cousin Beatrice sat behind me and I smelled the Sen-Sen on her breath. A Chicago quarterback with little presence of mind and no mobility in the pocket stepped up into it nevertheless and threw the ball forty yards. The spectators' roar went up, announcing that the ball was in the air, and Spider flew after a flankerback at least eight inches taller than he, and easily as fast. I marveled, as I always did, at Spider's shift from backpedal to forward run, but I feared for him. My feet moved.

"Ever make out?" Beatrice had asked me on a Sunday afternoon in the lightless bedroom.

I had tightened, and stared ahead into the jittery square of colors — Pluto the Pup pursued by a bulldog toward the edge of a high cliff. "Huh? Me? Beatrice, I'm only ten years *old*."

"I did. In this guy's car. In the back seat."

"The back seat?"

Pluto was over the cliff, but the bulldog, wearing a lethally spiked collar, had his paw on Pluto's tail, which stretched halfway down the cliff while Pluto sweated and gulped, hanging.

DEE-FENSE, the fans always shouted when the Giants' huge line crouched on all fours at the goal line, DEE-FENSE. But they weren't crying it now: they were roaring excitement and dismay as Spider fled toward where he should have been a half-second sooner.

"Let me tell you, my blouse wasn't exactly closed."

"It wasn't?"

"If you say anything, I'll murder you."

"Me?"

"Little creep. You know what french-kissing is, creepie?"

Pluto was grinning with fear as he climbed up his tail toward the top of the cliff. He knew, I knew — I had seen the same cartoon perhaps twelve times before — and even Cousin Beatrice probably knew that the bulldog soon would take his paw from the tail's end, that it would snap into Pluto's desperate behind, that Pluto would climb hand over hand a few graspings more before he realized that he was pulling on air, and then he'd fall.

"French-kissing?"

She did not, as I wished years afterward that she had, offer a demonstration. She sighed Sen-Sen at me, spoke my name — "Creepie" — and let me watch Pluto plummet into Mickey's arms, driving them both a dozen feet into the earth. Spider, in desperation, ran up the flankerback's legs, sending them both to the ground in a tangle; the ball sailed on, the official threw his flag, signaled Pass Interference, and it was first-and-ten on the Giants' six-yard line.

"Baloney," I told the official, hoping for Spider's sake that the interference was inadvertent, not a sign of his desperation and a tribute to the wisdom of *The Times*, but I knew how Spider's legs felt, reasoned that he'd saved us from a Chicago touchdown, then smiled when the sing-song DEE-FENSE rose as the Giants settled on the line of scrimmage to wait for the Bears.

The doorbell rang, the Bears' fullback went over the top on a broken play, gaining perhaps a yard, and the doorbell rang again. I kept my eye on the television screen and went backwards to the door. The Bears, always gritty, ran the identical play. Still backing, now with my hand on the knob, I saw them score the touchdown, then turned to the door and pulled it in, said something like "Hello" to Sarah, who was standing hipshot, holding my overnight bag. Her smile reminded me of Pluto's smile as he hung from his tail on the cliff, or of my own.

In the dance of embarrassment that followed, I tried to discover the pebble-grain spring binder gleaming on her person, but I couldn't. The dance was composed of only a few steps — the back-away, the shuffle, the weighted poise, the nod of awful politeness. We both performed each, if not in unison then surely in the same painful silence. I backed from the door, she entered, she lifted the bag, she placed it on the unbuffed parquet floor, she moved to the side, I strode to the set, she placed a hand about her throat and from that hiding place moved sideways, marking time, while I kicked at the newspapers and motioned toward the chairs. And then, in a marvelous uncoordinated sidling, we managed to sit, and puff, and then each move, as if surprised by a third party, when I rocked forward from the almost-inescapable Workbench folding chair to offer iced tea and then fetch it.

The clothes she wore were the clothes she had worn, and my vision was of Sarah wandering the woods with my bag in her hand, or walking all the way from Ossining in a savage penance, or pacing her livingroom all night, circling the bag, to gather courage for her trip. I wondered if she had brushed her teeth yet; I wondered if I ought to offer her my shower and a clean towel; I wondered if I owned a clean towel; I wondered whether the Giants' big damaged fullback could move the ball enough to let the defense — breathless Spider — rest awhile. "Sex," Sarah was saying, "is often overestimated as a factor in situations like these."

"I beg your pardon?" *Creepie!*

Her hand was around the front of her throat again, and the hand was smaller than I remembered. The nose was still all right.

"That beautiful speech you made," she said. "I don't think anyone has ever said anything about me like that in public. God. All I kept saying was, 'You don't mind.' "

"I apologize for the speech."

"But you *were* jealous."

"Sarah, I was."

"And you were angry. You were thinking about when we watched those children in the playground, weren't you? That none of it was a date. That's what you wanted it to be — a date. And you were thinking I'd spent that time with you so I could give you Milton's book. And you were thinking about sex. Milton and me."

She sat back, having said what I would not have mentioned, and she crossed her legs. The denim skirt, wrinkled and not terribly clean, flared; I stared at her thighs. My feet moved.

"It was your nose, Sarah."

She made a hiccup-noise and laughed with her lips wide. She had brushed her teeth. The composition of her face escaped her control, and the white lines of concentration above her nose and around her mouth disappeared into the smooth tan. She shook her head. "Don't even *tell* me," she said.

"I couldn't. You'd have to know Cousin Beatrice. Ontology recapitulates cartoon. And Cousin Robbie and his busted leg." I stared at Sarah's legs, then dipped into my iced tea, forcing my nose down to the glass, which was the only available shelter.

"If I knew you for one more afternoon, none of this would be crazy. I mean, I'm crazy — I almost understand you."

"Do it, Sarah."

"Listen. Milton was my husband. I let him give me the place when we split up. He's very well-off. I needed a place. But I don't take alimony. We're friendly."

"Can I ask if you sleep with him sometimes? You know, for comfort?"

"Very insightful. Very much none of your business."

"Give it an afternoon, Sarah."

"And he asked me to ask you —"

"So you did. Okay. No problem."

"Really?"

"No," I told the iced tea. "I hate him. I hate grownups who spend their days worrying about the kids. *The kids* can take over buildings and burn down laboratories, let them take care of themselves. He's talking about nursery schools for the six-foot-and-over crowd. Milton the Prophet."

"You don't know what he prophesied." She was blushing so hard, I flushed too. "You want to know what he said?"

"Only if it's about me, Sarah."

"It is."

"You talked about me?"

"I did."

"Is it wonderful?"

"I guess you'd think so, if you were pursuing me."

"Sarah, I am. I really am."

She stared at me, her mouth partly open, the white lines dancing into and away from the corners of her lips. Then she closed her mouth, swallowed, opened her mouth to speak. I stood so suddenly, I surprised even me. The iced tea splashed to the floor. She flinched, recovered, stood to meet whatever I was going to do — I had no idea, the point was to *move* — and she walked toward the door, taking car keys from the pocket of her skirt.

I was too proud to be begging, "*What*, Sarah?," but I said it anyway. She walked out the door, I walked to the television set and turned on the final moments of the first half: Bears 13, Giants 3. Homer Jones was running flat-out on a desperate pass-play the Giants shouldn't have been trying from their own twenty-yard line. The doorbell rang. The pass was intercepted by a rookie with whom the announcers were very pleased. The Giants had to hold for a minute and a half, and I didn't think they would. The doorbell rang again. I couldn't select the direction I should face. Chicago would work on the Spider's side of the field, I knew, and I felt weary on his behalf. *Why* was sex over-estimated? What were situations "like these"? Watching the set, I moved backwards toward the door, then spun, charged, pulled it in: the usual shadowed corridor, the elevator's whine and click, the usual no one there. I heard the spectators' roar.

But on Monday afternoon, I was in action again, walking along the high green fence of the Brooklyn College athletic field; Allie Sherman had played there, then had gone on to coach under Jim Lee Howell, before he succeeded him as head coach of the Giants. It was all clear sky and rows of trees, children ran and shouted across the street at P.S. 152, and, diagonally across the street, tough boys cutting classes at Midwood High School watched the traffic on Bedford Avenue and smoked cigarettes while pacing off their defiance.

I swung my briefcase onto the campus, and its weight provided enough momentum to draw me through doors and up steps. It was true that I should have been at 138th Street. But, I told myself, you can't fight a loaded briefcase, can you? Sarah shared an office with two men. Each wore gold-rimmed granny glasses, and each wore hair to his collar, and each specialized in flannel shirts and khakis and work shoes. I told them apart by their whiskers: the American Lit man wore a Tolstoy beard, while the Medieval man kept his trimmed to Dostoevsky. Neither spoke when I entered, though American Lit looked up from blue-books to nod. Sarah was staring.

I dropped my briefcase ungently and opened my mouth to declaim. Her chair scraped backwards with violence and she held her hand in the air to silence me, walked forward, pointed to the door. I pointed back to her. She stopped, slumped her shoulders, squeezed her throat, stooped to pick my briefcase up, and led me into the corridor.

A very tall and slender redheaded boy with freckles all over his face said, in a deep voice, "Professor Hartley, I need to talk to you."

"Not now, Harry," she said.

"Professor Hartley, I'm in bad trouble."

"Harry, nobody knows the trouble *I* seen."

A kid in a dashiki of orange and black clattered to a halt beside her, his bronze face knotted with disgust. "Honkette," he said.

"Oh, no," she said.

"You sing that song when you been black this long!" He

pointed to his face and swaggered off. Harry followed him, loping.

"What's a honkette?" I asked her.

"A female honkey. That's what he calls me. I don't teach black writers in my seventeenth-century course. It's okay, really. He really likes me. He just finds me revolting, sometimes. Why are you here?"

"I'm giving you one more chance, Sarah."

Her whoop of laughter didn't stop any students in their strides, but it carried me and Sarah toward the top of the stairs, where she handed me the briefcase. "Now," she said.

"You look very handsome in slacks," I said.

"And?"

"Will you take a walk with me?"

"No. I have to teach."

"Will you meet me after your class?"

"No. I have a meeting."

"Will you meet me for dinner?"

"No."

"You have a date?"

"At our age we don't *have* dates."

"The Blue Mill, on Cherry Lane. Six, seven o'clock? You know how to get there? It's around the corner from my building, where the street curves."

"I won't be there."

"I'll be the man on all fours."

"I won't *be* there."

"You don't have to tell me what you said to Milton. You don't even have to tell me what Milton prophesied. Show up, say seven o'clock? I can understand how you don't want to get married again. I was married too. It can be very trying, can't it. But what we have to do —"

Her face suddenly swelled, tears ran from her eyes onto her reddening cheeks, and the white lines were back, and were wider than before. She raised her fists to her chest, and her neck and shoulders shook. "I don't *want* this," she hissed. "I don't want your romance. I don't want dinner. I don't want any more love. I do not want *you*. Your innocence, your fake funny little-boy innocence and your bad jokes and your little proclamations and all that rhetoric you dish out like Bible tracts. *No*."

"You're saying you won't have dinner with me, Sarah?"

But even I was ashamed by then, so I took my briefcase and went out to Bedford Avenue and sat for a while at the bus stop in front of the school. Then I crossed to the P.S. 152 playground, where I watched a middle-aged man running the perimeters of the high link fence with his dog. And then I paced the street until my briefcase felt too heavy, so I stood with my back against the fence and I read through notebooks about texts-in-preparation. A lot of high-school children were released, and I watched them. Then, behind me, at the far end of the playground, the elementary school was dismissed, and I turned to watch the littler children run. A police car passed for the second time, and I tried to look unlike a pervert. And when some high school boys began, in the elementary school playground, to throw a football and then choose up a game of touch, I carried the briefcase to the entrance at the middle of the block and went inside. I saw them watch me as I set my sportcoat on the briefcase and rolled up my sleeves, tore off my tie; it was enough, in playground language, to signify that I wished to be included, and when I re-tied my shoes and walked toward the cluster of boys and lifted my eyebrows, one of them pointed to me, and I was in.

The police car came by for the third time and pulled to

the curb. I thought, as the officer watched me miss the tag on a short skinny boy who went for an easy touchdown, of the officers in Cambridge long before. But I was orderly and sober — I was very sober — so I ignored them and after a while they drove away, the one on the passenger's side shaking his head.

What called the play, when she came to stand on Bedford Avenue, holding onto the fence, looking through its diamond-shaped links at me, was all of my life. I hadn't been able to backpedal for the sake of a girl's attention since the day I decided on collision with my former-wife-to-be, and my heart pumped dangerously. I dropped back from the line of scrimmage on the blacktop field, and as the speedy runt I couldn't beat ran a down-and-in pattern, I stopped running backwards and went for the interception. He caught the ball, though, long before I was there. I made a note to explain how leather soles can cost you a touchdown. I flailed at him. He threw a hip toward me, pulled it back, cut away, went for the score. I whirled and went down.

The boy, panting but unsweaty, trotted back to say, "Okay?"

"Old age," I told him.

He pulled on my hand as if he were heavy enough to help me up; my pride drew me to my knees. "You playing?" he asked.

I limped on a tender ankle, shook my head, thanked him for the game, then winced on my way back to the briefcase and grownup's clothes. Sarah had worked her way around the corner to stand outside the fence, opposite my things.

"That was not graceful," she said. She wore a scuffed blue raincoat which, in its shapelessness, made her look like someone determined to be sad.

"It's time for the Spider to hang 'em up," I said, heaving for breath.

"I meant everything I said," she announced.

"I've been waiting here to see if I could ask you about that."

"I figured that out." She pointed toward the campus. "I watched you from the office window."

"Gave the guys something to talk about, did you?"

"They don't talk. They think."

"With me, it's the other way around."

"I figured *that* out. But nobody could be as dumb as that. So I figured a little more. It's possible you're interesting."

I was limping to the schoolyard gate, and she walked slowly on the other side of the fence, keeping my pace. "Did Milton think so too?"

She put her hands into the pockets of the sorry coat and said, "He predicted from the way I talked about you that we'd get involved."

"That's it?"

She shivered as if in the winds of a terrible fate, and I was insulted even further when she said, "That's enough."

So I told her, "This is awful for my confidence."

"Listen, pal. Anybody who plays a child's game with such enthusiasm, and so little talent, shouldn't *have* too much confidence."

We had come to the gateway, and I suppose we each had to wait to see which way to walk, and whether in someone's company. "You know something about playing defense?" I asked her.

She was closer, then, and I could see the white lines. In its long slender way, it was the proudest of noses. She said, "Yes. I'm an expert. And it's work, not play."

"I'm an amateur," I said.

"I know."

"Would you come in here, Sarah?"

"Why?"

"This is where the amateurs hang out."

The police car cruised slowly past. As he came abreast of us, the cop on my side made a motion with his hand, and the car speeded up to turn with Allie Sherman's school-day fence and disappear down Campus Road. The boys behind me cried in alarm, and I knew that the ball was up.

"No," she said.

"I have to come out there?"

"I wish you would."

"You really do?"

Her face was pale now. I couldn't see the lines because they'd taken over, all background was gone.

My ankle was stiffening, and I was awkward when I went through to the street. I dropped my briefcase and held the sportcoat out in my hand, hoping to be hugged. But Sarah stayed where she was. "I have to go back for my books and my bag," she said.

"And then dinner?"

She nodded, not smiling.

I lay the coat over my arm. "Sarah, things are going to be good. I promise."

"Your ankle hurts," she said. "I'll bring the car around. Wait here."

"Now, you come back. All right?"

She was walking toward Bedford Avenue and school.

"Sarah?"

I leaned against the fence and watched her cross the avenue and enter the campus. The kids cried out, and I hobbled to turn and watch them surge and protect. Between their plays, I looked to see if the police were returning. I tried to think of innocent phrases in case they did. And, just in case the little car appeared, to bear us on a nervous ride to Manhattan — "You don't mind" — and just in case it did not, I practiced long silences. Dee-fense.

Making Change

When Don Sturdy got lost in Glacier Bay, he was
with his Uncle Amos and his other uncle, Captain
Frank. They were guided by an Indian who had studied at
Columbia University. They were written about by Victor
Appleton, who had also written the Tom Swift stories, and
whose books were shifted in the sweet easy night from arm
to arm by Vinnie McManus, who was dressed in khaki
shorts, and khaki knee socks held up by red elastic loops,
and a collarless khaki shirt on which, among other insignias,
was the one that showed him to be the librarian of Troop
Eight, Oneida Council, Borough of Brooklyn, during the
year of the energy crisis, 1948. He was coming home from
the troop meeting at the Tompkins Congregational Church,
two miles from his house, with the usual haul of pre-War
books that no one but he, happy librarian, cared to read.
When he later decided on graduate school at Columbia, in
1958, one reason was that someone he knew had gone there,
perhaps someone in his graduating class, though the name
eluded him. Vinnie thought he recalled that his misplaced
classmate was some sort of outdoorsman.

But now, at twelve, he walked home in the silence of
Brooklyn at night. There were few cars parked at the curbs,

and few people walked about at eleven o'clock, and most
of the houses he passed were dark. The moon was bright
and faceless. He looked past it at the stars and was fairly
certain that he could see space, as opposed to the far at-
mosphere of earth. He thought it possible that he might see
vehicles in space, but tonight he didn't. He felt the usual
awe, and wished that when he looked up past the moon
and through the night-time, he might see further, clearer,
might remember better what he saw, might analyze its nature instead of forgetting it all the instant his face came
down to the sidewalk, the trimmed lawns, the wide stucco
or brick houses set back from the street so that hedges might
be planted, since in the suburbs — that was Flatbush, then,
a suburb for the up-and-coming — one planted box-yews,
or hawthorne. As he crossed Newkirk Avenue, he was forgetting that he had looked into infinite space. He was thinking of his books.

He had already, at Wilner's on Foster Avenue, drunk a
nickel rootbeer and eaten a couple of candy bars. So all he
stopped for in his darkened kitchen was a swig or two from
the milk bottle and a couple of fingers scraped through icing
on the dessert cake. He tiptoed up the wooden stairs to his
room. He heard his mother stiffen on the sheets and breathe
differently, and he knew that she'd been waiting, as usual,
while he had prowled the Troop Eight library shelves. He
didn't call out because he didn't want to acknowledge that
he'd robbed her of sleep. He didn't call because he wanted
the night to himself. He went into his room, shut the door,
stripped his uniform off and, in tee shirt and briefs, under
the bright light clipped to the bedstead, in the rankness of
a boy's room kept closed a lot, he started to read. If he fell
asleep while he read, he wakened with no sore chest, and

no racing pulse, and no panic because he didn't know, for an instant, what he'd been doing before unconsciousness sealed him over like mud. Now he was frightened that way because he was forty-six years old and scared both because he'd suddenly reached that age, and because he'd forgotten a lot about how he had achieved it.

But when he was twelve, and the Troop Eight librarian, and pretty much his own only patron, Vinnie McManus read Canfield Cook's *Wings over Japan*, or R. Sidney Bowen's *Dave Dawson with the Commandos*, or Noel Sainsbury's *Billy Smith Exploring Ace, or By Airplane to New Guinea*. It was something of a spell, and something of such an intensity that much of it had fled by the time the book was done. He could reread them every few months and lose little of the experience. What he needed, he supposed thirty-four years later, was the immersion in another world, a world that was manageable because in print and on a page and held in the hand, and yet full of what one couldn't be, or what one wished to be, or was afraid to be, and that still was attainable at least in the cool bed, in the ripe airless room, head propped on the doubled pillow rolled beneath his chin as, with elbows and forearms sometimes growing numb, he turned the pages. It had to do with little worlds and pages, he thought now. It had to do with control and absolute dream-stuff. It had to do, he realized, tying his bow-tie and preparing to be guest of honor at the St. Edmunds High School Library Fall Book Fair, with what made people write as well as read. It had to do with need and greed and desire. It had to do with taking, and nearly always feeling almost out of, control.

Julie was already at school. Julie was fifteen. Julie would be ashamed of him because his tweed sportcoat was not

only old, but was permanently wrinkled like a hairy ele-
phant's hide, and it had three colors of button on the front
— one that had come with the coat, one that he himself
had sewn on after Deborah's death, and one that she had
sewn on not too long before she'd left him. Julie's high
school librarian, Sheila Stewart, would sleep with him, and
quite probably would leave him too, but she would not sew
buttons on. What she did was run a big school library, and
show kids how to find the keys to life in *The American
Heritage Dictionary* and *Facts on File.* And what she did was
spray her body, after work and a glass of wine and a shower,
with something called Rive Gauche. What she did was drive
him, more than ten years older, toward noteworthy sallies
of lust. And what she had done, admitting first that she
would seduce him into it because the budget had been slashed
but she needed writers for her book fair, was to convince
him to attend, and talk with the students about how he, a
novelist of middle age and some success, did whatever it
was that he did. Vinnie had agreed, warning Sheila that
his daughter would be horrified, but still agreeing to appear
before the high school students because that was what Sheila
needed, and Sheila was what Vinnie needed, and it sometimes was satisfactory to stand before some people — almost any people — and tell them, who would never read
his books, that he nevertheless did write them.

Into the briefcase he had kept since his graduate school
days at Columbia he shoved galley proofs, bound and un-
bound, sheafs of Xeroxed page proofs, dummies of cover
designs, manuscript pages that were heavily corrected, a
page of sample type.

Before he became a Boy Scout librarian, his favorite library had been the Brooklyn Public Library branch on East
12th Street and Avenue J. He remembered the creak of the

wooden stairs and then the explosive cracking sounds along the second-story wooden floor as he walked in search of books like *Angry Planet*, or *Navy Diver* by Gregor Felsen. He had read *Navy Diver* so many times that his parents finally bought him his own copy for the Christmas of his tenth year. It was about a boy from Iowa who became a deep-sea diver for the U.S. Navy. He remembered the dark blue cloth cover. He remembered the hero fighting on the floor of the sea with a Japanese diver, and dropping his sheath knife. He remembered asking his parents, separately, to skim the relevant chapter and see whether they could find a further reference to the knife. He was upset, and his father asked him why. "It's U.S. Government *property*," he told them, and they were charmed for the rest of their lives by his concern. That was faith, Vinnie thought. That was real belief. That, Vinnie thought, leaving his house on the lake six miles from St. Edmunds, which was three hundred miles *and* a far cry from Brooklyn, New York, that was a sign that he would write books. He didn't know why. But he knew that it was something that had to do with control.

The house on the lake was big and not pretty, but Vinnie was sure that he wouldn't leave. He had loved his wife in this house, and she had left him in this house, and he had locked his daughter out of this house for a night, leaving her with neighbors — something to do with control — while he got sick-drunk and close to comatose and finished his heavy drinking forever the night after the morning he'd learned that Deborah had died of something as outrageous as blood poisoning — staph, the coroner had called it, but Vinnie had called it blood poisoning and always would — in another man's bed in Allentown, Pennsylvania. Here, in the worst of winter, when the lake was frozen and the wind beat at the house, he was happiest. He was snug here, and when Julie was inside and the fireplace was full of light, and she was doing homework upstairs, Vinnie McManus was a happy man, and he knew it.

He was happiest when he worked; Julie knew that and had grown up with the knowledge, and she didn't much care. It was fine with Vinnie that she didn't, just as he didn't mind that Sheila attributed madness and assorted Irish vagaries to behavior he considered quite moderate. He knew, finally, that she relied on words for the transmission of helpful information, while he, a writer of false facts, was proving himself to her, every day, untrustworthy because successful at lying. Sheila fought the allegiance to facts, and Vinnie resisted his resistance to them, and they managed to admire each other and fight, he thought, surprisingly little.

He thought he should tell the students, it was only when he sat at his very old manual typewriter, banging heavily on the keys, working in something of a blur — not thinking, to his knowledge, but reacting, as an athlete might to a thrown ball — *that* was when he was glad. At the end of his morning's work, his old Air Force tee shirt would be soaked at the armpits. Tell them about Balzac, steaming in the heatless room, Vinnie reminded himself. And why not tell them of Joyce, who also scorned his church, and who also destroyed a family, he thought. And Melville, hearing his son die in the night. Did he really hear him commit suicide, or did he discover his body at dawn? Tell them anyway. But in pursuit of what point, he wondered. Something, he knew, had been shoving out of his brain, like a splinter working from the flesh. Tell them about *that*, he hectored himself, steering around the far end of the lake and turning onto the last miles of road before St. Edmunds.

He had forgotten the lecture, though. He was thinking

about the public library, and how they had hired him, at fourteen, part-time, to shelve books and sweep the floor, and to sometimes check out books and accept the fines for those that were overdue. The first weeks had been his finest hour, and a great relief from his job as delivery boy for a small pharmacy on Avenue J. It had been the start of a career. He hadn't known what career, but he'd known it would have to do with books. Much as he loved softball at the Caton Avenue Parade Grounds and punchball at Wingate Field and stickball at whatever street he was on when the pink Spaulding was bounced and sides chosen up, and much as he thought with his penis and schemed about feeling up girls, he would have to live a lot with books, and very seriously, and he knew that even as he burned with acne and as his voice went deep one morning on its own, and he started the crawl toward adulthood.

So there he was, in the library after school and on Saturdays. It was an immigrants' neighborhood when he was in his teens, and the wealthier commuters to Manhattan were just moving in. The old Jews brought their milk crates to the library each afternoon and sat on them in the sun, before the brick front, where the heat was best. After school, he worked while the old people outside gossiped and traded stories about the Polish lady who sold pickles, and Yasbin the kosher butcher, and the unreliable goy fishmonger, and the lady who ran Ebinger's and sold ladyfingers as well as the sponge cakes for charlotte russe. "The Jews," his mother had said once, "know how to talk about you better than any race of my experience. When they run you down or sing your praises, whichever, and they will do both, you can actually feel it sometimes, and even when they're jabbering in their Jewish language too." So the little people in dark clothing and, despite the sun, pale faces, sat outside the library wall and told each other tales. Their children and grandchildren were to be found inside, taking out *Return to Jalna*, by Mazo de la Roche, and novels by Graham Greene that always looked depressing to him, and essays by T.S. Eliot — "We are a highly educated neighborhood," his mother told his father, as Vinnie checked out her copy of *Winesburg, Ohio*, which she never liked well enough to finish. His father was dutifully taking out, he thought he now remembered, a life of John Barrymore that remained unopened until it was returned overdue, and Vinnie had to pry back the cover to calculate his father's fine. He'd felt disloyal, doing that: his parents were simply bringing custom to their son.

But as a librarian, you had to make change. You punched the keys on top of the counter, and a bell rang, and the belt-high drawer slid out toward you. In the depressions in the drawer were coins. Fines, at two cents a day, made for uneasy calculations, and Vinnie had never in his life performed an arithmetic exercise with confidence. Bored or annoyed patrons, waiting for change, didn't increase his ease. He often made mistakes and then lost his count, and then he lost his courage, and, blushing and stammering and making hopeless jokes, with not one intact number in his mind, he would count money out in a slow-motion panic until the penalized patron would say that Vinnie had given back enough. His parents told him to count from the amount due, back to the amount given him. He didn't understand. His father, who believed in the possibility of anything, given the application of sufficient energy, told him to practice. Vinnie practiced. Twice asked, by different librarians, what he was doing at the cash drawer, he had answered, "Making change." "*Stealing change*," the third questioner, a part-time clerk, had said, reporting him to the head, and getting him fired the following Saturday morning. He hadn't cried until he was outside, and he hadn't doubted that he still would spend his life surrounded by books, and he didn't miss kneeling to shelve, or making change for patrons, but he did have to take the subway to the Grand Army Plaza branch near Prospect Park — there, he could borrow books anonymously, and with no shame — and he hated the time it took, and he didn't return to the neighborhood branch for a couple of years. When they all went to see a film in which Victor Mature was sent, head down, from his homeland, a country near an unnamed sea, on the shores of which everyone sported in a kind of toga except for Mature, who wore thonged sandals and a leather bathing suit, Vinnie had whispered harshly in the darkness to his parents, "I know a little bit about exile."

At the St. Edmunds High School, he parked as close to Sheila's old Chrysler as he could. That was the sort of gesture, she had told him, that attracted her — "Pure dumb romanticism" — and that intimidated her too, because it was almost like bowing and kissing someone's hand. Vinnie was sure she said that because she thought he wanted to hear such remarks. He did.

The school was a large H, and the library its crossbar. About fifteen hundred students usually went in and out of the double doors at either end, and Sheila and her three assistants — para-professionals, they now were called — usually spent as much time in policing the Picts and Vandals and controlling traffic as in showing kids where to look up famous waves of immigration. But today the students were kept from the library except on assignment, and today there was hard, clean light from a bright sky through the tall, broad windows, and there was the usual pathos of much care taken in a school. It was like a frowzy child dressed extravagantly by anxious parents, and with no hope that it really would be loved by others as they loved it now. There were flowers in cheap vases on tables, and snapshot photos of some of the authors tacked onto molding and corkboards, and there were signs, on the harsh broad-grained paper peculiar to schools, that welcomed visitors to St. Edmunds' High School Library Fall Book Fair. At the far end of the library, past tables and stacks and strange-looking TV sets — computers, he realized: the computers Sheila had talked so much about — there was a round table with a coffee urn on top, and there was a stack of nested plastic cups, and there were men and women standing nervously away from one another, but leaning at one another from the neck up, as if to vouchsafe the intimacy that most of their body denied. There too was Sheila Stewart, racing with Julie McManus to see who would be the next woman to leave Vinnie's life.

Sheila was nearly six feet tall, and she had long legs and big hands and feet and the strong back of an athlete. Her hair was cut short — he liked to brush it back against the grain with his spread fingers; the fine brown hair always looked finer against the coarse black pelt of his hand and arm. She was broad-shouldered and wide-hipped, with a funny flat ass that embarrassed her more than her size 10 shoes. As she was dressed now, in a plum-colored skirt and a stone-colored shirt and a corduroy blazer of somewhat darker plum, she looked elegant and at ease with her body.

She intercepted him before he reached the table. "You are *so* good to do this," she said, and he sensed that she'd almost reached forward to kiss him. He felt foolish, because even the incompleteness of such an intimacy from her was enough to please him. "Your daughter is outside with her drug dealer, but she knows you'll be here."

"I told her last night, or — no, I told her last week."

"Really? She said she never heard about it. Of course, she says she never heard about the book fair either."

"She's awfully damned detached, Sheila."

"Oh, she's in space, Vinnie. We should have been talking about that."

"We should?"

"Okay, chum. You ready? Listen — I owe you a big one. One from Column A and one from Column B."

By the time he realized that Sheila was promising sexual extremities, and while he had just begun to wonder what he should want and ask for, she had towed him by the arm toward the group of coffee-drinkers and had begun to introduce him. Here was Mr. Dunbar, whose little book on local blacksmith shops of the past was rather a hit with the vocationally-oriented and more rural students. Yes, Mr. Dunbar had photographed the old barns and smithies himself. Mr. Dunbar was the man in thick glasses who had tiny hands and feet. Vinnie meant his smile, because such a small man writing about such big people was, to Vinnie, the sort of triumph you try to watch for. Miss Wallach wrote poems. She wore a bleached moustache that was nearly as heavy as his, Vinnie thought, and she had no neck. She wore a white Dacron pantsuit — the sort that is puckered all over — and she looked pregnant at sixty or sixty-five. *"Haiku,"* she told him, in a deep and confident voice.

"Pardon?"

"It is a Japanese verse-form, comprising seventeen syllables, with —"

"Ah," Vinnie said, nearly bowing, and sounding to himself like Warner Baxter as Charlie Chan, "Ah, *Haiku*. How fine."

Sheila coughed because she was choking on her giggle, he realized, and she introduced him to a very slender middle-aged woman whose moustache was darker than Miss Wallach's, but more well-trimmed than Vinnie's. This was Mrs. Pescaore, who was also dressed in white, but the white trousers and tunic of perhaps a Nehru, or a practical nurse. She would dance interpretively to Miss Wallach's *haiku*.

Vinnie said, "Ah."

A young woman, not more than twenty, was the ostensible editor of a locally published book of recipes using cheddar cheese and other dairy products. She was Miss Niscayuna Agriculture, the prettiest farm-maid in the entirety of Niscayuna County. As she spoke, Sheila looked straight ahead, and therefore at nothing except a shelf of the Encyclopedia Americana.

Other authors would be present during the latter hours of the day, Sheila said, but their guest of honor, Mr. Vincent McManus, who would speak in the auditorium while the others met with small groups, had now joined them, and they would soon be ready to begin. Vinnie realized that she was also speaking to a semicircle of students who had appeared. There were six of them, blushing boys and girls in ties and good dresses and linen blazers and polished shoes, and they were taking coffee cups, and pouring coffee, and standing attentively, and in general behaving like servants in a parody of drawing-room customs. These would have to be the children who wrote for the school literary magazine. And of course they were. One, Vincent saw, held a paperback copy of a novel he still regretted publishing. But he'd a note due at the bank and had needed the low advance his former publishers — now digested by a German machine tool company — were willing to pay right away. It was called *You Know Who I Am*, and its best scene was swiped from Farley Mowat's *Never Cry Wolf*, he could now admit to himself: the drunken protagonist, staggering from tree to tree near his rented country house, urinating to claim the territory as his own, while an upstate snowstorm blew the pee off-track. The boy who held the book was covered with severe acne, from his neck and around his ears to his forehead. He seemed to blush constantly, and perhaps he did. Vinnie wanted to touch his shoulder or even hug him. He looked away from the boy, though, so as not to cause him discomfort, and he found Miss Wallach, who wrote *haiku*, staring at him. He looked down at his shoes, and he realized that he'd put on boating shoes instead of the going-to-business shoes he'd polished that morning while he sat on the edge of the bathtub. Sheila would let him know later, he thought, how superb she felt his scuffed and listing deck shoes looked with his good gray flannels and his blue tweed jacket with three colors of button. He smiled at the thought. Miss Wallach must have thought that he was smiling at her, for she herself smiled. She smiled what was nearly a simper. Her poetic sensibilities were aroused, Vinnie knew, and he feared that she would be giggling with him for the rest of the long celebration of books and writers and the people who were said to read them. He nodded back politely and tried to fetch himself more coffee, but the boy with acne preceded him, though without speaking, and had it poured by the time Vinnie reached the table.

Sheila was behind him, whispering. He could smell her breath and feel the wind of her words at his ear. He was pleased, and he was confused — for Sheila had said, "The pusher's with her too." The first time, he'd been certain it was a joke. High-school people were always joking about their students' sex and drugs. This was the second time, and perhaps she'd said something oftener, and he had failed to listen. He turned to ask for more information, but Sheila said, "We're starting, and I owe you a big one. You decide what it should be." She blew a soft kiss as his head came around, and then the St. Edmunds High School Library Fall Book Fair was in motion, and so was Vinnie.

He was taken by two students down the noisy wide hall. They were on their way to the auditorium, where Vinnie would give his talk to the assembled upper grades. It was addressing all those disgruntled, conscripted and absolutely uninterested students that terrified him. He knew well enough from failing at the job of raising Julie that, while you could lie to an adolescent for a while, or frighten him for a while, or even impress him momentarily with feints and gestures and footwork, you truly couldn't interest a teenager for more than six minutes — often, sixty seconds was the limit — unless your primary topic of conversation was something along the lines of "Why You as a Teenager in a World of Sexual Fullness, Drugs and Abusive Elders are Fascinating, and Why I Feel so Sorry for You." And what had Sheila meant about Julie? Surely, a father would know. Oh, Jesus, Vinnie thought, and then he thought it in his mother's voice: "Oh, Jesus God above in *blue* heaven, will you listen to the fool?" And then he thought it in his father's: "Oi may live on a street that's overrun with Greeks and Jews who celebrate Easter on a different day than us, but you can't lie to a liar: the parent is the last of them all to know." Baloney, Vinnie told himself. The old man never talked like that except when he was drunk with the mick friends from the office, the drunk micks from Sears and Roebuck, talking like immigrants while they told stories about their favorite baseball teams and noble boxers of the past. Vinnie remembered one of the men weeping, on a Friday night, as

Making Change

Joe Louis lost to Rocky Marciano. They were at the auditorium doors, and walking in, and he was congratulating himself on his ability to cloud the issue. It's a gift, he would tell the students: being obtuse is a gift. And, meanwhile, there was the matter of Julie and this other party to whom Sheila had referred. My daughter doesn't use drugs, he said as they walked the aisle to the front of the auditorium. My daughter may not be using drugs.

On a cruel chilly night, about a month before, when the wind over the lake had been whistling all of Saturday, and when the pines near his house had rattled so violently that it sounded like a seething, and he'd said so, and Sheila hadn't replied, Vinnie, cooking up tea for them in the kitchen, had called out, "Hey. Sheila Stewart!"

"Yeah, Vinnie."

"Hey! Stewart!"

"Vinnie: what."

"Do you love me?"

"So what, Vinnie?"

"No. Do you *love* me?"

"Vinnie, I do. And what does that prove to you?"

"I wanted to know."

"But you don't know a thing you didn't know before."

"Sheila, you sound like the Jebbies, you know that? All your Jesuitical doubletalk and logic-rattling? It's like being a kid again."

"Vinnie, you're not Catholic. Your grandfather was Orange, and your father was born in Newark, New Jersey, and you never talk about 'Jebbies' unless you're trying to sound like an Irishman, which you do when you're embarrassed. What's the matter?

"I'm embarrassed." He took the dishtowel from his shoulder and spun it around, then went back into the kitchen for the tray of milk and sugar. "I'm feeling needful. When do you leave?"

Sheila, crouching in front of the fireplace, looked up. "Do you think I'm leaving you?"

"No, not now," he said, putting the tray down, then stooping near her but looking only at the gray logs he'd split a year before. "No, I mean that I think you're restless. I think you're a little bored about servicing doctors' kids who get bored with the alphabet. Helping pregnant girls find books on morning sickness and not asking them why they don't come in months ago for a Planned Parenthood booklet."

Sheila's hair was in a ruffle of static, and she smoothed at it like a long, nervous animal. "The all-wise eye of the novelist," she said. "Are you trying to impress me?"

He got up slowly and went back to the old ironware pot and the chilling tea. "I wasn't trying to be a smart-ass, if that's what you mean."

She shook her head and blinked, saying, "Never mind. I was a little abrasive."

"Because you hate to be labeled. And you hate to be pinned down in words. And you hate it when I sit there and tell you what you feel."

"Which you just did, Vinnie."

"I'm sorry."

"Though you were right, too."

"Then I'm sorry for that."

"Shut up," she said.

They sat in the old house on the lake, and the water and wind outside made the noise of water in a kettle being boiled, and the fire beat at the chimney flue like a lake at its shore, and they sipped at the tea which Vinnie always

208

served them with milk and sugar, though neither of them used milk or sugar. It was old-fashioned, she once had told him, serving tea like that. He did it every time after that, and she then had told him that he repeated elegant gestures because he wanted to remind her that he was more formal than she, and also older. He had told her he didn't want her to forget the disadvantages of being involved with him. She had told him she wouldn't. And to prove to her that he wasn't frightened that she would remember his age as a difference between them, he served tea with the sugar and milk that neither of them would use. And he remained scared, while proud of his courage: the Ernest Hemingway of the teapot set.

And that night, after he had shut up and stayed shut, and after Sheila had sat, waiting for him to speak, and after he hadn't spoken, she said, "It's very hard, living with a man like you."

"That's what Deb said."

"Deb," Sheila had said, as if sneezing without a handkerchief. "Deb. I wish you'd use her name. Deb. It sounds like some kind of newspaper thing on the garden page about debutantes. The St. Edmunds, New York, Debs' Ball. Deb."

"Deborah," he said obediently. "She made the same case, though. It's hard living with a man like me. Actually, what she said, at one of our lower ebbs, maybe at dead low tide as a matter of fact, was that being married to me was like fucking a book. End of quote. I leave the mechanics of it up to you."

"I can't complain. I wouldn't want to. So don't ask."

"No. I guess I'd be afraid to, anyway."

"But you are not a man who's easy to live with. I was thinking about it. Living with you, more or less, at least more than on weekends. I wasn't proposing it, Vinnie, but

I was thinking about how it would be with me and you, and that led to me and Julie. So I practiced, one afternoon. She was in the library with this boy she hangs around with — Jerome? Do you know Jerome?" When Vinnie nodded his head slowly, then shrugged, he knew that Sheila knew he was lying. She said, "He's very tall and broad-shouldered, and he uses about a pint of aftershave lotion every morning. He dresses well, as he should, since his father owns both of the movie houses. Got him? Jerome Gregg? He keeps putting his hand on your daughter's ass. Oh, relax, Vinnie. They screw standing up in the library, if we let them, some of those kids. Not Julie, no, but she likes him, because she puts her hand on his ass too when they walk in the halls with their arms around each other."

"I don't like the age we're living in," Vinnie said.

"Sweetheart, I sometimes don't like the century. But they do grab each other's bottoms, these kids, and your kid's one of them that does it, so you're stuck with fingerprints on her little behind."

"I don't like this," he said. "Writers, you know, we're wild people. We live dangerously all of the time, except for me. I don't go in for enough absinthe and heroin and racing cars and killing myself. My agent thinks that's my big problem. I diminish my marketability by not killing myself enough."

"No," she said, "but we're talking about your daughter, not you. Remember? I called your daughter into my office and we split a can of Coke and we talked. She's very jealous of me."

"That would figure," he said authoritatively. Then: "Right?"

"Probably," Sheila said. "Are you jealous of her boyfriends?"

"Probably," Vinnie said. "Sheila. Should I be worried about Julie?"

"I don't know anything specific you could stay up nights about," she had said. "But you'd be nuts not to worry, I guess. She's fifteen, she can conceive and lactate. She's another sitting duck."

"Quack," Vinnie had said into his teacup, and they'd started to laugh.

That was what Vinnie thought of after the introduction by Mr. Bowers, who seemed to hate teaching English, as well as English itself and his students and this honored guest who would be addressing these combined classes on the subject of, if anyone cared, what it was like to be a writer. As he looked at two boys entering into an arm-wrestling match on the divider between their auditorium seats, Vinnie could only think of *Quack*.

"I write because I can't do anything else," he told the students. Some of the girls looked at him with what seemed to be pity. A few looked interested. Most of the students were trading things back and forth — he couldn't tell what — or calmly discussing matters of what seemed to be greater moment. He noted that his voice carried poorly in the large hall. The walls had bright mosaics. They seemed to represent a great many scenes of misfortune.

A big handsome kid in the third row, the sort who goes to parochial school and is loved by nuns for being their Bad Boy, and who then attends public high school and is shocked to find how hard he must work to make the non-virgins give him passing grades, called out, "Why don't you learn a trade?" There was general laughter. Mr. Bowers sat, in the rear, with his legs crossed and his gray suit unbuttoned and his eyes closed tight. There was another teacher beside him, a woman, who stood up and walked out, locating the pack of cigarettes in her purse just before she was through the doors. A third teacher, tall, very bony, with several fingers missing on each hand, was waving and snapping what fingers he had at the noisy students. They ignored him with the same tranquility they displayed in ignoring Vinnie.

"I like to write," he said, and he knew that he must finish very quickly because he was boring a lot of people. He didn't blame them. His ribs were running with sweat. He told them what Sheila had said they would want to know. "I usually wake up very early," he said. "I usually have breakfast with my daughter, or at least I say hello to her, or at least we sometimes argue over who makes the coffee that day." He chose not to see the ongoing arm-wrestle or the mouth-motions of the handsome Bad Boy in the third row. He remembered what Sheila had said were the categories, and he heaved his life in little mounds and shoveled them into the areas she'd mentioned. "So then I go into work. I have a long table, it's about six feet long, in a little upstairs room that looks over the lake. I don't look at the lake. I have my desk so it looks at the wall. I just keep some photos and things on the wall, but it's mostly blank. I look at the wall a lot. It's like my mind." He waited for the laughter, but of course it didn't come, so he went on. The sweat was on his forehead and chin now. "I try not to look too hard at what I wrote the day before, and I try not to think too hard." Pause. No laughter. Proceed. "I write sometimes from notes. I sometimes make notes in this little ledger-book I carry as a notebook. I'd love to be making notes about dollars and cents in it, but instead of that I usually have things about ideas I want to work from. I write until my characters get going, and then they take over and I put down what they say and do. I don't have a real outline, nothing long and involved. Plots hatch as the characters make their decisions. I write for a few hours and then I find out that I'm very, very tired. In some ways, it's manual labor. It's very hard. And you feel all washed out when you're done. Empty, but good, because you made up a whole world if you got lucky, and it's mostly dumb luck. Well, you have to have some talent. But mostly you need energy. You need the energy to keep working for months and years, no matter what. But you also need luck. And if you're lucky, you've made up this little world. You can watch it on the pages that you're writing, if you're lucky. And for a while, you believe in it. It gives you something to believe, so in that respect it's gorgeous, it's really thrilling. It's like heaven. It's *sex*. You have —" He looked up, because the big room had suddenly gone quiet. The two big boys in the middle were still arm-wrestling, though, and their faces were very red.

"Well," Vinnie said. "You usually spend a large number of years without a publisher or an agent, and then you get one. That's some of the time you need the energy I talked about. You just keep on going. And then you have an agent, and you send the stuff there, and your agent sends it to editors, and sometimes you find one who wants to turn your manuscript into a book. They start out by picking a typeface and designing a book. A book designer does that." From his briefcase he drew a wad of paper, found the sample pages, and held them up. "Then they set the book into type, and they print it on these long pages here" — he rummaged, then waved a batch — "which we call galley proofs. You make your corrections on these and send them back. They make changes according to what you said and they run off page proofs. That's these. But meanwhile, for all the world to see, they're sending around your uncorrected galleys, bound in this kind of binder here" — he

waved it at them, and a few of them looked; they were
chatting again, and arguing, while the Bad Boy squeezed
the thigh of the pretty girl next to him, and she slapped his
hand, but not hard, and the jocks, their faces crimson now,
continued to arm-wrestle — "and they go to reviewers,
magazines especially. They need a lead-time of three months
to get a review of your book into print. If they want to do
one, of course. And then yer book's out and then, me lads
and ladies, it's a *foin* bog yer up to the waist in, Oi can tell
ye." He held up his last book, a collection of stories his
publishers hadn't wanted to do, but had printed because
they were loyal and were prayerful that his next book, a
novel still in progress, would make some money back. A
few students, the sad acned boy who owned *You Know Who
I Am* among them, looked up as he waved his book. The
two boys who'd been arm-wrestling were on their feet now,
and one had his arm around the other's neck while, with
his free hand, he was punching him in the face. A lot of
blood ran from the pinioned boy's nose and eyebrow and
mouth. It jetted at one point, and then the caught boy pulled
loose and braced himself and kicked the other boy very hard
on the thigh and then flush on the kneecap. Vinnie thought
that he was remarkably agile to do all that in the aisle of a
school auditorium. He saw, out of the corner of his eye,
that the pretty girl whose thigh had been squeezed was in
fact his daughter, Julie. He hadn't realized that she wore
so much eye makeup, or sat so close to boys. The Bad Boy,
still smiling, was closing Julie's fist around something. Her
fist fell into her purse and returned, clutching money. She
counted it into the Bad Boy's palm. He watched her mouth
move. And eight. That's nine. That's ten. Mr. Bowers had
leaped onto the bleeding student, cracking the boy's head
against the metal armrest. The other boy lay on his back

and slowly shook his head. A girl in a pink sweater stood and screamed. Vinnie looked away from his daughter, because he didn't want her to feel spied upon, and he packed his briefcase as the students, commanded by the teacher with few fingers, were dismissed.

In the hall, slower-moving flotsam in the loud bright stream, Vinnie was caught by Julie, who hugged his arm to her side. His briefcase was pinned against her recently-squeezed thigh, which pushed it back against his knuckles. They walked in step toward the library. She was going to be taller, she already came to his shoulder, and she seemed to him much older than she'd been last night or this morning at home, when she called goodbye without coming into his bedroom.

"That's a terrific-looking shirt," he said to her.

"Thank you. It was on sale, about a year ago."

"And I didn't notice?"

"You were beginning to get very involved with Sheila."

"Are you going to be like Sal Mineo or someone, and be mad at me for that?"

"Who's Sal Mineo — oh, the greaseball. He died, Daddy."

"I meant, are you becoming a neglected adolescent of the customary sort?"

"Oh. Well, I'm pregnant and I'm snorting coke, Daddy, but otherwise things are fine. Don't worry." She laughed at the speed with which his head swiveled, and then he felt constrained to put a clown's face on — tongue out, eyes bulging, moustache dancing up and down on a terrified lip — and she laughed again at the show, while Vinnie felt like twice a fool.

"Oi *can*not be bothered, ye know, wit the dairty laundry of yer small life."

"Oh, I know," she said. "Poor me."

Julie was thin as Deborah, with the same disappointingly thick neck, which ought to have been swanlike to match her body. Her nose was long, like Deborah's, her eyes large and dark like his own, her legs more sturdy-looking than Deborah's had been. She was as pretty as Deborah, it seemed to him, and with more delicate expressions — probably from always wanting to woo her parents away from their fights — so she smiled readily and often looked happy. She saw him looking at her, and she stopped him there in the hall, this large child in jeans and a smocky shirt, and she reached her face up to kiss him on the cheek and under the ear. The second kiss was confused, he felt, as though she were kissing a boyfriend. He wondered whether she had done it on purpose, or was merely mixed up. Either way, he was wholly hers, and his eyes filled up because he remembered what it seemed to cost a kid to admit to having parents, and then to acknowledge in public who they were. "Yer a foin decent gal to yer fadder," he muttered at her.

At the library door, over the noise of the students, she said, "Don't worry about your lecture, Daddy. They'd talk through sudden death. You were terrific. Gotta run! Gym class! See ya! Bye!"

While he was telling himself that his daughter could not possibly take drugs, Vinnie walked into the library in time to see Miss Wallach, with the moustache, rattling pages and beating her foot to the rhythms established by her small partner, Mrs. Pescaore, who was trailing white rayon handkerchiefs. Of course, it was an enactment of *haiku*, and in a bold and manly voice the poet read, to flittings and dartings and sudden droopings of the neck by her partner:

Making Change

Constant rain! Dark sky!
The storm arrives in my heart.
Sun runs on mouse feet.

The students standing in a circle about them suppressed laughter, somewhat more effectively than Vinnie, as Mrs. Pescaore did her bit to imitate the sun's mincing flight. Sheila waved from her place at the far end of the long library where she was supervising a demonstration by one of her guest authors. It seemed to have to do with nails and horseshoes, and Vinnie actually didn't want to know. Great writers want to know these things, he cautioned himself. All you want to do is avoid parties and not kill yourself. A wonderful writer would kill himself. A permanently great writer might do it at a slow party. To turn down an invitation to a party, one of his colleagues once had stated, is to turn down an invitation to life. Refusing to kill yourself at a party, therefore, would be the act of a churl. A professional, he chided himself, somebody who was just competent, would at least be taking *notes* now. But what Vinnie did was to get himself a plastic cup of bitter coffee and watch the day tick, with a little happy smile on his face, as if he were listening to someone just out of sight; it was the way he worked at hoping, during public events, that no one would come and talk to him. You should have been an Eskimo, he snarled at himself, alone in the night for ten or twelve months. There he stood, nearly fifty years old, an honest-to-goodness working writer whose books were extant and sometimes even read. You stand here like a teenage boy at a dance. Your daughter is older than you are. Go someplace and live alone, he thought. Thinking of solitude, he thought the word *gay*. No, it was a name: Gay. Gay who? Why *Gay*? And, like the slowest-moving freight train, aching its way upstate from the Long Island Railroad yards in Brooklyn all the way up along the Hudson, past commuter stops — Ossining, say, and Beacon, and Pough-keepsie — and then across the Rhinebeck freight bridge to the other bank and then west from Albany through Syra-cuse, through Utica, through little towns where red lights flashed and bells clanged to hold up traffic while the train went past, it arrived, thirty-four years later and still fresh: Gay Little, the Alaskan Indian, educated, like the writer Vincent McManus, at Columbia University, and the de-pendable guide for Don Sturdy and his uncles Frank and Amos during their adventures at Glacier Bay. "Hot *damn!*" Vinnie said, cutting three syllables off the weather report of another *haiku*, and bringing eyes upon him. He didn't care. He was grinning with real pleasure, even as he realized how great a part the distant past was coming to play in his life.

It grew very cold on the night of the book fair, and Vinnie sat in the livingroom, in front of a hot fire, looking at the old books he had dragged in from the storage room in the garage. The red of the Tarzan books was less brilliant than he'd imagined, and the paper of course was chipped, like soft stones, and over them all — the green of the Dave Dawson books, Lucky Terrell's terracotta, John Carter's fading Martian crimson — there was the smell of mildew, which Vinnie thought of as rot. He had always told himself that he kept the Troop Eight library books, or a lot of them, because no one else had wanted to read them; they'd been light on the trip home from Scout meetings, but very heavy on the long haul back. He wondered why he still kept them, though. Julie had never cared for them, although she had liked the chastely sensual picture of Dejah Thoris, John

Carter's beloved, in the front of *A War Lord of Mars*. He wouldn't read them again, Vinnie knew. But he also knew, and just as certainly, that to throw them away would be like chucking out people who no longer were in great demand at parties. And it might, he finally admitted, be like saying that the boy on the street beneath stars and mile-deep mystery no longer lived. Sheila rang the bell, as she always did, then let herself in with her key, as he liked her to, and then called out. Vinnie felt rescued.

But he knew that Sheila was going to thank him, and he didn't want her to. She was going to apologize for his experience in the auditorium, and she didn't need to. "I was so worried about you lads," Uncle Frank Sturdy said, "that I lost all interest in looking for a blue bear." He closed the book. It smelled like an old attic, and his nose was irritated. Sheila was also going to tell him something more about Julie, he figured. Julie who was not recognizable to him from the third row of the auditorium because she changed her face when she arrived at school, and because she sat with her leg pressed against the leg of a world-class Bad Boy whose face qualified him to become a robber baron or high-priced hostage taker, or welfare drunk who whipped his wife with a leather belt on the buckle of which was a truck insignia. He had watched her, through a mist of stage fright, parental disbelief and general myopia, as she counted money out to the kid who wore a tall, slanted pompadour as if he were imitating James Dean. She wasn't lending the boy money, because you offer it in a wad when you lend it. She was either counting out change or buying something from him. And if Sheila, who knew everything, said the boy was Julie's pusher, then Julie was probably buying dope from the kid. She had made a joke about cocaine, he remembered. She wouldn't be buying cocaine from that big, wicked, handsome and totally untrustworthy boy with the 1950s hairdo, he thought. Because she's my *Julie*, he simpered at himself. That's right, and tell them the other part. You might as well. Because — go ahead — because my daughter wouldn't *do* that. Thank you very much. The sun on mouse feet becomes the daughter quacking wise. He went through to the kitchen of the big house and walked up the narrow back staircase, avoiding Sheila, whom he could hear calling along the first floor. At Julie's door he smelled it before he knocked, the incense that itched in his nostrils like the rotting book he had held. He knocked, and when she didn't answer he opened the door wide enough to find her dead from an overdose on the bed.

She wasn't on her bed, or on her floor, so she wasn't dead from an overdose — of what? — at least in her room. He noted that her room was, as usual, neat and pretty and still signaling that she was partway between her lives: a jumble of undusted dolls was on the bottom shelf of her open cupboard, not on the top shelf but still in sight; if the Def Leppard poster was over the bed, a Babar poster was near her open closet; a little stuffed doll of Pooh remained near her mirror on top of the bureau she had used since she was nine.

The top drawer of the bureau was ajar, and he was going to open it all the way and find her cache of mind-altering substances or, in row upon row — laid out like the five-hundred-pound bombs that the Air Force had trained him to help shove up into the bays of B-52s — reefers. Call them joints, he told himself, in case you talk to her about them. When he was in high school, a joint was a schwantz, a penis, a joint of meat. American boys liked to talk about their penises as if they were twelve-pound legs of lamb, tons of gristle, *joints*; this made them feel better, later in their lives, when what they sported went numb, or little, or merely held its peace, as was, from time to time, its wont and need. Joint, he thought, seeing the rows of bombs, and remembering how they had stuffed them up and into the airplanes, and he thought of Julie, and of stuffing, and of *joint*, and he was somehow pleased, in all the suddenness of thinking about so much at once, that he could react with horror and the prurient *frisson* — he did, physically, shudder — of the father who lived alone with his baby girl. He was more worried about Julie in the sack with young James Dean, he admitted, than he was about the dangerous drugs she might in solitude administer to herself. He was jealous. He was an intensely selfish man, he concluded. He thought he smelled the marijuana in her room — *tea*, they'd called it in college — as he speculated that she had been masking it for a long time with the incense and perfumed candles that he had dismissed as adolescent mysticism. He went no further toward the bureau or anything else. He remained standing on the threshold of her room. That was where he belonged. He backed away and shut the door, and he went down the front staircase, wide and interrupted by two broad landings, and he called out to Sheila.

Her broad-brimmed man's felt hat, worn to dazzling effect, was still on the knobbed coat rack that he and Deborah had put in the hall. Her trenchcoat was hanging there too, but Sheila wasn't about. In the livingroom, he saw that his big fire was reduced to steam and hissings as the sap in a green log boiled. The kettle was on the stove in the kitchen, and he turned it off and went outside through the back door, which she had left off the latch. Why come clothed for autumn, leave your garments at the front and walk out the back?

To follow Julie, he thought, not knowing why he'd thought

it, but nodding as he walked. If he were writing it, that was what he would write. He went back for Sheila's coat, put on his own raincoat, and walked through the house and out the storm door of the kitchen, which led onto a small porch, past an herb garden that was dominated by neighborhood cats and rarely productive, then down the flagstoned steps, four of them, over a terrace of wind-burnt lawn, and down a steep incline, through apple trees that never had taken. And then he was on the gravel, and then the sandy soil that met with a narrow maintenance road that ran over all the back lawns around the lake. Beyond that, there was the water and the wooden pier. The water was torn by high winds that blew in gusts. He walked in the darkness and cold until he found Sheila standing near a wide maple tree, off to the side of the maintenance road. He hissed, as if at villains, so that she wouldn't be startled when he came up behind her. She turned, saw him, received the coat and put it on. Then she kissed him near the ear, just under it. He wondered why.

"How did you know I was here?" she whispered.

"Is it Julie?"

"Yes. Damn it. I don't really know if we should be here. I don't think we should."

"Is it drugs?"

"Probably," she whispered. "At least."

Finally, he had the courage to look over her shoulder and beyond the tree, and there was the car, parked not ten feet from them, on the rutted maintenance road that came out from its intersection with the main road to St. Edmunds. "Sheila," he said, "the trouble is — Sheila: I wanted to say that I couldn't imagine what's going on in there. The trouble is, I can. You understand?"

She hugged him. He felt her nod.

"If that pretty-faced little shit is doing an abortion on her with the dipstick off a '57 Chevy, I imagine it. I already imagined it today. Understand?"

The lake banged at the pier, and he heard wind, like sheets of water, slamming at the long car parked in darkness in what was just about his own backyard. The lights from his kitchen and other back rooms didn't reach them or the tree or the car. But they did dilute the darkness a little, and he might be able to see something of what happened in the car if he went forward, he thought. He didn't, of course, know all that he might see. But he knew some of it. He must stay where he was, though, just as he stayed on the public side of Julie's threshold in the house.

But then he thought he saw a motion in the car. He thought that someone was beckoning. It was a whiteness, and it might be a hand. He wondered if Julie might know somehow that they were there, and might be calling them. He wondered if she might be motioning her father forward. He was going to ask Sheila, but when he turned he saw that she was walking back to the house. He went nearer to the car. He waited for Sheila to insist that he come home, but she was out of sight now, and the car was closer. In the weakened darkness he saw that the back-seat window was fogged. But there seemed to be a head pressed on the window. The hair of the crown of someone's head that rubbed the pane was cleaning the window off. What had seemed to be a hand beckoning was really a forehead upside-down, floating above the sweaty, matted, curling hair of someone whose head, hard at the window, was moving in a frantic steady rhythm, back, and back, and back. The head pushed even harder, and the forehead rotated higher up and then back. And there, upside-down, staring at him with no vision, offering no recognition, there was Deborah, making love, on her back, in the rear seat of a car, her face nearly reversed. Deborah floated there, eyes huge and white in a pale face, the body arched. And of course it isn't Deborah, Vinnie McManus thought, it's her daughter. It's my daughter. And Julie's face — it was a terrible white moon, familiar and infinitely distant — came rising through the window's fog. He turned away from the eyes, and he ran to the house.

Sheila was on the back steps, waiting.

"What I wanted to say," Vinnie said. But he stopped. If he were writing this, and really believing it and in control, he would catch his breath and say to Sheila, "Well, then."

And she, just as easily, would say, "How's life?" Perhaps she would say it with — for the sake of light relief — a hint of pasteurized Yiddish, so that Vinnie might feel as if he were on Avenue J, returning from the library, lugging books. Or maybe walking home in the dark from the Troop Eight meeting room, his wrist numb from the weight of the books he had checked out to himself. He would remember staring into a high black sky and past the moon, waiting for signs of extra-terrestrial life, wishing he could see farther and remember longer what he felt as he looked into all that cold light, in pinpoints, coming toward him from long ago.

"I believe," he would say, "that I could be a little melancholy if I really let myself go." Sheila would bend her head down.

Then she would sit up and say, "Oh, you poor dumb bastard. Vinnie, you poor dumb son of a bitch. You break my heart, you know that?"

But he was not writing this one, and in the darkness, not that far from them, his daughter rose beneath a boy. The wind came up the lawn to the steps where Sheila sat, looking past him. Vinnie straightened, as if he were going to speak,

but he didn't know why he'd done that. And then he did.
He'd understood that he wasn't, for a moment, thinking of
Julie. And he had wanted Sheila to know this, because he
wanted to show off his lack of self-absorption. But then he
realized whom he had in mind: a slender, acned, bashful
high-school boy who had patiently stood, holding a copy
of Vinnie's book, and waiting — Vinnie knew this — to
talk about how he too was a writer, and in love with stories
and with owning the handmade worlds inside them. It was
nothing to boast of, though, to the silent woman who sat
before him, out of his reach and unwilling to offer the
consolations of only language. He had forgotten the boy.
He had walked past him and away, and into his own history.
In Vinnie's imagination, the boy's face flamed with embarrassment and loss. He saw the burning face. And *that*,
he wanted Sheila to know, was on his mind, was also on
his mind, though he said, as the wind shook windowpanes
above them, "Well, they've a *foin* dark night fer it, haven't
they?"

Stand, and Be Recognized

I delivered Lenny just as I delivered a hundred or more pieces of mail during the War. And I sent the letter that brought him into mourning and risk. I wrote it care of the school in Rome, saying that when our Opel hit the doe, the deer stood still and the car ricocheted off the road, then across it, and up an incline of shale. We rolled back, I told him, and then we stopped, and I was certain that before I fainted I saw the bone of Ariana's forearm slide through her flannel sleeve.

Lenny Levine, in 1971, was teaching American servicemen's children abroad because his country had tried to draft him twice, before he took up teaching and was therefore classified Essential to the National Effort. I knew that if he came home he would invite conscription. But I sent the letter, and five weeks later he flew from Rome to Boston, rode the bus to Montpelier, Vermont, saw me in the Trailways waiting room and butted me in the chest. Weeping, he said, "I'm here. I'm here."

He wept again as I drove us in my Volkswagen bus, and

he sniffled at the end of the drive, outside Irasville, at the house that Ariana had bought for us after her mother drowned off Providence, drunk on white Burgundy and widowhood. I fried old ham and poured neat whiskey for us in the damp kitchen. Lenny was letting his whiskers grow again; his pale face was framed as if in a locket by the sparse red hair and beard. In his greasy suede sportcoat, he slouched in a chair and studied the room, and I knew he was thinking that if the lights were brighter, he would see the old canisters Ariana had bought, and the William Morris wallpaper, the stripped chairs she'd refinished. Lenny wore the dimness of the room like a quilt, he pulled it upon himself as he leaned one shoulder at the wall and huddled, peered.

And then as I served us he chattered — because, I guessed, he was frightened of what he had done, of how much safety he'd renounced, of what emotions I'd require. He talked about Italian girlfriends and war-loving officers and nuclear artillery shells and his trip to Venice. "There was this boatload of German tourists on Murano," he told me. "They all marched into one of the *fornaci*, one of the factories where they blow the glass? I'm standing there with them, we're all lined up on a kind of bleacher, three tiers of steps, and this sweaty little guy opens one of the ovens — I didn't *know* they were Germans, did I say that? So he opens the furnace door and all this heat comes out. There are these middle-aged people around me in very good lightweight tweeds, and when the oven door opens up, they sigh. They *love* it! And I'm standing with them, and they're moaning. German tourists always moan when they appreciate something. And all of a sudden I think, wait a minute, hold it: all these people are swooning for an oven. They have to be Germans. And they had to be there when it happened.

They damned well probably were *there*. Now, I knew they weren't about to pick me up and put me in the oven —"

"Alice in Wonderland," I said.

"What?"

"No, I meant — which one is that? Hansel and Gretel, I guess. Is that what I meant?"

"What you meant was I'm telling you a lot of stories because I'm afraid you're about to tell me something about Ariana."

"More ham?"

"No, no more. More whiskey."

"I don't think so," I said. "Not for me. I want to drive tomorrow. Are you coming with me?"

"Sure. Yes. That's why I'm here."

I was cleaning my nails with a paring knife. I looked past Lenny, along the wall at which he leaned. Lenny turned to look there, but he could see just a pair of muddy black boots, a long propped shotgun, a corner. "You're here because of Ariana," I said.

"Where are we driving?"

"I've been doing mail runs," I told him. "I go up to Montreal, sometimes other places. I did Toronto once. I take letters from people in the States. I deliver them to people who didn't want to get drafted. And then I take mail back. I take it into Vermont, New York, sometimes New York City. Sometimes I drive to Boston. Tomorrow I'm going to Utica, some towns near there. Would you like to come?"

"That's why I'm back, Bill."

"No it isn't, dammit. Now, I want you to tell me the *truth*."

"But why?"

"Why?" My anger made me feel that if I took a breath

and bellowed, I would say something pivotal and salient. But I had so little to say. And this was my friend, I told myself. This was my friend; I wanted to tell him I remembered that. And I wanted to hit him, then. I stood, and I was much bigger than him whether I stood or sat. I decided to at least tower. And finally I poured more whiskey for him and said, "Find a bed, Lenny. I'll wake us up."

"I thought maybe we'd talk a little," he said.

I shook my head. "We did."

So he gave up, finished his whiskey and asked, "Any room's okay?"

That was a question I'd been waiting for. I took considerable pleasure in saying, "Ariana was sleeping upstairs in the little room, the second door on the right. You're welcome to it."

I enjoyed his silence, and then his little syllable: "Bill?"

"Lenny, goodnight."

But he persevered, and he fooled me. "It was something I used to teach to the seniors. Chekhov said, if there's a shotgun at the beginning of a story, you should make sure it gets fired by the end. You remember that?"

"You duck out of the army, and all those cannons, Lenny, and you end up teaching children about shooting off shotguns?"

"It's about story-telling," he said. He looked so dirty in that suede coat, so sparsely haired, so like a gosling, so lonely in a kitchen he had known at other, brighter, times, that I wanted suddenly to talk about college and the years afterward in New York, and our long silly drunken conversations, our truer sober ones. But instead I moved toward the kitchen door and put my hands above its frame, leaning in at him, but staying away. I said, "You do keep on not telling me what you're telling me."

Lenny closed his eyes as if he were a stutterer who had to measure out sound. "Don't do anything rash," he said.

That was Lenny: words, little wisdoms, the fearing for the worst. I heard myself say with great calm, "I had a concussion. I wasn't conscious. I couldn't tell them. She was out too. Nobody knew. The bone tore through the skin. They were afraid of infection. They gave her a lot of penicillin. She's allergic to it. I could have told them. They didn't wake me up to ask. She's allergic to penicillin and she had a reaction. So she died. Her throat closed. Everything closed. Now: you think, is this it? You think I'm going to take a breech-blocked shotgun that's fifty years old and put it in my mouth and try blowing my brains out on account of a woman's secret allergy?"

Lenny was panting as if he had run up the stairs. "I'd consider it," he said.

"Maybe that's why we're here. Because I know that you would," I lied. "Would you go to bed now, please? And stop telling me Russian stories and German stories and Italian stories and fairytales and lies?"

It was supposed to be my time of grieving, just slightly his, and we were supposed to understand that and not talk about what we understood, so he rose and walked to me and squeezed my arm, and I squeezed his, and then he went up. I knew what he would do — turn on the lamp in the room she'd been using, and see the mattress on the floor, its sheets and blankets mounded, and see no clothes in the closet, and see no pictures on the walls, and no sign of Ariana or anyone else. He would stand in the room that was abandoned and he would fear to lie on the mattress. I went upstairs and got into the bed we'd moved from New York in a rented truck, years before. I heard him walk softly downstairs to sleep on the livingroom sofa. I knew he'd pause, on his way, and stare in the darkened kitchen at the shotgun I would never use. And that was Lenny: he was the man who indicted me — the man whose indictment I nearly wanted to share — for having no desire to load a gun and suck on the muzzle and make my story neat.

The weather was good for driving — a low, overcast sky with little glare on the Albany Northway and New York 20 — and the driving was simple and fast. In a New York town called Schuylerville, we delivered a letter addressed in a hand so looped and dark with effort, we both expected hysterics from the addressee, Mrs. Adolph Yoder. But she smiled and shook her head, as if her hiding-out son were a naughty fourth-grader, and before she read the letter, she served us iced Kool-Aid. "Isn't this war con*fus*ing?" she crooned. At a house on a hill outside Cooperstown, we slid a letter underneath a door. Circling back to Route 20, near an abandoned gas station, at what used to be a diner, we presented, to a very old unshaven man who chewed tobacco and didn't speak, three envelopes, numbered in sequence and held together with a hinge of masking tape.

We drove as far south as Norwich on Routes 12B and 12, stopping at Deansboro and Madison, where a short woman in a trailer park turned her back and told us to leave the letter in the mailbox outside her mobile home. She said, looking away, "You'd think grown men would have a regular job."

Between deliveries, we stopped at bars, eating kielbasa and pickled eggs and drinking beer, filling ourselves each time as if we hadn't stopped before, as if we had performed hard labor and were emptied. We were driving north again when it was well past dark, and Lenny had told his stories about Salerno and Lake Como and Rome, and I had told a number of stories about how Ariana had paid for the house and we had lived there, as he knew, on her mother's money, one year raising two pigs and killing them, thereafter planting a garden each year but keeping no stock.

On Route 20, outside Madison, I turned onto 12B, and Lenny said, "That leaves the big envelope for Clinton."

I said, "That's the last one. But first we pause for replenishment."

"We just did that, Bill."

"I want us to wait a while for the Clinton delivery. The woman we're delivering to doesn't always get home until later on."

"That's custom-tailored service."

"Service is service," I said.

So we stopped in a town that was a large crossroads lined with shabby small houses that were close together, many for sale. A long high factory sat on a river that ran through the town, and its open windows let out light and the surf-sound of machines. The streetlamps, instead of shining the blue-green radiance of highway lamps, cast a hard brown-yellow glare, and the town was an old tinted photograph at night. Men on the street wore white undershirts and stared. The women we saw looked older than the men, but not as old as their children.

At the clapboard Antique Mirror Bar, the only functioning part of a closed hotel, we parked the van and walked on stiff legs. Inside, we drank beer in a booth across the large room from an ordinary bar counter backed by the customary mirrors. We looked away from one another at the wallside booths; we commented on the size of the glowing jukebox, the silence of the bartender and his only other patron, a small man in a yellow slicker who drank something green at the bar.

"I'd like to commend us," Lenny said. He left the booth and returned with two double-shots of whiskey.

I took one and said, "That sounds like the beginning of a comment."

"No, it's the beginning of a commendation. Which is different."

"Not with you, it's not. Let me instead remind you of the night you became impotent in Hanover, New Hampshire. You remember that? It's a worthwhile recollection, which I prefer to a commendation, because it is definitely *not* a comment."

"I was never impotent in Hanover, New Hampshire. I was impotent at a small hotel on Torcello not too long ago, and I was less than efficient about a year ago in the Vaucluse. But never in Hanover."

I signaled to the bartender, raised the shotglasses, and he reluctantly brought more drinks. "Yes," I said, enjoying myself. "Hanover, New Hampshire. You were upstairs with a nurse, the one who had beautiful brown hair. I was downstairs, I don't even know whose house it was. We were supposed to spend the night studying for something. A classics course we were flunking, I think. So, you were up there, and all of a sudden I heard you singing your sad little song — 'I can't *do* it!' Right? Remember? And the nurse you were with, she had amazing brown hair, I remember, she screams back, 'Honey, you sure can't!' "

Lenny didn't laugh. He nodded, smiled, stopped smiling, and said, "I would like to commend us."

"I'm not going to be able to stop you, am I?"

"I'd like — no, you can't. I flew about ninety-seven thousand miles to say this. I'd like to say, we are the only two men I know who can do this."

I looked at the room.

"And without talking about her," Lenny said.

He lifted his glass; I held mine on the table. The door opened out and the women arrived, entering single-file and in silence. They wore red shiny warm-up jackets trimmed in white cloth. On the back of each jacket, in small and unevenly-applied white letters, was KADETTES. Their slacks were tight on their calves, and they wore ballet flats or sneakers. The one who carried the largest bowling-ball case, made of bright red plastic, wore curlers in her hair beneath a pink translucent scarf. It was she who went to the jukebox at once and put the money in.

Lenny said, "What year is this?"

"This is where I want to go when I die," I said.

The women stood at the bar and drank beer. They smoked a lot, quickly dipping toward their cigarettes to sip the smoke. And songs I hadn't heard for years came out of the wide high jukebox, and everyone listened to Jerry Lee Lewis and Paul Anka, to cha-chas and mambos and mostly to songs that required the Twist and the Lindy, or the Jersey Bounce. "This is better than being in the world," Lenny said.

And then, while the leader towed a taller, thinner woman by her red satin sleeve, another member of the team put more money in the Disney-glow jukebox. The women stood at the end of the table and smiled at Lenny and me with shy but certain expressions — *Only Dance* — and each held out a hand. Without speaking, we moved to the center of the room, bobbed our heads at one another until we agreed to the beat, and then began.

We thumped on the soft boards of the Antique Mirror Bar with our knees cocked, our elbows locked, eyes avoiding our partner's. We turned, stamping, gripping moist hands, then releasing, then gripping again, pulling hard, each trusting the other to support the bent weight hanging as we spun, shoulders banging down as heels did, to signal or celebrate the rhythm, or the act of dancing, or the silence in which we agreed to move.

There was no arrangement for the tenure of each dance. Women in red satin jackets walked up as they wished, tapped a teammate on the shoulder, moved, head nodding, into the music and then the dance, and then danced with Lenny or me. The music was constant, and each member of the team danced with one of us several times. Lenny and I huffed and blew, but the women, though sweaty, only smiled or frowned with effort, the women made no sound. So there was the music of the Lindy-Hop, the squeak and shuffle of shoes, and the panting of men.

The little person at the bar in his yellow slicker turned, twice, to look over his shoulder at us, then went back to his drink. The bartender watched a small soundless television set at the corner of his counter, set in among beef jerky and potato-chip packets. Chuck Berry roared.

Then the music stopped. Lenny said "Thank you" to everyone. No one replied. The women reassembled at the bar, a couple of them nodding to Lenny and me, one offering a small wave at shoulder-height. They worked at their hair and lips, pulled the hems of their red satin jackets, the cuffs of their sleeves, and then, each retrieving a bowling-ball case from the floor among bar stools, they left.

"The guys are coming home from the four-to-twelve shift," I guessed. "They'll make dinner for them now."

"I believe it," Lenny said. "I believe anything."

From outside the partly-open door, a woman called, "You're welcome, boys," and the team giggled as the door closed.

Lenny said, "I believe it."

I brought drinks from the bar, and we sat in the booth,

sweating, drinking warm whiskey and chasing it with cold beer. "There are nights like this, anything like this," I said, "and some fishing, and sometimes I go out with a gun that isn't breech-blocked and I shoot something, and sometimes I see a couple of movies in a row."

"And then go home and watch another movie on TV until you fall asleep?"

"Unless it's a sad one. I turn them off."

"Right," Lenny said, "or an offensively happy one. Right? For me, anyway. If Gene Kelly starts in kissing her, and she smiles with tears in her eyes, then I fall apart."

I put my hand on Lenny's wrist, squeezed it, released it, wiped my mouth, and said, "That's all I'm telling you, Lenny. Fill in the rest. You know me well enough, all right? That's all of the details for now."

"We can do that," Lenny said. "You and I are the only guys I know — you know that wasn't true about Hanover, I don't remember that at all. But the time I was talking about on Torcello did happen. After I got your letter, about the crash."

"That did it to you? Are you surprised I'm not surprised?"

His pale face reddened, and I thought he might cry once more. But he said, "I wonder if this wouldn't be a good time to deliver the last letter."

"Oh, fine. Fine. You don't care about sleeping in the van, do you?" I was almost sorry, then, for having written to him. But there was, as he had pointed out, the last delivery.

"One more drink and I can sleep on the roof," he said.

"You probably won't have to."

We stood in the Antique Mirror Bar and waved at the bartender, who didn't wave back. "Nobody answers you in this part of the country," Lenny said. "Have you noticed that? They do not perform the little motions of grace to strangers around here. I believe they live on human flesh."

The little man in the slicker, drinking his green fluids, called, "You be careful, boys."

I said, "You too."

"Oh, hell," the little man said, "I always am. You don't see *me* churning around with no half a dozen girls in pajama tops."

So at half past midnight, pitching up hill roads in a northeast backwater, Lenny calling out names on rural mailboxes, as if I didn't know where to go, we came to the small farmhouse on the broad plain that sat above the valley we'd driven through. Route 12B below gleamed gray in hard moonlight and looked like a nail that lay on a board. Up there, the land was silage crop, golden even at night with the coming-on of autumn, blown by steady winds. The house was at a crossroads, in a square of shaved lawn, flanked by balding maples. The leaves rattled, insects called through the slamming of our car doors, and it wasn't long — we hadn't yet rapped at the metal knocker — before an upstairs light went on, and then a parlor light, and then the light above the door.

She said, "I guess I got more mail."

I said, "My friend's delivering with me."

She wore a bathrobe meant for a man, and her feet were bare. Her hair looked shiny and tight, it held to the curve of her head the way her large toes gripped at the floor. Her nose was narrow, nearly beaked, and she looked like someone — she always did — fresh from inconsequential angers. "Hello, friend," she said.

I said to Lenny, "This is Miss Waldren."

"You can call me Loretta, friend," she told Lenny. "The man who writes to me is not my husband. We never made agreements, really." She looked at the mailing envelope I held out. "I don't think I want that."

"The guy who sent it thought you would," Lenny said.

"Do you think he's a victim of something?" she asked him.

Lenny said, "I don't much care what he is. I hope he doesn't die of something in Asia sometime. He's in the dead letter department already."

"Well, that tone of talk doesn't make much sense," she said. "And nobody's dead, for heaven's sakes." Then she looked at me and raised her eyebrows up at her own mistake and shook her head.

Lenny said, "No, huh? Says you. But how about this — we came about a hundred and fifty miles the long way around to give you that?"

She said, "All right. Then I'll take it from you." She was looking at me. I wasn't able to turn to look at Lenny and dare him to say something more.

I stood in front of her, waiting, and then Lenny went back to the van. I watched him lean against the door. She raised her eyebrows, this time for fun, and she went inside.

Lenny called, "You bastard. You son of a bitch. How am I supposed to handle this?"

I turned around and folded my arms. It was all I could do.

Lenny said, "Sure." He climbed into the van. I went inside the house.

Next morning, I woke him very early, bringing a thermos and a brown bag filled with cinnamon toast. I threw the envelope from Canada into the back of the van and, as we ate and drank, I drove. We listened to the radio, we watched the traffic form, we didn't speak.

Turning onto the Northway, I looked at him. Lenny said, "Get much?" and I sprayed a mouthful of coffee onto the instrument panel.

"It was awkward for you," Lenny said. "It serves you more or less right."

"I'm sorry, Lenny."

"You're so sorry, you're taking that poor bastard's letters back to him, right? All of the way back to Montreal? Do you think he'll find that form of penance touching?"

"She doesn't love him," I said.

"Dammit, Bill, didn't you read *Civilization and its Discontents?*"

"Nope."

"Neither did I."

We both tried to laugh again. We listened to a Phil Ochs song and looked at the cars. And in a little while, I said, "You know, you realize this: I'm not the one around here doing penance."

"Leaving me the penitent?"

"Lenny, you're the guy who came over an ocean for her. You're the one who rode the bus. You're the one who couldn't get it up, and you are the one who is stuck so deep into grieving, you have to hang onto Ariana's husband who she probably would have ditched. Might have. I don't know. But I'm right about this. You loved her for so long."

Lenny looked out the window.

I put my hand around the back of his neck and I squeezed. He bent forward. "I like it that you loved her," I said. "It's fine."

"Do you love Miss Waldren?"

"We're friends. We get along. You don't understand it all, about me and Ariana. It's confusing."

"You brought me over, didn't you, just so I could see her? I believe that's called confession, in certain churches. Except I'm not —"

"No! You keep on having what you had for her, Lenny. I'm driving you to a bus station, Lenny. All right? I'm taking the ⸱amned envelope north, and that's my problem, and forget it. But you get onto a bus and go someplace for a while. We're friends."

"Who?"

"I'm talking about you and me."

"Okay."

"And we'll connect in a while."

"You are not about to shoot yourself, that's pretty apparent."

"And it isn't the reason you came here."

"Part of it."

"All right. Part of it. But you know why you really came here."

"Because you wanted me to," Lenny said. And a few minutes later, he sighed and said, "Listen, why don't you save me the carfare and get me over the border into Canada? You can drop me off up there. Because I'm sure to get drafted if they catch me in the States. I'm not Essential now. Get me over, and I can stay up there for a while."

"You wanted to come home, Lenny."

"Fine."

"Lenny, you *did*."

"You can carry my mail back and forth."

"I didn't force you home, Lenny."

He said, "That feels better, doesn't it?"

Stand, and Be Recognized

II.

I'm here. I left Canada because I was tired of people who said *oat* instead of *owt*, and because I didn't like ice hockey, or anyplace named Mastigouche, and because too many people complained to me about acid rain that came from the States, as if I didn't get rained on too. I didn't eat dogfood in Canada: I worked, and made good wages. I wrote some pretty bad stuff for the kiddy shows on television — they took my sour prose as wry charm — but I worked, and I drank fresh milk and ate marbled meat. But what I *felt*, at night, on some of those nearly-in-Europe Montreal streets, was the misfortune of those old people who eat dogfood because they're so poor.

As a matter of fact, I never saw anyone eat dogfood. But I did hear a lot about people who did. It seemed to be America's fault in general, and mine in particular, that they had to, no matter what country they lived in. It was like the story I heard from a terrifically handsome woman named Rosa. She told me that her way of working against the Vietnam War was to walk these kids, draft-dodgers, over the bridge at Niagara Falls from New York State into Canada. The customs officers weren't apt to stop newlyweds, at least that's what the anti-war workers thought, and they often were right. Rosa never got caught. And she used to walk these trembling, green-faced little American boys over the bridge, and then she'd wave and deposit them there, they'd seem like a married couple with one of them looking for a bathroom. And he'd be gone, and she'd walk back after a while. She'd have a drink first, if she could, she told me. She came to Montreal to look one of them up once, and we met, and she told me this. We got friendly. She never found the guy, and then the war ended and we were all a good deal older. That's the story she told, and I guess if that's true, and I don't see why it shouldn't be, if something like the *war* was true, then I believe it, and I believe about the old folks eating Alpo out of cans.

It doesn't smell that bad, when you first open the can. I was on my way out of Canada, traveling down on 133, aiming for 89. I wanted to find out if I was part of the President's amnesty. No-one had told me, and I didn't know who to ask anymore. And if you asked the wrong person, and you weren't pardoned, you might find out in federal jail — that's where the counterfeiters beat on the draft-dodgers because of their pride in our flag.

I was hitching in, because hitching was a habit, and so was saving money up, and this man in a very sedate Ford Galaxie 500 of some age who picked me up had a little white dog in the back. When we stopped at the Vermont state line, and I was sweating out the border patrolman's eyes, he fed his dog, and I smelled the stuff. It made me think of stories about old folks eating dogfood, and it made me think of Rosa and how she remembered things. And it made me — all that remembering, regretting as I sometimes did that the body kept the brain alive at its pleasure and the brain had no independence — it made me think of Bill Gruen, who used to be my friend. This was particularly true when his wife, Ariana, was alive, since I loved her dearly. I mean: I was in love with his wife. But I'd loved him too, until I found out he was sleeping with a lot of new women-friends. Those infidelities, along with my long-term jealousy, made it seemly that we step aside from one another. I went up to Canada, and I hid out from the war. He stayed in the States. He used to run mail to and from some of the people hiding in Canada. But we met only once after his wife died and I had found out about his private life. I guess we were fairly deft at not meeting.

And while I was sitting next to the decent, fat, dog-bound and sentimental salesman of cigars who was driving me in a long Ford toward anyplace south of Canada, I realized that I had no one to come sidling silently home to. I realized how much I regretted that I had outlasted my family — except my sister, who wished not to speak to me again, and whose husband agreed. There weren't friends, no-one I'd want to sit next to, describing exile in Canada. Ab*oat* my time there, I had no solid feelings yet — except that I was homesick, and uncertain of what distance I could make toward home, if I could name it and then get there. So I thought of Bill Gruen. I might have hated him. And, surely, he felt some kind of salient and possibly dark emotions toward me. But we *knew* one another. And I had a great need, then, to be known. I got out of the Ford near Swanton, Vermont, and I stomped around in my worn-down boots, dragging my old duffle bag behind me like a kid who'd been thrown out of camp. I found a bus station, and I sat around and drank coffee until it was light enough to see the cars, and be seen, and then I thumbed and walked and thumbed and walked, from Swanton to St. Albans, St. Albans to Georgia Plains, and then all the way through Winooski and Burlington to Montpelier, where I could look for locals going west on the small roads toward Irasville, and the only person in America whom I thought I might know.

I had hitchhiked half-asleep, then had slept for real in a stranger's car. He delivered herbicide for Agway, and he didn't care, he said, what it killed or polluted, as long as his wife and his chickens were all right. I saw this short, round, freckle-faced man who had remarkably long arms, my Agway driver, waking up in an old four-poster bed, his chunky wife alongside him, and the two of them under a living blanket of Leghorns and Rhode Island Reds. I laughed, and then he woke me, or I'd been awake and then he spoke, but, anyway, I had made it into the gut of northern Vermont, which in summer looked green and frisky. It had always seemed on the verge of dying out, like a giant creature that had eaten its food supply and that waited in hunger for the vegetable world to decide on its fate. Grass was always sparse there, it had seemed to me when I was living in Canada, writing for kids about Uncle Nelvin who talked too much and fell down a lot. I thought of the grass in Vermont as thin, like the wisps on a balding person's scalp. And yet here was the lush dark green I associated with France or the flat fields in the south of England. Instead of meadows where rocks were the crop, I saw rye and corn fields, and a lot of growth I couldn't name, and from a distance it all looked healthy and thick. The road to Bill Gruen's house was still a stony track, and dust kicked up almost before my boots thumped on the surface. There were midges to swat, and a red sun to signal high heat, and a massing, around the sun, of thick clouds.

I had forgotten how, as you came closer to his house, the brush grew denser and rose higher around the road. It felt as though the air supply lessened in that dark and green and brambled channel that approached the house. I had forgotten how, beyond the long and narrowing road that rose with the land, there were foothills crouching, so that air had a hard time moving out when a low-pressure front oppressed this part of Vermont, as it surely was doing right now. I nearly couldn't look forward, but I could look up, as if I walked in a trench, and there was the sun, rising to catch up with me, and as red as infection. The clouds closing in around it looked purple and matted, transparent but growing thick very quickly. I was sweating, and I was nervous because of the time that had passed without our speaking. Five years before, I had come back to the States from Italy, where I'd skipped the draft by teaching — Essential Service, they called it — the kids of military people stationed near Rome. I had come back because I thought Bill needed me after Ariana died in a manner too ridiculous to think about. But I do not think about her dying. I don't think about that. My return had meant the end of my deferment, and a sure trip to Southeast Asia. I returned to comfort Bill. That's what I told him. That's what I pretended to believe. We both knew that I'd come because Ariana was who I loved — a reason for going away to Europe, and a reason for returning to mourn. And Bill, on one of his runs through northeastern country to deliver mail from draft evaders in Canada to their parents and girlfriends and wives, had stopped off to screw someone, a fine enough woman I'm sure, and I had withdrawn my trust. Like a prig at a bawdy party, like a miser at a shaky bank, I'd taken away the deposits of friendship made over years and years, and I'd stuck in Canada while Bill went back to the States. And here I was. Without a right to be where I was, and without too much of a reason I could state without shame. I was here to be recognized. *Halt! Who goes there?* Me. Me. *Stand, and be recognized.* Me.

Then the high hot bushes ended, the path spilled out into a low hilly lawn before the small woodframe farmhouse that was backed by a meadow and then the hills that caught the air and kept it there in muggy weather, and that held the house in something like a palm. Even the hills were knotted like knuckles, and even the lawn before me was like the thick ridge of muscle at the base of a person's hand. I stood, therefore, at the edge of the wrist and I stared up the narrow path, worn only by feet and not tools, that went to the house; it was like one of those lines you're supposed to read so you know the future, but I didn't know whether the pebbly path was called Career, or Life, or Love, or Hope, or just something to do with breakfast. I was hungry, hollow with trepidation, and waiting for someone in America to look me over and say that of *course* that's who I was: the famous and oft-remembered me.

What I saw was a belly I thought I recognized. It was in front of the house, and part of a body so still and slender and dark that in heat waves, and next to the doorway's vertical lines, it had seemed to be a piece of the picture I saw, and not a living thing, that belly's body. I looked again, and I saw, below a stomach that ever so slightly protruded, a small red rag of cloth. I saw very long thighs, knobbed knees, though not unsightly ones, and slender calves. I saw the rag again, the belly again, lean stomach and ribcage and small breasts in matching red rag, and then a set of braids, and dark hair tight on the scalp. The face, at that distance, looked like a child's, perhaps a teenager's or that of an older adolescent. The nose looked bobbed, which for a nose in my generation is not an unusual state: it was something of a national hobby in the late fifties and early sixties, cutting down the beaks of upper-middle-class girls. It was a ghost. It was Ariana.

I thought that if I went closer — or, probably, just closed my eyes and focused within the little stereopticon of my madness — I would see, it was returning now, that the suit was made of terrycloth. Ariana had sewed that suit, I remembered. So, naturally, her ghost would be wearing it.

In that regard, this was a practical delusion, I thought, since clothing could be recycled and natural resources saved. *Who goes there?*

"Bill?" the ghost called in a high, nasal voice. The voice tried to emulate softness and calm, but it sounded worried. I wondered if a man who thought he saw a ghost could make it think that it was frightened. It moved, and for an instant it was gone in the lines of the cracked gray door and its unpainted sills, the sun-scarred creosoted cedar shingles of the house, the densities of heat that rose in the air around the dooryard. Then it was back, and calling for Bill again. It seemed to be looking directly at me, and it did seem, really — *really?* — to be scared.

I thought I was going to fall over. I was standing in the dreadful downward push, like that of a hard hand, that the heat and mugginess exerted. I held the duffle bag on my shoulder, still, and my lightweight jacket was knotted around my waist. Inside my boots, my feet felt ankle-deep in water. I wanted to tear my clothes away, but instead I sat down, on top of the bag, and unbuttoned my shirt to nearly the waist. It looked at me steadily, the ghost, and its legs didn't move. I studied its nose and its stomach. It called again for Bill.

The door opened out and he came. It was Bill, tall, though shorter than I'd remembered him, yet big enough to tower over most men, which was something he liked to do in markets and bars. He was burly as ever, covered with graying blond hair and whiskers, wearing only shorts and sandals, so that the hair all over his body glowed with sweat in the sun. He looked annoyed. That was something of a permanent expression, I remembered, because he was near-sighted but refused to wear glasses. He swiped at midges as if they were persecuting him. He saw her. He saw me.

He looked. His tensed shoulders and big arms relaxed, then slumped, and he smiled, the wonderful smile that made people less frightened — me included — in his vast and often grouchy presence. He smiled and held his arms out as if we would hug like fellow bears, which we often had done, drunk and sober, in trouble and out, over many years. Then his arms went to his waist, and he said something — my name, I thought — out of the corner of his mouth. The ghost nodded — the woman, someone like Ariana, I thought, as I walked toward them, someone very like Ariana but not resembling her nearly enough to be her twin, just a woman who was long and slender and whose belly was doppelganger to hers: belly-ghost, I thought, laughing a belly-laugh. Which was when Bill did walk over to me and seize my shoulders and hug me, as if he'd decided that, no matter what I wanted, I would be embraced. *Stand, and be recognized*, I thought, as he squeezed me against his smelly wet chest. Well, I was.

"Lenny Levine!" he called to her, as if confirming what he'd earlier whispered. "Lenny Levine!"

I stepped back, wrinkling my nose and wiping sweat off my lips. He nodded, as if to confirm that as usual he wouldn't bathe until forced to by the niceties of a trip to town, or by local pressure.

The ghost — well, she wasn't one, was she? The woman who looked at a distance like Bill Gruen's long-dead wife: that was all. The woman came closer, after squatting awkwardly for a shirt that lay on the lawn. As she walked, she buttoned it over her and rolled up the sleeves. It was a huge shirt, Bill's, of course, and she looked more interesting in it than diminished by it. Don't men want to possess a woman by wrapping her in their large clothes and thereby making her little, more easily owned? It was a bobbed nose, a nosejob, we'd called it at home when we were high-school kids, and it was a lived-in face. Bill was older than I was, and she was closer to his age than mine. She was very pretty. In spite of the heat, however, her face was frozen: she smiled, but not above the nose; she talked, but not with flexible lips; she asked me questions and heard what I said, but her forehead and eyebrows never moved to signal that she cared. I envied her such coolness in that temperature and humidity.

Her name was Kelly. I hated her name. Everyone was being named Kelly and Erin and Shaun, spelled Shawn, and they wrote me letters care of the program, asking idiot questions about whether Captain Goldfish was as much of a Pike-er as I'd said. They signed their letters Kelly, and I knew they would have to grow up into airline hostesses or footsore hookers in Saskatchewan. Her name was Kelly, all right, and she wasn't glad to be interrupted in her working vacation with Bill. She took photos for a living. Well, she took photos, and for a living she taught students at the University of Vermont how to take photos for course credits. She was an artist, Bill made clear. I was to see her portfolio later. Neither she nor I had spasms at the prospect.

The house was almost cool because of its screened windows and because of the ash that served as shade trees. What moving air there was came in the shaded rear windows and moved across to the front. But the sun was still a hot red circle and I sat and sweated, dripping, yawning with fatigue and apprehension. They pointed me toward the bathroom, though I quickly remembered where it was, and I took a cool shower, enjoying the smell of a household's soap and drains and hair and old shampoo that clung to the shower tiles. Someone lived here, even if one of them was wrong, and it was a house. I wanted one. I had enough money for a down payment on one, and it was there, in the small cramped bathroom that Ariana had used and that someone named Kelly, enamored of strawberry gels, had usurped, that I decided on my course of action. I would stay a while with them, until I felt American again, or accustomed to being in the States, and then I would leave them to one another and go somewhere cooler — maybe Maine, or someplace near the White Mountains in New Hampshire, and I would buy myself a small house and a lot of land, and I would live there until someone came who loved me, and we would sleep in a four-poster bed under chickens, and I would never have to think about television, or children named Kelly, or people going *oat*, and I would write a book about being an expatriate so close to home. When the money ran out, I would write radio ads, or travel folders, or even teach a language course — Italian for beginners, say, at a Berlitz franchise in Peterborough, New Hampshire. *Ecco i miei bagagli. Ci sono solo effetti personali.* I stood under the shower head as, with closed eyes, I saw one of my students presenting his luggage at the border for inspection — just personal effects, he'd say, with my hand-made accent. I did have a future, a plan. *Viaggio solo.* But what the hell. Here I was. *In camera mia non ci sono asciu-gamani!* I stuck my head out and shouted for towels, please, and Kelly came, her smile a piece of ice, *ghiaccio*, on her lips. I had a plan, though. I was going to be alive in America, and live in a house with one hell of a bathroom, and one day teach Italian and make love under chickens to someone terrific in a red bikini.

And be a jerk. By the time I was dressed in khakis, and loafers without socks, and a cotton tee shirt that said RCMP BALL BOY — our station had played the Mounties to raise money for a children's hospital — I was depressed again. I put my sweaty clothes back in the duffle and shut my jacket and toilet kit inside of it too. I was ready to move if I had to.

Kelly had dressed in baggy shorts and had tied Bill's shirt high up on her stomach, so that we were treated to her youthfully middle-aged muscles a-ripple. Bill had washed his face in the sink, I thought, because water still dripped from his beard, and there was soap in his ear. He was carving with a Pukko folding knife at pencils, probably just because he needed to do something with his huge, beat-up hands. He was a man who had to work away at the world, and with dangerous tools. If he wasn't breaking something because it needed removal, or building something only marginally necessary, or shooting something down, or digging something out, he became nervous. He had to feel useful. He was one of his implements, and he needed to feel that he was utilizing himself in such a manner as to earn her praise. But I was thinking of Ariana, for whom he used to show off, and whose love he had felt it was required he must daily earn. Now he was with Kelly. And here she was. She was scooping frozen lemonade from a large, long can.

"Lenny, will you have lemonade?" she called from the old trough sink.

"Thank you," I said. "Yes. I will. Thank you."

"I'll put two spoonfuls in then," she said. "I won't have any." And that's what she did. In a small stoneware pitcher she dropped two tablespoons full of frozen lemonade concentrate. She put the tin back in the freezer of the old Kenmore refrigerator, and then she stirred the concentrate in the pitcher.

"Very economical," I said.

That made her smile. She had beautiful teeth and a wide

mouth, and when she meant her smile it was lovely to see. I understood how attractive she must be for Bill. Of course, there was also the fact that, given the right atmospheric conditions, she could pass for the ghost of his beautiful wife. How proud she seemed about saving money, too: that might be a source of her beauty, not a defrosting of reserve. Time was money, after all, in America. Next, I thought, I'd be telling them of the threat to Canadian forests posed by pollutants that American industry released into the jet-stream. *Who goes there, dummy? Stand.*

I stood. I sipped at the artificial citrous taste — she'd put no ice cubes in the pitcher; I had seen, when she opened the freezer, that there were two trays of ice, so she was saving them — and I walked from the kitchen past the hall and toward the foot of the old, narrow stairs. Up there was a room in which I had wanted to sleep after Ariana's death. I wondered if Kelly kept away. It seemed to me that she could make good use, economical use, of Bill's need to earn his salvation in the daily world. Salvation through sex after performing useful acts, it might be called. Sex withheld, it might be called, until the acts were performed.

He had followed me. He stood in the doorway and put his hands on the molding at the top of the frame. "Whaddya think," he said, his Scandinavian eyebrows, all woolly and peaked, jumping on his face like wings. "I mean Kelly. What's your verdict?"

"Beautiful," I said.

"For a lady in her advanced condition of age — you know she's almost as old as I am? Who's better looking than her?" His tongue rolled in his mouth as if he were going to butter her up and pop her in. "She's got to be the best damned looking woman in the whole northeast."

"Are you guys married?"

He shook his head. "She can't get a divorce. Her ex-husband, he's still her husband, but I can assure you he's ex. He won't give her a divorce. He calls her up and whines when he gets broke. Doesn't matter. Good stuff's good stuff, married or not. Her father was head of the glass museum, you know. Did I tell you? He's still about as important in glass as Ansel Adams is in photography." He whispered: "And what a piece she is."

I remembered, then, that he had used to talk of Ariana in the same way, and with the same phrases. She, then, at the start and even past the middle, had been good stuff. She, then, had been a tempest in bed. The things she knew, the things she *did*, he would sing. And she too had been one of the five — he'd never named the other four — most beautiful women in all of the American northeast. Well, Kelly was Number One now, Kelly the gorgeous, with her fake nose and her ghostly stomach and her two scoops of concentrate, and save the ice for later, and I would have to stop. I would have to: I hadn't been invited, and I'd felt a need to intrude, and he had been my friend.

I think that I might have made some somber announcement about the confirmed death of a friendship after long illness, had Kelly not come in behind Bill, with a fine smile on a face that was red with pleasure. There was a sincerity in her eyes that made me think I was a liar and fool. She stood on her toes and he stooped, and she whispered in his ear. She was flushed, as if she'd been baking. Bill said, "It's naptime, isn't it?" He stretched and yawned. I remembered the terminology. In their good days, Bill and Ariana had taken frequent "naps" — which meant that strangers and friends had to move a discreet distance away as they went

upstairs to make love. It had been important to them, the
announcement, and I used to wonder if they had much sex
when no one was about to know.

I said, "I'll take a walk down to the river, the little stream
in the meadow. I'm not sleepy right now. I think I'll drop
my feet in there and cool off and make some plans."

He smiled at me, and there was just the glimmer of a
much older man, who would dodder after lean flanks and
nosejobs until he was dead. I closed my eyes because I knew
that I'd mourn him if he were dead, just as I mourned,
while he stood before me, radiant with health, ready to rut
on the floor of his farmhouse, so much that had to do with
his being alive. They started up the stairs, and I went out
to the hot buggy meadow.

Behind the house, I saw where I had worked with Bill
and Ariana when they'd first moved in, cutting pipe for a
sewage runoff into the giant concrete cistern we'd sunk. It
was rumpled land, I saw, as I walked it again. Although it
lay in flatland surrounded by hills that blocked it from good
breezes and, in winter, collected snow, the land itself was
corrugated into millions of one- and two- and three-inch
hills and their valleys, and I tripped as I walked through
high grass and the clouds of gnats and other little bugs that
flew up like living dust at each step. Where the garden had
been, where Ariana had worked herself into tears of fury,
and a passion for rows of order in her life, and rows of
babies in her fallowness, I'd always thought, nothing grew.
The fence was there, chickenwire on old pine sticks, so Bill
had made at least the empty outline of it whole again, and
maybe in her memory. There was no produce. There were
stones and dry clods and blown pollen that didn't take, some
weeds with tightly furled brown pods, and some black long
leaves where something had flowered some years past her

dying and that now lay like flags along the sad surface that she'd dug at so hard. *Il giardino*, I would tell my students, moving my lips like a drunk old husband in a bad Italian movie: *jar-'dee-noh*.

In the meadow, a hundred yards or so from the little hill and garden behind the house, the stream ran in ox-bow shapes beneath its shallow bank. I didn't dangle my legs, but I did lie on my back under the sun, surrounded by the wideness of the unused fields, as ripe for crops as the garden was blasted and black, and I pulled my shirt up to my neck to catch the sun on my fish's belly, and I closed my eyes. I would leave tomorrow and spend some money on clothes and maybe one of those swanky small bags that travelers carry, and something light to wear on my feet, and I would go to Logan Airport in Boston, and get myself fetched overseas. Either Venice airport, and then the *vaporetto* to my favorite place, Torcello, where in the church on that island the Christ is a pagan's dream of dying gods, all rolled eyeballs and thick blood — or the Santa Maria del Fiore in Florence, where there is a Last Judgment worthy of the notion of *last*. Yes, a pair of white running shoes, maybe, that I would wear on the plane and while I walked around, before I settled into — wait a minute, I told all the little chirring, chugging, peeping, whistling insect engines that were loud around me: Wait. I'm talking about going all the way back, back overseas. What about Peterborough, New Hampshire, and the Berlitz franchise for nervous tourists? That's it, dear: he says *Passaporto, prego*, and you smile and hand it over, and then you say *Viaggio solo* to tell him you're traveling alone.

There seemed to be a difference of opinion among the staff in Expatriate Control.

It was the lemonade, I realized, that had me as wild as

anything — everything? — else. It was the cheapness of two scoops of frozen lemonade concentrate instead of, say, a whole pitcher of lemonade with ice cubes and fresh-baked cookies and a kiss on the cheek and a roll in the hay, and maybe she *was* Ariana's ghost. Because even though I hated her, and resented her intrusion, and despised Bill's unfaithfulness to the dead, I was as covetous of Kelly as I'd been of Ariana. Could all this mean that the common denominator between these women was their husband and boyfriend? Was I queer for Bill? I thought not. On the other hand, I'd never thought I'd live that long in Canada, either, and anyone who could live in that enormous small town of a nation that long, talking *aboat* American imperialism, could just as well be lusting after men when he never thought he would. All right, I told myself, sighing up into the sun, put the sexuality issue on hold, but don't ignore it. At your age, and at your station of life — which is to say: being too old, with too little achieved, and with too few prospects — you mustn't ignore any clues. All right. But meanwhile, and of course keeping this famous open mind, consider that you've come a long distance over a good many years, to see someone who knows you. You know him. You knew him. Be patient. Find out.

Where's the bathroom? The question was asked by Ariana, who was wearing one of those crinoline-lined wide skirts of the fifties. It was gunmetal gray, with a pink felt poodle on it. The blouse was a matching pink, with piping on the collar that matched the body of the skirt. She wore long black ballet slippers, and in her ponytail were pink ribbons. Her fingers were bleeding. Her eyes were bloody holes with little glass beads in them, and they looked like the Christ in the medieval cathedral on Torcello. *Where's the bathroom?*

she asked, and from her angry tone I realized that we were having a disagreement. I tried to tell her where it was, but she didn't understand my Italian. I tried English, but all I could say were the embarrassed laugh-noises that no one really makes, but that are represented in *Archie and Veronica* comics by bubbles emanating from teenaged mouths with *Heh Heh* inside them. *Heh Heh*, I told her. In the dream, I knew as I spoke that it was necessary to cry to her something more important. I couldn't and, anyway, her eyes were so bloody, her fingers were dripping, and she was angry at me.

I woke with sun in my eyes and I closed them and fell asleep again, to the sound of my voice: "She isn't angry. You're having a nightmare. Anyway, she's dead. Go back to sleep." When you live alone, you're the only one who can wake you from hard dreams and send you back to sleep again without them, and that's what I did. I wasn't deep in sleep, I was riding sleep's surface and remembering, as I lay along it, how once, wonderfully, Ariana and I, in the Gruens' apartment in New Haven, with sun rolling in from the fire escape, had sat together while Bill went out to buy something for dinner. We were on a little sofa that we'd pushed up close to the window so that we could put our feet up on the window's low ledge and still see pedestrians across the street. The neighborhood was filled with students and poor people, so the radios throbbed like drums in the early evening as we sat, our shoulders touching, and each at once, I think, grew aware that they touched. I moved away and looked at her. She was smoking cigarettes and looking at the street. I moved back, and she must have felt my shoulder lie along hers again, but she made no sign. I stayed that way, seeing nothing of what she saw outside, and breathing shallowly so that my body wouldn't jump and make her understand that we — no other description will do — were intimate.

I felt her: tough muscle that moved easily under the skin. I smelled her: harsh cheap bath soap, the Balmain perfume her mother brought her from Paris, the scent of her shampoo, which was something used on infants' hair and which had the delicate fragrance I associated with the innocence in little bodies. When she spoke, I smelled her mouth: cigarettes, the spiciness of coffee we'd been drinking, and her body itself. Her body smelled like cooking herbs I've held on a hot bright street in Provence.

Then she moved, she tilted her head back, breathed out smoke and rocked in place beside me in the big room that overlooked an ordinary street. She said, in her low voice, "Were you glad when Bill left?"

I stood, as if I'd done something daring and offensive and must move. I watched her. I was certain that my face was bright. Hers wasn't; she was calm, and she was clearly enjoying herself. I was certain I looked young to her. I said, "You mean was I happy to be alone with you? Why are you *asking?*"

"You're right," she said.

"No, no, *I* don't mind. I didn't mean I minded. Yes. You know that. Don't you?"

"You're right," she said. But she was smiling such an innocent smile: I seemed to give her such pleasure that she smiled broadly enough to make my chest squeeze. That was it. My entire body winced. "You're right."

"I don't mind. I'm — always glad to be with you. This isn't what I mean."

She was wearing a shirt she'd made from some very coarse homespun-looking tan cloth, and her jeans were faded almost powder blue; they made her thighs look softer than her torso, and I wanted to put my hand on her leg, just to touch her, to see whether her legs were as tender as they seemed. "I know it isn't," she said. She smiled, and the sun and her clean hair, the hazy filigree of her drifting cigarette smoke, everything made her words feel warm as I heard them. "I know it isn't." She beamed, as if with pleasure. "I wonder," she said.

That was it. We spoke on other topics, not hastily, but carefully, and in a manner that was considerate to everyone, but especially to me. She did, always, try to take good care of me. But I waited on the precipice of her statement. I carried her smile, and her hair, and her exhaled smoke, the stiffness of her shirt, the softness of her jeans, the glow of her language and its promise unfulfilled: I bore them all with me to Rome, and I bore them back when Ariana died; they went, as surely as my GI duffle bag, from the States up to Canada and now down to Vermont, and they were with me in the field that she had owned, they were over me as surely as the sun and heavy air and little flies.

I heard jays and crows fly up and make their protests, so I knew that someone was coming. I heard Bill grunt as he walked past me on the corrugated field to plunk something heavy in the stream. It would be beer. Bill conducted business in a context of alcohol. I looked at Ariana's smile and I knew what I could easily have known at other times, but had decided not to. No: I hadn't told myself that I could know. But now I did, and I knew it for absolute truth as I lay in the field, and I know it now, as I say this to myself again. While I had always carried with me the possibility, the outside chance that we, had we tried, might have loved, Ariana hadn't wanted me to think that way at all. She had seen me as wounded and youthful and sweet. She had en-

joyed my deference, my supplication, and my quiet love —
it had been flattery, it had been whatever she needed. She
hadn't, however, needed Lenny Levine. And I had carried
with me from place to place and time to time what was
finally nothing more than a mistake.

Bill came up and he nudged me from my almost-dream,
which had turned into more of an almost-waking, by prodding me with his foot. He pushed me with his toes and I
opened my eyes.

When I moved my mouth to tell him, again, that I was
going away, and as I tilted up to prop myself on an elbow,
my skin felt taut and stretched and mildly burned. The sun
was balanced on the top of the hills before dropping behind
them. The air was starting to swirl and make the meadow
slightly cooler. From the stream, Bill pulled up a couple of
cans of beer, which he opened for us. He sat beside me,
on his haunches, and he smiled.

The beer was cold and it tasted good; I was glad to take
some pleasure in it. "Where did you say you were going?"
Bill asked.

I shrugged, sat, pulled my shirt down over the sunburn
and bugbites, then shrugged again. "It isn't clear yet," I
said. "You know, you sometimes feel like you should really
be getting on your way, but you don't have any plans? I
think either New Hampshire or Venice."

He laughed and laughed, as if I'd made a good joke.
Maybe I had.

"But there's someplace else," I said. "It was the wind
picking up that made me think about it. I went there when
I was teaching in Rome. I took a train down there, and then
there was a bus that went to a market town in the south of
France, Salon de Provence. A pretty place. They have a

fountain inside of a huge bushy tree in the market square, and I used to sit there and drink pastis until I admitted that I wasn't Hemingway and anise gave me the runs. But you could get a bus out of there that went to a place called Les Baux. It was once like a country up there, with most of Provence right under it. A giant castle, walls all the hell over the place. Some king named Philip, I think, had it leveled, just to make sure everyone knew he was the only king they had — he was the Lyndon Johnson of France. Well, the chapel's still there. It's built right into the rock of the mountain. They have shops and even art galleries there now. When I went, it was like a carnival up there, and kids were running around, and tourists, and all that pretty Provencal cloth — didn't I send some to Ariana from there? A scarf or something? There were some doorways left, you know: arches going into rooms where all there is isn't there anymore — just doorways and some stones. And the chapel. It was so dark and low. And off to one side, they'd left it the way it must have been when knights with big noses went in there to really believe in God and be scared. Cold, and dampness, and darkness, a low ceiling. There was a little stone cross, and that was it. It was the second-best church I ever was in. It made me cry. Good churches make me cry," I said, starting to sniff and get teary, "so I got the hell out and drank white wine and looked down on everything from way up. That place and Torcello. Don't I seem to be going on about churches today? Well, in my sleep, anyway. Never mind."

"You're in what the military would call a traveling mode," Bill said.

"I think I'm mobile again."

I drank more beer. He sat, then, and stretched out his

legs, which were in brown duckcloth carpenter's pants, all loops and toggles and pockets and flaps, and held together with big rivets. He said, softly, "What was Canada like?"

"Oh," I said, "it was okay, if you like nothing-special. It's a nothing-special place and everyone there is determined to do something about that. You're okay there if you aren't black or Pakistani or something, and if you can say *oat*, and piss and moan about America — American TV, American books, American industry, American foreign policy. They spend so much time, in Montreal, anyway, trying to be either France or not-America, they don't know *who* in hell they are. It was like living in a doctor's waiting room. It wasn't bad. It was long."

"So how come you stayed there? I mean, besides the draft? The war."

"That's a lot to say besides about. But I didn't know where to go, was one thing. I didn't know what they'd done about my passport. And then it was expired. And I had to learn how to save money. Which I did. I'm loaded. I've got traveler's checks all over my person and inside my shaving tackle and everyplace. I can go where I want to, for a while. Anyway: there wasn't that much going on out here that I missed, I guess."

Bill said, "And you were pissed at me because I wasn't faithful to the memory of Ariana Gruen."

"Come on, Bill. I mean, she was dead. I'm sorry. But she is. Right? And you can fuck whoever you want."

"We were in trouble before she died. You know that. It didn't make it easier when she died. It was tough on me. You know about this thing, guilt?"

"My people brought the industry to America, remember? Anyway, that's why I came in from Europe."

"Nah," he said. He walked to the stream and brought

two more beers back. "You came on account of her. It was on account of her."

I drank my beer because he was probably right and because there wasn't much to say.

Bill said, "I might marry her some time."

"Kelly?"

He nodded.

I said, "Great."

"She's a little shy," he said.

"I'd have thought she was a little resentful."

"Nah," he said. "She loves you. No, it's when someone from before her time comes up here, she feels like she's competing with Ariana."

"And she is."

"I guess that can't be helped," he said.

"She looks like her. A little like her, anyway."

"Really? I'd never have thought so."

"Well, something like her."

"Two legs and a crotch," he said.

"And Ariana's bathing suit," I guessed.

Bill looked down at his beer. Then he looked up and smiled all his teeth and his big wet lips. He waggled his eyebrows and blinked his small bright eyes. "I never said I wasn't careful with a dime," he said.

"Very practical," I said. "What the hell, why not? Why not? Why *not*?"

He raised his can of beer and toasted me. I raised mine and toasted him back. Our beer cans clanked, and we drank. It was what we had done, years before, over and again. For we had achieved much of our friendship in the silent and persuasive rituals of bars and activities connected with the consumption of alcohol. We hadn't talked much, after the first year or two of knowing one another. It had been a long and easy silent friendship, and the assumption always had been that we'd progressed past language. As we toasted and drank, I understood that we had evaded language, out of embarrassment and probably emptiness. We had danced a dance of friendship, and the music had been habit, and — just as now, I realized — we had spent a lot of our time in not discussing what was difficult and maybe therefore important in the lives of adults. I was moved when I understood how easily the silent companionship that men grow up in search of, that they admire in films and books, can turn into the silent politeness of strangers who sit at the same long bar and drink.

We went back, and Kelly was out on the lawn, this time in crisp chino trousers and a soft halter top at which her nipples prodded. I watched her nipples for a while, and then I got tired of the stimulation. So I cut back on my focus, and I watched her and Bill set deck chairs up on the lawn near a folding table. On the table went a bottle of inexpensive gin and a small bottle of domestic vermouth, and half a bowl of ice cubes — Kelly would be saving the rest, I thought, for something important.

Bill made a fire at the brick fireplace near the end of the house, feeding it hardwood that popped and cracked, and as he let the coals accumulate, we made martinis and ate synthetically-flavored garlic-and-sour-cream potato chips, diving right into getting drunk enough to act at ease with one another. Kelly, with all the graciousness you could ask of someone set to entertaining an uninvited and relatively undesirable guest, passed the package of artificial chips toward me once or twice, and she even made my first drink. She gave me one ice cube, but didn't protest when I took a second without asking permission. The fire hissed and exploded, and dusk settled over the bowl of hills, and then the meadows, and then the lawn; the insects changed pitch, or maybe different ones began to sound, and it nearly was night. The vermouth was oily, the gin was sour and strong, and, if I used my imagination, the little ice available to us did reduce the temperature of our martinis. We drank.

Bill was telling me, soon, what a simply brilliant photographer Kelly was, and how at faculty meetings her colleagues were often heard to praise her at the level of extended song. The bugs at night were worse than the ones that had bitten me in daylight. I remembered where Ariana had kept bug spray and, without asking permission, I went to the door, reached around to the low shelf just inside the kitchen, and found an old orange can. I brought it back to the table, sprayed my arms and neck and face, spat out the residue that had leaked onto my tongue, put the can beside its cousins, the garlic-dip-chips, and made myself another drink. I smelled like a drugstore, or a gas station. I held my breath while I drank. Bill checked the fire, then decided to delay cooking by piling lots more wood on. He'd have to wait for more coals he could heap up, which meant another couple of drinks. Kelly was trying to channel the conversation back to her teaching and her photography, and Bill was eager to cooperate — his little eyes swiveled and danced as he watched us, hoping for the best, no doubt expecting only the worst, and drinking and talking, and working, in general, quite hard.

I was asking about his car, an old Ford Bronco that guzzled gas. He was telling me about a used International Harvester with a winch on the front. We were going on about body rust when Kelly stood and stretched. I had hitherto seen such moves in films, but never on a live person before me. Having composed a face that generated concern about the starving children of the Indian subcontinent, or perhaps certain lost manuscripts of Thomas Mann, she continued to stretch, so that she gave each breast its turn and each nipple its due; then she gave notice of her flanks and her loins, and then she sighed — all those hungry kids? I stopped talking and I watched her and, as she sat, I said, "Yes?"

"I didn't say anything," she said, smiling.

"I thought you did." And she had. For Bill had shut up as she'd begun to move, and he now dutifully concentrated on the topic she had raised. And now that she was sitting again, now that his leash had been tugged, he didn't know what to say. So he added more gin to his glass and he drank it.

Kelly smiled at me, all fang. I showed her a tooth or two in return. We talked about the Presidential election, and I expressed my regret that Richard Nixon wouldn't be available for service to his nation once again. "I miss him," I said. "He's been in my life or on the fringes of it as long as I can remember. It's like not having Satan anymore. How am I supposed to remember who God is if I don't have the Devil for purposes of comparison-shopping?"

Kelly said, "My father feels the same way, about the first part of what you said. He misses Nixon too. Except, he thinks he was railroaded out of office."

Bill said, "He tried to kill Lenny by drafting him, he *did* notch up a couple of hundred thousand bodies to his credit. Anyway, you don't believe that, Kel."

Kelly said, "I'm talking about my father, strange one. Of course. Lenny, my mother's in the DAR, you understand? That's her chief attraction for my father. He thinks it was the blacks and the Jews who railroaded Nixon out. My father has a lot of trouble with Jews," she said, staring at me and not blinking.

I sprayed bug stuff up into the air, as if there were an

all-out attack of giant flies. Bill panted loudly, like a large dog, reminding us that anti-Semites were a joke, and here we all were friends.

I said, "Yeah, I know a lot of people who've got trouble with Jews. They're called bigots. Or assholes, maybe. In Europe they call them either the village mayor, or Sir, or fascists, depending on who does the calling. They've got them in Germany — you vere surprised, *fraulein?* — and Italy and France and Rumania, where they do a first-rate job of hating, I can tell you, and let us not forget the oft-victimized but always stalwart Poles, who could do you a valve-job, lube and change the oil on a Jew before you say *O Gott.* And of course we have the DAR Americans."

Bill panted, poured more gin, and escaped to check on the fire. He was too responsible to us, though, to stay away, and as Kelly was describing for me this document her father owned several copies of, and as I was howling like the second large dog on their property, but with a certain cheer-fulness, I have to admit, Bill returned and sat down on his beach chair to pour more gin, then fled for the kitchen, saying, "Ice."

By the time he lurched back with an ice-cube tray, the final one, by my count, I was explaining things to Kelly. "*The Protocols of the Elders of Zion* was imported by Henry Ford. He did business with Czarist Russia to buy thousands of copies because he was so impressed. He didn't under-stand the book was a fake. He didn't want it to be. But it wasn't, it *isn't*, an actual account of these vicious old rabbis sitting around and cackling into their beards and drinking the blood of small Christian children as they plan to control the currencies of the world. It is possible that many distin-guished people have believed this, including Ezra Pound, maybe, and your father, maybe, and several selected members of the general staff, and conceivably Richard Nixon. But it isn't true. George Wallace knows it isn't true. The American Nazi Party knows it isn't true. The KKK thinks it might be true. And your father knows it *is* true, is that right? Are you kidding me?"

Bill dropped ice into our glasses and Kelly said, "Save some, sweetie."

I said, "Hitler did believe it, of course. Fine, that was his job. He was supposed to behave like Hitler. Okay. But how can your father — how, after they killed all the damned Jews in Europe, nearly, can your father *talk* like that?"

Kelly was blithe. I have to give it to her: she was the blithest. She said, "Daddy's hard to convince. It takes a lot to change his mind. You have to understand: he hardly ever met a Jew until he went to college, let alone a good Jew."

"A good Jew?"

Bill said, "I'm gonna smear a lot of mustard on some very thick chuck steaks and broil them over the fire and we are gonna have a *feast*."

"Kelly," I said, "a *good* Jew?"

She turned toward me. She smiled with all of her mouth. She nodded her head. And that was all, for she was blithe. " 'Scuse me," she said, still smiling, "while I go in and make us a green salad to go with the steaks."

"A good Jew," I said to Bill.

He said, "Look. It's how she was brought up. She didn't *decide* to think that way."

"You don't think that way."

"You should know better than to talk about that to me, Lenny."

"Yeah, but you're living with this woman, Bill, and she has some kind of dividing line in her life. Good Jews, bad

Jews. Doubtless we have good blacks and bad blacks, good spics and bad spics, bad Indians and dead ones, semi-tolerable Greek Orthodox — Bill: what've you got in your *life* now?"

"I love her, that's all. So forget it. All right? Some people have bad breath and other people keep living with them. Kelly was brought up by dumb people, that's it. She's working it out. This'll help her. Lenny: she did a whole photographic essay on people in New York, she must have half a dozen Hassidim in there, these old Jews with braids."

"I think Goebbels had a Jewish wife, Bill. Braids and all, little leather party dresses, wooden shoes. He still liked the smell of Jew-smoke."

Bill was too gentle to hit me in the face or body. He flailed with his paw at the tumbler I was holding. He pressed his lips together and his eyes narrowed and he batted at me with his arm straight out, his torso unmoving. He wasn't malicious. He was trapped, he was desperate, and he had no more words. I went to my knees, and I was hurt. The glass had apparently shattered when he struck it, and the shards were in my fingers. I was on both knees, then, seeing bright lights go on and off as Kelly called, "Wow!" Bill went down onto his knees too, snuffling, holding my sliced hand as he picked the glass out as well as he could while we both panted and trembled. "Oh, Jesus," he said. "Don't bleed to death, all right? Don't die." He stood and raised me and herded me into the house. Kelly was at the door, and she looked pretty because there was that pink flush under her slow-baked front-lawn tan, her nostrils were wide with excitement, her eyes were immense, I thought she was going to swallow the night. I thought that I was going to faint, and I made that announcement. Bill shoved me onto a chair and then pushed my head down between my legs with such strength, I felt one of my vertebrae threaten to pop, or so I thought. I leaned all the way forward to save my spine, and I went off the chair, face-first onto the floor. I lay there and tasted blood in my mouth from a slice of the lip I'd apparently caused when I threw myself down.

Bill laughed, a forced and purposeful "Hoo" like the sound a man in the spin of good times might make. But there was nothing funny, only Lenny Levine being ridiculous, and I didn't join in, and he stopped. I became aware of odors — cheap, store-bought dressing for the salad, and the damp rancidness of the unswept wooden floor, and the sweat that came off Bill's big body, and the sweat that came off my own. They sat me up where I was and leaned me back against the chair. I let my head rest on the seat while Bill held my hand still and Kelly, with tweezers and then hot needle, took splinters of glass from my palm and my fingers.

"Leave my thumb," I remember gasping. "Take the others off if you have to *ow*! But leave the thumb."

"So you can hitch," Bill said grimly.

"You guys are crazy," Kelly said, as one might remark of the antics of a ladies bowlers' team. I wanted to take my bloody palm and smear it on her face. I smiled, though, and nodded.

"That's what always got us through, Kel," he said.

"But then we got old. We grew up. Remember?" I said. "Bill? You remember what Ariana told us? You remember that? In New Haven? You went out and you came back — *ow! ow!* — with Chinese food? I think you were in the place on Chapel Street. You sat down across from me and you took out these about fifty eggrolls and a quart of cream soda, and Ariana made herself a cheese omelet and told us we'd be okay acting like that as long as we didn't get older.

Dammit, Kelly! I'm sorry. *Woof!* Thanks for trying to be gentle. Are you trying?"

"No," Bill said.

"What, hon?" Kelly said, and she knew what he would tell us.

"I don't remember, that's all."

"Well," I said, "what the hell. What's eggrolls."

"I'm sorry I swung like that," Bill said. "I panicked."

I said, "Me too."

Kelly said, "Ariana was probably right."

"I don't remember that," Bill said. He let my hand go and he helped me up by my arm. Kelly was pouring Merthiolate on the palm and daubing it on the fingers. Her hands were shaking more than mine, and I think it was pure excitement. I think that she was galvanized by the picture she must have retained: her big Bill, her own, swinging his massive arm in a wide, powerful arc to swat the buzzing Jew-boy and smite him where he'd lighted. Bill was shaking too, I could see him vibrate — even his knees were going. He couldn't breathe right, and he was pale. I knew how much he regretted hitting me, though the blow was also a gift to Kelly, and he'd treat it as such to woo her, and he'd take her praise with thanks. That was Bill. That was how he bought the affections of women. American men were famous for doing that, I had been told by Europeans, and Bill was all of an American man. I wondered, of course, if I purchased my loves by getting hurt.

He hugged me. We used to be conspicuous in that regard. People in bars would sneer when we got joyous and squeezed one another's shoulders. We did do that, and he did it now. We went outside, my thanks to Kelly and her response colliding in the air between our turned backs. We sat at the table again, and he spilled gin as he poured it into the yellowish vermouth, trying to make a proper martini and start our evening off all over again on a ceremonial note. I couldn't look at him, even when he shakily left the table and went into the house, then returned with gauze bandage and adhesive tape. He wrapped my hand, patted my cheek and then my shoulder, and he raised his glass to signal our toast.

My hand was throbbing, and the gin wouldn't help. My head was starting to throb in rhyme with my hand. I raised the glass and then put it down. I said, "I'm sorry. I didn't mean to come here and criticize your — I was going to say wife. But you know what I mean. I hope it really works out terrifically for you. I do."

He sat at the folding table on his lawn and watched me walk inside. He probably thought I was going to drop my wriggling benediction onto Kelly too. But I hadn't gone in search of her. I went in — the flashing lights I'd seen were still behind my eyes, and I'd finally decoded them — to find her camera. It was one of those large 35mm professional instruments, sleek and black and, in the right circumstances, as menacing as a gun.

"Hi!" she said brightly, showing the most affection she'd displayed to me — I was her subject, now, not just an intruder.

I picked up the camera, which was near some cellophane-wrapped lettuce on the counter next to the sink, and I fumbled at it.

"What are you doing, Lenny?"

"I'm trying to open your camera, Kelly, and get the film."

"No, don't do that."

"You're right," I said. I put the camera on the softwood floor and stepped on it as hard as I could. Kelly wailed. I jumped on the camera, and something popped open while a lot of delicate glass and machinery crunched under my feet like bugs. I saw a piece of film and pulled at it, and the spool unwound into a twisted mess that was torn up the middle by something projecting from the shattered box. I held it up and said, "Good shots, Kelly. But of course you had a good Jew to work with."

After which pivotal brilliance, I went into the hallway and found my bag, tied my jacket around my waist, and walked past my friend, Bill Gruen, who sat at the table and didn't act surprised. I went along his lawn, and down his road, and through the clouds of midges that seemed to never cease their swarming onto anything that moved. My eyes grew accustomed to the dark, my hand hurt worse, my feet chafed because I wasn't wearing socks, and I was alone at home in America, well-met by the only person alive with whom I had much history, and greeted by the ghost of what I'd sought.

It remains for me once more to say the obvious. I'm an American in Europe, residing on the cheap above a trattoria run by Spaniards in Venice, close to the Rialto Bridge. I earn a living as a teacher of English to the children of wealthy Venetian restaurateurs, summertime guide for British tour groups, and occasional travel writer — "Northern Italy Without Pasta!" — for American food magazines. I get by. Sometimes I take a few hours and sit with a bitter coffee at the Locanda Cipriani on the Island of Torcello, as now, and I watch the gasoline shimmer on top of the canal.

I walked away from Bill Gruen's house in Vermont and, by the time I'd stopped hyperventilating, I counted myself lucky that he hadn't come after me to batter at me for insults to Kelly and her equipment — or, worse, to ask me to stay.

I didn't expect to catch a ride, but I did. An old guy in a new pickup stopped for me and made courteous conversation before I left him at Montpelier. He had a son, he said, who worked at IBM in New York.

I went there too, though not to work for anyone. I made Manhattan a full day later, and I checked myself into the Waldorf-Astoria because that was the fanciest hotel I could think of when I caught the cab at the Port Authority bus terminal. I felt that I owed myself some luxury, and I graciously accepted the gift. I stayed there in a cool peach-marble room for a week, enjoying the air-conditioning and good showers, room service, and even the barber, who washed my hair and shaved me as gently as you'd like to be stroked by a stranger. I bought a first-rate pair of running shoes and some lightweight trousers and shirts, and even a suit that Brooks Brothers fitted for me with a minimum of fuss. Then I moved over to the West Side, after soliciting the advice of a cab driver, and I checked into the Royalton, a very dusty, very shabby, but un-verminous hotel, where they did scrub down the bathrooms and change the sheets, and where the bill was low. I went to a joint on West Forty-fifth and had my picture taken. I applied by mail for a passport, knowing that if it took a long time, then I would not have been pardoned, and had better make my way up north, and at least into Montreal, if not all the way to the Gulf of St. Lawrence. I went to a lot of films and I saw a revival, in Greenwich Village, of a Harold Pinter play that made my jaws ache just under the ears, as if I'd been sucking on lemons. A week went by, and there was no passport in the mail for me. I bought myself a paperback copy of Hugh Honour's Venice book because I thought that I might hack a living as a guide of some sort, and Honour knew everything I'd have to say about the pictures in Venice. It was well into the second week, when I was truly considering fright and flight, that my passport came.

At Macy's I bought myself a canvas suitcase. I picked up some toilet supplies, and some paperback books, and more shirts, a seersucker sportcoat and summerweight dark slacks, and then I was off for the Pan-Am office, where I booked my plane. I left, two days later, for the place where ghosts are said to be more at home; even the buildings in Europe are constructed as if to house them. Though certainly I knew as I went what I'd learned on coming home — that you cannot be haunted by the ghosts of your choosing. You take what you get. It's up to them.

I shuffled from the departure lounge at Kennedy Airport to display my passport and tickets at the Pan-Am gate. Ariana seemed more mine than she'd been. But she was air, she was argument, and there was no consolation in possessing her with words. The bored young Pan American Airlines clerk, skin the color of saddle leather, eyes very dark and very intelligent and consummately bored, sat sweating in his dark-blue uniform in the wet heat that crushed New York that summer. He looked at my tickets and he took my passport. I waited for him to stare at the little glued photograph and compare it to my face. His job, I'd forgotten, was only to be certain I had the proper date in my passport booklet. The music of a long-defunct Broadway show was playing from the speakers in the ceiling as he looked at the passport, but not at me, and then nodded to no one in particular, returned the little book, and motioned listlessly that I could pass. *Eccomi qui.* I'm here.

TOO LATE AMERICAN BOYHOOD BLUES was set by PennSet,
Inc., Bloomsburg, Pennsylvania in Linotron Janson,
a recutting made from type cast from matrices long
thought to have been made by the Dutchman Anton
Janson, who was a practicing type founder in Leipzig
during the years 1668–1687. However, it has been
conclusively demonstrated that these types are actually the work of Nicholas Kis (1650–1702), a Hun-
garian, who most probably learned his trade from the
master Dutch type founder Dirk Voskens. The type
is an excellent example of the influential and sturdy
Dutch types that prevailed in England up to the time
William Caslon developed his own in-
comparable designs from them.

*The book was printed and bound by the Haddon
Craftsmen, Scranton, Pennsylvania. The paper was
Glatfelter offset, an entirely acid-free paper.
Typography and binding design by Dede Cummings.*